ANCIENTS

A DARK DRABBLES ANTHOLOGY

Compiled & Edited by D. Kershaw

Also available from Black Hare Press

DARK DRABBLE ANTHOLOGIES

WORLDS
ANGELS
MONSTERS
BEYOND
UNRAVEL
APOCALYPSE
LOVE
HATE
OCEANS
ANCIENTS

Twitter: @BlackHarePress
Facebook: BlackHarePress
Website: www.BlackHarePress.com

Ancients, A Dark Drabbles Anthology title is
Copyright © 2020 Black Hare Press
First published in Australia in August 2020 by Black Hare Press

The authors of the individual stories retain the copyright of the works
featured in this anthology.

*All characters and events in this publication, other than those clearly in the
public domain, are fictitious and any resemblance to real persons, living or
dead, is purely coincidental.*

All rights reserved. No part of this production may be reproduced, stored in
a retrieval system or transmitted in any form or by any means, electronic,
mechanical, photocopying, recording or otherwise, without the prior
permission of the publisher and copyright owner.

Paperback: ISBN 978-1-925809-69-5
Hard Cover: ISBN 978-1-925809-70-1

Cover Design by Dawn Burdett
Book Formatting by Ben Thomas

Where once we danced, where once sang,
    Gentlemen, The floors are sunken, cobwebs hang,
        And cracks creep; worms have fed upon
            The doors. Yea, sprightlier times were then
            Than now, with harps and tabrets gone,
                Gentlemen!

Where once we rowed, where once we sailed,
    Gentlemen, And damsels took the tiller, veiled
        Against too strong a stare (God wot
            Their fancy, then or anywhen!)
            Upon that shore we are clean forgot,
                Gentlemen!

We have lost somewhat, afar and near,
    Gentlemen,   The thinning of our ranks each year
        Affords a hint we are nigh undone,
            That we shall not be ever again
            The marked of many, loved of one,
                Gentlemen.

In dance the polka hit our wish,
    Gentlemen, The paced quadrille, the spry schottische,
        "Sir Roger." And in opera spheres
            The "Girl" (the famed "Bohemian"),
            And "Trovatore," held the ears,
                Gentlemen.

This season's paintings do not please,
    Gentlemen, Like Etty, Mulready, Maclise;
        Throbbing romance has waned and wanned;
            No wizard wields the witching pen
            Of Bulwer, Scott, Dumas, and Sand,
                Gentlemen.

The bower we shrined to Tennyson,
    Gentlemen, Is roof-wrecked; damps there drip upon
        Sagged seats, the creeper-nails are rust,
            The spider is sole denizen;
            Even she who read those rhymes is dust,
                Gentlemen!

We who met sunrise sanguine-souled,
Gentlemen, Are wearing weary. We are old;
These younger press; we feel our rout
Is imminent to Aides' den, -
That evening's shades are stretching out,
Gentlemen!

And yet, though ours be failing frames,
Gentlemen, So were some others' history names,
Who trode their track light-limbed and fast
As these youth, and not alien
From enterprise, to their long last,
Gentlemen.

Sophocles, Plato, Socrates,
Gentlemen, Pythagoras, Thucydides,
Herodotus, and Homer, yea,
Clement, Augustin, Origen,
Burnt brightlier towards their setting-day,
Gentlemen.

And ye, red-lipped and smooth-browed; list,
Gentlemen; Much is there waits you we have missed;
Much lore we leave you worth the knowing,
Much, much has lain outside our ken:
Nay, rush not: time serves: we are going,
Gentlemen.

Thomas Hardy, *An Ancient of Ancients*

Table of Contents

Foreword

From the Etruscans, the Nok, the Sanxingdui, the Silla, and the Indus, the Egyptians, the Persians, the Mayans…

Ancient civilisations have long piqued our interest—from their gods, their rituals, their religions, their folk tales. For centuries, stories have been passed down the generations—from grandparents to grandchildren—thus keeping traditions alive.

Here in Ancients, international authors bring you a taste of those stories of old, carefully researched, to give you an insight into times gone by.

So, turn off the lights, lock the doors and settle in.

Wait…is that the reflection of Anubis you see in the window…?

Love and kisses
D. Kershaw & Ben Thomas
Black Hare Press

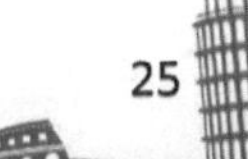

Love Sick
by A.S. Charly

Akhenaten stood at the top of the stairs, looking down to the gardens with his son.

"Your sister has grown very beautiful."

Burning anger lit Tutankhaten's heart. This was not how a father should look at his daughter.

All the words Ay had whispered to him, about how his father was bringing ruin to the country and its people by worshipping the wrong god, rumoured in his mind.

He would fix this, protect his people and his sister. With insanity filled eyes, he pushed his father down the stairs.

Ankhesenaten—no, Ankhesenamun—would belong to no other man, but him.

A.S. Charly loves to lose herself in fantastical worlds far away between the stars, filled with magic and wonder. She also writes and draws when her head is not stuck in the clouds. Her writing has been published in various anthologies and online publications.
Facebook: A.S.Charlydreams
Amazon: www.amazon.com/author/a.s.charly

Ivar Ironside's Journey to Valhalla
by Will Christian

My eyes open. Confused and dazed, I hear the chants. They shout my name!

But I'm bound and encased: what is this around me? My sword, my helmet, food. I try to cry out. My body is encased in linen so tight, not a movement or sound escapes.

Why are they chanting Valhalla? Who's dead?

Not me. I'm alive. My heart beats!

A whoosh and thud, the smell of tar and peat burning nearby. My mind clears as I remember the betrayal by Bjorn. Struck down by his hand.

I, Ivar, am the leader! But flame engulfs me, burning flesh.

Will Christian is a father of two writers and a husband to his beautiful wife (who paid him to write that). With a sense of humour that his eldest daughter calls "adorable and groan-worthy dad jokes with surprising creativity," Will can usually be found wandering the local beaches, writing poetry and drabbles, and wistfully daydreaming about the boat that his girls haven't yet agreed to buy him.

Everything Must Balance
by Stuart Conover

Thoth sat still in darkness.

Trapped in a temple once meant for his worship.

All the old Gods had long ago perished or fled this world.

All but one.

Thoth's egg had given birth to the cosmos.

His Ibis eyes gave him access to all knowledge.

The ultimate truth was all things must balance.

His egg gave birth to creation.

At the same time, it gave birth to destruction.

Countless eons had passed.

As he had given the cosmos life.

It was now the time of Anubis.

Soon, every soul would belong to the God of Death.

Including his own.

Stuart Conover *is a father, husband, rescue dog owner, published author, blogger, journalist, horror enthusiast, comic book geek, science fiction junkie, and IT professional. With all of that to cram in daily, we have no idea if or when he sleeps or how he gets writing done! (We suspect it has to do with having evil clones.) Stuart is a Chicago native and runs the author resource Horror Tree.*

The Warriors Impression
by Peter J. Foote

"Master Kun, why build a clay copy of me? I'm a soldier, I serve the Emperor with my spear and my body," Chen says.

The master artisan finishes sculpting the clay warrior before replying.

"Excellent!" Master Kun states and gestures to the bewildered Chen.

"Help me arrange the clay warrior in the kiln and I will reveal all." The pair fire the kiln and wait.

When cooled, they open the kiln and a terracotta version of Chen strides out. It seizes the spear out of Chen's hands and stabs him through the heart.

"Now Chen, you'll serve the Emperor forever!"

Peter J. Foote is a bestselling speculative fiction writer from Nova Scotia. Outside of writing, he runs a used bookstore specialising in fantasy and sci-fi cosplays and alternates between red wine and coffee as the mood demands. His short stories can be found in both print and ebook form, with his story "Sea Monkeys" winning the inaugural "Engen Books/Kit Sora, Flash Fiction/Flash Photography" contest in March of 2018. As the founder of the group "Genre Writers of Atlantic Canada", Peter believes that the writing community is stronger when it works together.
Twitter: @PeterJFoote1
Website: peterjfooteauthor.wordpress.com

Glauce's Dress
by McKenzie Richardson

When the early wedding gift was delivered to the palace, Jason's young bride hastily threw open the chest. Inside was a robe that sparkled as if firelight had been woven into its fabric. Immediately, she pulled it on, admiring herself in the mirror.

As she stared at her reflection, the faint smell of burning flesh permeated the room. The dress glowed bright for a moment, then erupted into flames. Before her eyes, skin blistered, peeled, and melted from her bones until there was nothing left.

Jason should have known better than to betray a sorceress. Medea always got her revenge.

McKenzie Richardson *lives in Milwaukee, WI. Her horror stories have been featured in various anthologies including Evil Lurks, Pandemic, and After: Undead Wars. She has also published a variety of poems and flash fiction pieces.*
Facebook: mckenzielrichardson
Blog: www.craft-cycle.com

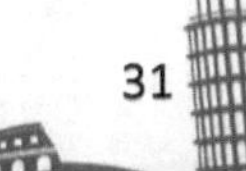

Buried Mars
by Shawn M. Klimek

"Engineers are inspecting the final tunnel segment now," Lansing reported. "Once they radio back that it's safe, the remainder separating Ares from Tharsis Station can be excavated manually."

Richard continued studying the borer instrument readouts. "I thought subterranean Mars was homogenous basalt," he commented.

"True, except beneath major topographical deformations," Lansing confirmed. "Mars has no tectonics."

"Then what could have caused these two pressure spikes?"

"A buried meteor?"

"So, a hollow meteor? See, the pressure drops to zero!"

"Let me see that!" said Lansing.

Suddenly, the radio spoke. "Not safe! Not safe!" the tunnel inspectors cried. "We've found a tomb!"

Shawn M. Klimek is the internationally published author of more than 170 poems and stories, in several genres. He is the author of Hungry Thing, an illustrated fantasy tale told in five poems. He lives in Illinois, USA, with his wife and their Maltese. Website: blog.jotinthedark.com
Facebook: shawnmklimekauthor

The Hounds of Actaeon
by Holley Cornetto

Actaeon broke through the forest into the glade. Bathing there were the most beautiful creatures he'd ever seen.

The loveliest of them turned. Not a nymph, no. This was Diana, and her eyes glittered with rage at his intrusion.

He ran. Bones cracked and twisted with each tormented step. He felt splitting pain as antlers sprouted from his skull.

Diana would have her revenge.

Another step, then a stumble. In the distance, he heard the baying of hounds. Two legs became four. Man became beast. He looked down the length of his body, now a stag.

The hunter now hunted.

Holley Cornetto was born and raised in Alabama but now lives in New Jersey. To indulge her love of books and stories, she became a librarian. She is also a writer because the only thing better than being surrounded by stories is to create them herself.
Twitter: @HLCornetto

In the Soil of London
by Galina Trefil

Slaughter lives in my backyard, under my house, throughout this entire street. It's the saucer that this city sits upon, rather like an unknowing teacup.

I saw it when we were digging to put in a pool: reddish-brown ash mixed in with pottery fragments and debris. Boudicca's Layer, it's called—the evidence of her burning this ancient Roman jewel into the ground.

What happened to the hands that formed this pottery, I wonder? Were they cut off or crucified by Boudicca's outraged warriors? Probably.

Go on. Touch the soil. You can almost still hear the victims screaming amidst the flames…

Galina Trefil is a novelist specialising in women's, minority, and disabled rights. Her favourite genres are horror, thriller, and historical fiction. Her short stories and articles have appeared in Neurology Now, UnBound Emagazine, The Guardian, Tikkun, Romea.CZ, Jewcy, Jewrotica, Telegram Magazine, Ink Drift Magazine, The Dissident Voice, Open Road Review, and the anthologies "Flock: The Journey", "First Love", "Sea of Secrets", "Coffins and Dragons", "Organic Ink Volume One", "Winds of Despair", "Waters of Destruction", "Curses & Cauldrons", "Unravel", "Hate", "Love", "Oceans", "Forgotten Ones", "Dark Valentine Holiday Horror Collection", and "Suspense Unimagined".
Website: galinatrefil.wordpress.com
Facebook: Rabbi-Galina-Trefil-535886443115467

The Wits Elixir
by M.A. Nolte

Red thing
and dead thing
—how they cling
together nicely
and so precisely...

Kvasir,
the late seer
without peer
in wisdom and art,
has sparkling-red blood.

Chuck-chuck,
flood of blood...
But no luck!
Dwarf Galar's looking;
yet it's still lacking.

Such shit
—where is it?
Where's the wit,
the ingredient
of his brilliance?

A cup
of his blood
and a mug
of honey... mix it:
the Wits Elixir!

Ah, oui!
This red tea
gives wits thee.
So Galar's done it;
now wisdom's bottled!

Beware,
gods in the air!
Galar swears:
your end's getting near,
with Galar's your peer.

M.A. Nolte *studied prehistory, preferred to read Greek mythology as a child rather than listen to fairy tales, and— argh—rather writes texts for gravestones than for an 'author's biography'. So here it is: Beware! M.A. Nolte is still alive— somewhere, somehow!*

Olympic Mishaps
by John H. Dromey

Back when Zeus ruled the roost on Mount Olympus, things did not always go smoothly. Although asymptomatic, the big guy was concerned—while disguised as a white bull—he might have exposed himself to mad cow disease. His angst was contagious.

Hermes had an identity crisis. Using his Roman name Mercury, he took up body surfing. Net result: he contaminated the surrounding waters and poisoned the fish.

Dionysus drank all the ambrosia.

And so on.

Hera suggested hanging numerous miniature paintings on tiny nails to help restore calm. Relief was in sight… Then Thor hit his thumb with his hammer.

John H. Dromey was born in northeast Missouri, USA. He enjoys reading—mysteries in particular—and writing in a variety of genres. In addition to contributing to the Black Hare Press series of "Dark Drabbles" anthologies, he's had short fiction published in Alfred Hitchcock's Mystery Magazine, Martian Magazine, Mystery Weekly, Stupefying Stories Showcase, Thriller Magazine, Unfit Magazine, and elsewhere, as well as in numerous anthologies, including "Chilling Horror Short Stories" (Flame Tree Publishing, 2015).

Quaint Little Things
by Umair Mirxa

Qadim hid in the shadows, quiet as he could, and felt a cold shiver crawl down his spine. Mohenjo-daro was supposed to be deserted, abandoned millennia ago, and yet…

It took all his strength not to scream.

"Quaint little things, aren't they?" said the wizened old man who now stood before him.

"Who…what are they?" said Qadim.

"The original inhabitants. Those who never left. Tonight is carnival, and you are expected."

"What? How can…"

"I don't know how exactly but each month, they summon a soul curious as yourself. Say it adds flavour to the flesh."

Umair Mirxa *lives and writes in Karachi, Pakistan. His first published story, 'Awareness', appeared on Spillwords Press. He has since had stories accepted for publication in anthologies from Zombie Pirate Publishing, Blood Song Books, Black Hare Press, Iron Faerie Publishing, Clarendon House Publications, Fantasia Divinity Magazine & Publishing, and The ReAnimated Writers Press. He is a massive J.R.R. Tolkien fan; loves everything to do with mythology, fantasy, and history; and wishes with all his heart that dragons were real. When he's not writing, he enjoys reading novels and comic books, playing video games, listening to music, and watching movies, TV shows, and football as an Arsenal FC fan.*
Website: umairmirxa.com

Diverting Catastrophe
by Wendy Roberts

Dennis grips the stone tight. He found it while touring the Aztec ruins. It spoke to him then. Warning him of an accident that would happen on the way home. He scoffed at the words, thought it some joke but took the old stone with the strange writing anyways, until he woke up two days later in some hospital because the tour bus flipped. Now he grips the stone until it cuts into his hand as it whispers how the plane carrying him and his family will go down and he drops out the window, hoping to change the outcome.

*Writing short stories and novels started as a past time for **Wendy Roberts** and has now become a full-fledged passion. She posts short stories on her website and can be found most days on Twitter.*
Website: flippinscribbler.com
Twitter: @_WARoberts

Life Must Be Heavy
by Sue Marie St. Lee

Salama screamed when Mekal dropped from the sky in front of her.

The next day, Salama followed her father to Bastet's temple where mummified Mekal would be laid to rest with thousands of departed felines.

Salama laid Mekal at Bastet's feet whose stony eyes beamed a blinding green light upon the panicked father and spoke, "Your sentence is death."

Lifting the father high, Bastet's beam propelled him to the ceiling, dropped him in the same manner he killed Mekal who now struggled to be free from his bindings.

*Born in Chicago, **Sue Marie St. Lee** currently lives in Oklahoma with her husband and Manx cat. A storyteller since learning to talk, her wild imagination caused reprimands from her mother. Her imagination persevered. Retired from Finance Management, Sue began ghostwriting until 2019, choosing to have works published internationally, in print and online, under her own name. Black Hare Press, Fantasia Divinity, and Spillwords Press are some of the publishers to feature Sue's work to date.*
Blog: suemariestlee.home.blog
Amazon: amazon.com/Sue-Marie-St.-Lee/e/B07WJFRF1L

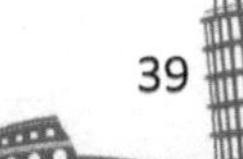

Unfeeling Dawn
by Laurence Sullivan

Watching from atop a mountain peak, Itztlacoliuhqui never sleeps.

Bringing the dawn with him each day, he resents the people of the Aztec Empire—able as they are to enjoy the sun he so unwillingly summons.

Somewhere deep within him, he remembers the warmth of that blazing orb, but his obsidian skin—unfeeling as it is—ensures it remains a distant memory…

One thought sustains him: stealing their lives away through famine.

Each year he has one shot at brushing away their bounty beneath a bitter blanket of snow. A chance to watch them waste away under the winter sun…

*Runner-up in the Wicked Young Writer Awards: Gregory Maguire Award, **Laurence Sullivan**'s creative writing has appeared in such places as Londonist, The List, NHK-World-Japan, Literary Orphans and Crack the Spine. He became inspired to start writing during his studies at the universities of Kent, Utrecht and Birmingham—after being saturated in all forms of literature from across the globe and enjoying every moment of it. He is currently pursuing a PhD at Northumbria University in the Medical Humanities, exploring literary portrayals of women's domestic medicine during the eighteenth century.*
Website: www.laurencesullivan.co.uk
Twitter: @LozzySullivan

Red Sun Rises
by Zoey Xolton

Blood dripped over the clouds of Heaven, spilling into the world of mortals below. The sound of war echoed throughout the realm like thunder.

The *yokai* marched upon the Ascended in countless legions, the demons' darkness a tangible, foul corruption on the air.

Just as the war seemed lost, and the gods almost overrun, Amaterasu—the goddess of the sun—rose above the chaos on gleaming wings. Throwing her arms wide, she screamed, and from her mouth streamed the burning, brilliant rays of the sun and the *yokai* army eviscerated.

The sun over Japan that day bled over the horizon…

***Zoey Xolton** is an Australian speculative fiction writer, primarily of dark fantasy, paranormal romance, and horror. She is also a proud mother of two and is married to her soulmate. Outside of her family, writing is her greatest passion. She is especially fond of short fiction and is working on releasing her own themed collections in future.*
Website: www.zoeyxolton.com

Freedom
by Ethan Hedman

The retiarius watched as his bloodied opponent was carried from the arena, still tangled up in his net.

"Another fine fight," his master called above the crowd's cheers, walking up from the pits with his guards alongside.

"My fifth," the gladiator said between heavy breaths, "and last. I'm owed my freedom."

"No." His master's face warped into a greedy grin. "The laws have changed since I acquired you. You'll fight again."

The retiarius felt the spirit of Liber filling his body, his glare blazing with divine fury. "A sixth fight, then," he whispered, thrusting his trident into his master's chest.

Ethan Hedman is a speculative fiction writer from South Florida, the land of heat, humidity, and hurricanes. His work has been included in a variety of publications, including Gunsmoke & Dragonfire, Unrealpolitik, and The Hamthology. Ethan's full bibliography can be found on EthanHedman.com, his little corner of the Internet.

Transitions
by Stuart West

The heavy sun's crimson light caressed her face; loving eyes fixed upon the new-born. Before them, the house he had toiled to build in advance of their son's birth stood complete but for the solitary stone, standing motionless beside the entrance.

Her gaze met his and they nodded silently. Together they advanced and he took up the great stone as she stooped, delicately placing the infant into the void within the doorway. He allowed the stone to fall. There was no sound. No cry.

He took her hand and they enthusiastically crossed the threshold of their new family home together.

Stuart West Stuart is a qualified archaeologist and chartered town planner living on an island archipelago within the hinterland of Thule. In his spare time, Stuart plays tabletop wargames for fun and competitively for his country; writes speculative fiction; and paints. Stuart has no cats - nor does he want any. Writing mainly Sci-fi, Stuart has been published in a variety of short story anthologies, magazines and journals - one day he'll finish the novel!
Twitter: @aosbatrep
Instagram: NorthernInvasion_Stu

The Wild Hunt
by Rowanne S. Carberry

Artemis dons her mask and pulls on her armour, thinking of the hunt ahead.

Armour clinging to every curve and she smiles.

"How is it that people still think a man heads the wild hunt?"

"Because my muses sing it so." Apollo laughs.

"If they don't stop, they will find themselves hunted."

Artemis looks outside—the moon is nearly full.

She lets out an ear-splitting cry. Unearthly sounds, the clamouring of a thousand hooves, and the voices of riders answer.

"See you at dawn brother."

She steps into air and onto her beast, her prey in sight.

They hunt.

Rowanne S. Carberry *was born in England in 1990, where she stills lives now with her cat Wolverine. Rowanne has always loved writing, and her first poem was published at the age of 15, but her ambition has always been to help people. Rowanne studied at the University of Sunderland where she completed combined honours of Psychology with Drama. Rowanne writes to offer others an escape. Although Rowanne writes in varied genres, each story or poem she writes will often have a darkness to it, which helped coin her brand, Poisoned Quill Writing—Wicked words from a poisoned quill.*
Facebook: PoisonedQuillWriting
Instagram: @poisoned_quill_writing

Roundabout Route
by John H. Dromey

The charioteers lined up in battle formation. On command, they started to advance slowly. First at a walk, then a trot, and finally at a full gallop. At that point, one chariot broke ranks. By going around in circles—out of harm's way—it avoided the bloody fray.

Afterwards, the driver of the errant vehicle complained to the armourer, "I'm now the laughingstock of the squadron, and I may be charged with cowardice and desertion."

"You're not to blame. By mistake, you were assigned a chariot designed for racing on a circular track. One wheel is bigger than the other."

John H. Dromey was born in northeast Missouri, USA. He enjoys reading—mysteries in particular—and writing in a variety of genres. In addition to contributing to the Black Hare Press series of Dark Drabbles anthologies, he's had short fiction published in Alfred Hitchcock's Mystery Magazine, Martian Magazine, Mystery Weekly, Stupefying Stories Showcase, Thriller Magazine, Unfit Magazine, and elsewhere, as well as in numerous anthologies, including Chilling Horror Short Stories (Flame Tree Publishing, 2015).

The Witch of Girona
by J.M. Meyer

Since I allow no slight to go unpunished, I am to blame for every misfortune in Girona. My spells whisper in the leaves blowing outside my neighbours' homes. The farmer who refused me eggs, his hen stopped laying. The milkmaid who ran in fear, her cow's milk dried up.

Today, I baited the Angel who sits upon the cathedral, waiting to turn me to stone. Tonight, the milkmaid exchanged milk, wearing my red cloak through town, for a love potion; the farmer hasn't noticed her. The Angel turned the girl into a gargoyle, sitting on the cathedral wall for all eternity.

J.M. Meyer is a writer, artist, and small business owner living in New York, where she received her Master's degree from Teachers College, Columbia University. Jacqueline enjoys writing speculative fiction and mysteries. Her favourite author is Alice Munro and her favourite film…is…anything horror related. Jacqueline also enjoys hiking with her dog Molly and the company of her husband Bruce and daughters Julia, Emma, and Lauren. Jacqueline's mantra lately: there's no such thing as failing, it's called learning.
Website: jmoranmeyer.net
Amazon: www.amazon.com/author/jacquelinemoranmeyer

Beautiful Evil
by Rowanne S. Carberry

The box opens, and Pandora hides. She watches as Pride peeks out. He looks around the room, a smile on his face.

She sees forms flow from the box, stretching out around the room.

Pandora stares—transfixed as Hate dances beautifully and Sickness sing her freedom.

Then, the most beautiful of all.

"There's someone here," he whispers.

The curtain's ripped away and Pandora is there for all to see.

"Thank you for our freedom," he says, placing a kiss on her forehead.

Her first, and last, brush with Death. She dies watching the beautiful evils she's released step into the world.

Rowanne S. Carberry *was born in England in 1990, where she stills lives now with her cat Wolverine. Rowanne has always loved writing, and her first poem was published at the age of 15, but her ambition has always been to help people. Rowanne studied at the University of Sunderland where she completed combined honours of Psychology with Drama. Rowanne writes to offer others an escape. Although Rowanne writes in varied genres, each story or poem she writes will often have a darkness to it, which helped coin her brand, Poisoned Quill Writing—Wicked words from a poisoned quill.*
Facebook: *PoisonedQuillWriting*
Instagram: *@poisoned_quill_writing*

The Favourite
by A.R. Dean

The pharaoh is gone. I stand with the other servants as the priest takes note of us. He stares at me; his ebony eyes flash with familiarity.

"Kuhmet, you were his favourite. You will join him." At his command the guards lead me away. I am silent until they seal me up inside the tomb.

The fires begin to die as the air goes thin. My nails rip out as I scratch the stone door in terror. I begin to scream into the darkness. I beg Nephthys to have me spared. She doesn't come as I am lost into oblivion.

A.R. Dean is a dark and twisted soul. Dean has spent their whole life spreading fear with the tales from their head. Best known for stories that terrify and show the evilest side of human nature. So, look for Dean haunting your local cemetery or under your bed, because they're here to spread the fear. Turn off your lights and enjoy a scare. Dean is being published in Black Hare Press' Beyond and Unravel Anthologies. Keep a lookout for more stories.
Facebook: A.R. Dean Author & Ghoul

Fruit of Boudica
by Nicola Currie

As the last of her men fell like rain and her daughters' lights were extinguished, Boudica took shelter in the merciful trees. Her final moments would not be taken by the Romans. They were all she had left and would be hers alone.

The poison did not sting, as she made her deathbed on the welcoming grass of her kingdom. As she drifted, she could feel the creatures of the wood attend her, as her spirit sank into the earth.

It is said that those who eat of the berries where she fell gain a warrior's heart, even now.

Nicola Currie is from Cambridge, UK, where she works in educational publishing. She has published poetry in literary magazines, including Mslexia and Sarasvati, and short stories in various anthologies. She has also completed her first novel, which was longlisted for the Bath Children's Novel Award.
Website: writeitandweep.home.blog

Hounds of the Wetlands
by Robin Braid

"I've got something."

By the pit's edge, Kirsty shook dirt from her gloves. "Roman?" she said.

"Pict, I'm sure." Calum's hands worked faster. "An armlet, bronze."

Kirsty crouched to watch as he lifted his find from the mud. "Fantastic craftmanship. See the animal engraved there?" he said.

A sudden sound, a chorus of growls, seemed to rumble from the earth.

Kirsty glanced up. "Did you hear that?"

Calum didn't answer. Instinctively his hand slipped through the armlet, its weight biting into his forearm. He dropped to all fours; head flung back. His eyes flashed amber at Kirsty.

"Run," he said.

Robin Braid writes stories of the mysterious and macabre. A resident of Fife, Scotland, he graduated from Dundee University with a degree in English Literature. When not working in his regular job he can often be found rambling over hills and glens in search of inspiration for further tales. Twitter: @robinbraid

Reliquary of the Ancients
by Daniel Bagley

Among the hallowed crypts and mausoleums, the apparitions of the dead wander in shattered silence.

Confused in their search for untold peace, they whimper and cry.

We ask, they speak…a never-ending cycle of question and answer.

Yet, for a civilisation that is bound to the spirit earth, their relics and machinery continue to click, a mark for their ingenuity beyond their recorded time.

Even the mere mention of their name remains lost, forever locked away in the vault.

What keeps them relevant to this day is the treasury they have left behind, a constant reminder that nothing lasts forever…

Daniel Bagley has spent the last three years finding his way through the world of literacy, to understand different styles and its various audiences. Dark fiction, for him, is a rarity among genres, because not many will explore its crevices. Of course, he sees it as a reflection of one's life, the journeys we have to take to seek redemption. Through the power of words, he finds it easier to unleash his emotions to convey my point. Despite its name, it's a genre worth exploring.

Ulama
by Maxine Churchman

His stomach churned. It was more than a game; it was life and death.

The losing team would lose their heads. The best player would be chosen as a sacrifice to Chaac.

Earlier, his mother smiled at him. "I will be so honoured if you are chosen my son. Play your best—for both of us."

He didn't want to die; certainly not for Chaac, but could he face his mother's disappointment?

The game began. The ball bounced towards him; his reactions took over and he knocked it back with his hip. His only thoughts were to win the game.

Maxine Churchman *lives in Essex, UK, and has recently started writing poetry and short stories to share. Her interests include learning to improve her writing, reading, knitting, walking, and teaching yoga. She is also planning a novel.*

The Morrigan
by Jasmine Jarvis

I hear them marching towards me. The clanking of their weapons, the singing, and nervous energy.

Soldiers heading into battle.

As they draw closer, I wade into the river; the moment I enter the water, it runs red, and battle-broken corpses appear beneath the river's surface.

The soldiers stop when they see me, the Morrigan. I don't say anything. I know they are scared. I raise my hand and point to the soldiers whose bloodied corpses are around me in the water.

One by one.

Silently pointing out those who are doomed to die in the battle.

Setting their fates.

Jasmine Jarvis is a teller of tales and scribbler of scribbles. She lives in Brisbane, Australia, with her husband, Michael; their two children, Tilly and Mish; their German Shepherd, Ripley; and indoor fat cat, Dwight K. Shrute.

The Flayed Lord
by Nicola Currie

I sew the final stitch and my costume is complete. As I wear it and step towards the altar, my brothers and sisters kneel, welcoming me into their congregation, a new priestess of the Flayed Lord, god of torture and new life.

I stroke the growing mound of my belly and feel a kick, my lord Xipe Totec already nurturing the joy within me. This one will not meet its end before its birth.

He will be a beauty like his father. I think of his father fondly as I clutch my robe and think of his skin. Still warm.

Nicola Currie is from Cambridge, UK, where she works in educational publishing. She has published poetry in literary magazines, including Mslexia and Sarasvati, and short stories in various anthologies. She has also completed her first novel, which was longlisted for the Bath Children's Novel Award. Website: writeitandweep.home.blog

Comfy on Yrkm's Bosom
by Joachim Heijndermans

It's not too bad here, all things considering. The sandstone isn't too hard. The view's nice. Besides, it's not every day you get to sit on Yrkm's titty. Not the real one, duh.

Down in the ruins below, the ghosts of Abbadyn walk the streets. They chant dead prayers, which I record. A thousand years they ruled the golden oasis, until Yrkm bailed to heaven knows where.

I look to the horizon. Sunrise hits the great statue of Yrkm, and me seated on her bosom.

A thousand years. Unbelievable. I hope she comes back, just for the chance to film her.

Joachim Heijndermans writes, draws, and paints nearly every waking hour. Originally from The Netherlands, he's been all over the world, boring people by spouting random trivia. His work has been featured in a number of anthologies and publications, such as Mad Scientist Journal, Asymmetry Fiction, Hinnom Magazine, Ahoy Comics' Edgar Allan Poe's Snifter of Terror, Metaphorosis, and The Gallery of Curiosities, and he's currently in the midst of completing his first children's book.
Website: www.joachimheijndermans.com
Twitter: @jheijndermans

Beside Bolivia's Lake Titicaca
by Vonnie Winslow Crist

Eduardo placed flowers at a colossal figure's feet.

"Tiahuanaco was built by giants," explained Abuelo. "But they offended the Sun, so Tiahuanaco was destroyed."

Eduardo nodded.

"These symbols are the giants' words." Abuelo tapped grooves in the statue. "Now, none know their meaning."

Next, they visited Gateway of the Sun. The creator god Viracocha stared down at them.

"Why does he hold condors, Eduardo?"

"Because they capture souls of the dead and return them to Viracocha."

"Remember what you have seen," said his grandfather.

"I will," promised Eduardo as sunbeams poured through the sacred gate like a pathway to eternity.

Vonnie Winslow Crist *is author of The Enchanted Dagger, Owl Light, The Greener Forest, Murder on Marawa Prime, and other award-winning books. Her fiction is included in "Amazing Stories," "Cast of Wonders," "Outposts of Beyond," Killing It Softly 2, Defending the Future—Dogs of War, Midnight Masquerade, Chaos of Hard Clay, and elsewhere. A clover hand who has found so many four-leafed clovers, she keeps them in jars, Vonnie strives to celebrate the power of myth in her writing.*
Website: www.vonniewinslowcrist.com

Gardener King
by Shawn M. Klimek

"Because the goddess of healing grows medicinal herbs, sacrificing a gardener seemed apt," explained the priest.

"Reasonable." King Enlil-bāni allowed.

"So, you see, King Erra-Imitti only placed his tiara on your head as part of the ritual. The status was meant to be temporary."

"Until I was sacrificed."

The priest wrung his hands. "Yes. But no one expects that now they're both dead. We're simply asking you to step down."

"I think not," said the ascendant Sumerian king severely. "Nintinuga has harvested one dynasty and planted another. All of Isin is my garden now…and I'll soon be uprooting weeds."

Shawn M. Klimek *is the internationally published author of more than 170 poems and stories, in several genres. He is the author of Hungry Thing, an illustrated fantasy tale told in five poems. He lives in Illinois, USA, with his wife and their Maltese.*
Website: blog.jotinthedark.com
Facebook: shawnmklimekauthor

Golden Touch
by Peter J. Foote

"Curse? How can this be a curse, daughter? I turn everything into gold with a touch." King Midas roars with laughter and pats his daughter's hand.

He tosses the cluster of grapes, flashing golden orbs bounce and roll throughout the throne room, resting against the boots of his guards and court officials.

"You have changed your tone, daughter. Does endless wealth excite you? Speak, give counsel! Is everyone in my court mute?" Midas shrieks, his cracking voice reverberating off the golden figures that were his royal court, his wizened fist clasping his daughter's golden fingers, alone in the golden chamber.

Peter J. Foote is a bestselling speculative fiction writer from Nova Scotia. Outside of writing, he runs a used bookstore specialising in fantasy & sci-fi cosplays and alternates between red wine and coffee as the mood demands. His short stories can be found in both print and ebook form, with his story "Sea Monkeys" winning the inaugural "Engen Books/Kit Sora, Flash Fiction/Flash Photography" contest in March of 2018. As the founder of the group "Genre Writers of Atlantic Canada", Peter believes that the writing community is stronger when it works together.
Twitter: @PeterJFoote1
Website: peterjfooteauthor.wordpress.com

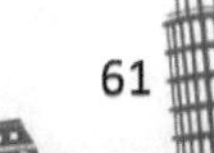

My Tongue
by Stephen Herczeg

"For life," they had said.

I agreed, prepared to lay down that life for the Pharaoh.

I held an honourable position as one of the Pharaoh's guards. Others shed blood just to be considered for such an honour.

But the Pharaoh died. I stood guard as the priests came for his body. They came for me as well. Pain exploded as the darkness took me.

I awoke, finding a Priest with tongs holding a writhing hunk of meat before me.

"My tongue," I shouted, but only a gout of bloodied words erupted.

"Prepare to guard the Pharaoh, for all eternity."

Stephen Herczeg *is an IT geek based in Canberra, Australia. He has been writing for over twenty years and has completed a couple of dodgy novels, sixteen feature length screenplays, and numerous short stories and scripts. His horror work has featured in Sproutlings, Hells Bells, Below the Stairs, Trickster's Treats #1 and #2, Shades of Santa, Behind the Mask, Beyond the Infinite, The Body Horror Book, Anemone Enemy, Petrified Punks, and Beginnings. He has also had numerous Sherlock Holmes stories published through the Belanger Books—Sherlock Holmes anthologies.*
Amazon: amazon.com/-/e/B07916SQQS
Facebook: stephenherczegauthor

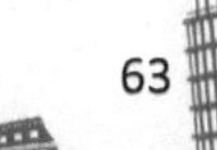

The Blood of Beginnings
by Chris Bannor

Pangu's death had created a beautiful world and Nüwa walked in the bliss of such wonders, but as time passed, she grew lonely. In her solitude, she formed humans and watched them blossom.

But no world was perfect. The pillars cracked and ferocious beasts devoured the people that had kept her company. Rains flooded the plains from a broken sky, fires burned unquenched in other regions, and monstrous birds annihilated her children.

The goddess could weep.

Instead, she prepared her knife. The great black dragon would fall first to her blade as she set forth to remake the four pillars.

Chris Bannor is a science fiction and fantasy writer who lives in Southern California. Chris learned her love of genre stories from her mother at an early age and has never veered far from that path. She also enjoys musical theatre and roadtrips with her family but is a general homebody otherwise.
Facebook: chrisbannorauthor
Website: ChrisBannor.com

Shamash's Return
by Monica Schultz

Eddie traces the fading letters with his gloved fingertip, struggling to pronounce the dead language. With each word, his body sways. Sweat prickles his skin despite the airconditioned room.

Zap.

Eddie yelps, cradling his charred finger. The fluorescent lights moan, complaining, before they surrender to darkness.

Yet light remains, burning into Eddie. He squints against the glow.

"You dare to stand before a god!" Shamash thunders.

Eddie's knees buckle. His skin blisters as he shields his face against the sun god's wrath.

"You humans have disobeyed my law. No more! I will not rest until all nations bow before true justice."

Monica Schultz *is a full-time Mathematics and History teacher from Ipswich, Australia, with a passion for writing fantasy. When she isn't busy finding "x" in the latest equation, you can find her curled up with a young adult book and a cat on her lap.*
Website: https://monicaschultzauthor.weebly.com/
Instagram: @monicaschultzauthor

Monumental Mourning
by Ethan Hedman

Tremors shook the ground before a thundering crack rang out over the plateau. A cloud of crumbling limestone and dust billowed outwards as the Sphinx rose from its haunches, freed at last from its perpetual slumber. It arched its back in a colossal stretch before circling in place, observing its surroundings.

Droves of panicked tourists fled as the Sphinx eased into the rhythm of a prance towards the towering tomb of its caretaker. It pawed gingerly at the base of Wer-Khafre, curling into a ball against the structure, wanting nothing more than to see its long-departed friend again.

Ethan Hedman is a speculative fiction writer from South Florida, the land of heat, humidity, and hurricanes. His work has been included in a variety of publications, including Gunsmoke & Dragonfire, Unrealpolitik, and The Hamthology. Ethan's full bibliography can be found on EthanHedman.com, his little corner of the Internet.

For Sparta
by L.P. Hernandez

Sometimes they survive.

They fall, twisted limbs breaking on the rocks, flesh torn to ribbons, gurgled cries dying in the ears of their departing mothers.

Sparta must be strong—they whisper to the Hunter's Moon.

Mother's footsteps crunch over autumn leaves. I wait for the cries to soften to a whimper, to nothing. Then I emerge, the light of the moon stinging my eyes, to claim my prize, its innards steaming. My stomach churns, mouth flooded at the prospect of pink flesh.

My scars sparkle with moonlight, gnarled fingers like tree roots seize the now still babe.

Sometimes they survive.

L.P. Hernandez is an author of horror and speculative fiction. His stories are featured in many collections, including Tavistock Galleria, Black Rainbow, and Monstronomicon. His work has also been adapted as audio productions on the NoSleep Podcast. He is an NYC Midnight Short Story Challenge Finalist and was awarded second place in the 2019 Writer's Digest Annual Writing Competition.
Website: www.lphernandez.com

O Great King of Asia
by D.J. Elton

Once strong, muscular, magnificent, he is now a withered, increasingly insignificant party, a guest in the palace of Babylon. This king, although outnumbered, never lost a battle.

He calls out in his sleep, remembering his home, Pella; his Persian nemesis, Darius; and his mother, Olympias, from whose womb he came, a thunderbolt.

I clean his body, as he now just sips water, before he vomits. The festive wine spiked with white hellebore and foul water from the River Styx. He cannot tolerate solids.

One eye like the dark night, the other like the blue sky. Alexander's heart is already dead. Adieu.

D.J. Elton is a writer living in Melbourne's west. As a child, she came from England to Australia, on the last boat down the Suez Canal, where she underwent a sacrificial dunking ritual in the court of King Neptune and has never looked back. She likes creating speculative microfiction and short stories, as well as random essays. Her work has been published in several anthologies, and she has written a historical fantasy novella, 'The Merlin Girl.' When not playing with a pen, she likes most of all to go to the green country.

Big, Deep Water
by Ralphie Graves

Boom! The percussive shockwave rippled over foggy waters.

Boom! Thirty-two oars sliced the sea, jetting the longship ever farther 'cross foamy waves. 'Twas a proud voyage, and several rowers grinned excitedly from their benches. This was their first time allowed along for raids—unbloodied, sweet summer boys venturing to be called men.

Their smiles died away with the drum as the Captain keened an ear; it sounded like something large swam aside. Two black, writhing tentacles crept upon the deck.

The men drew their swords, prepared to feast in Odin's hall. The boys paled as the cry took up.

"KRAKEN!"

*From within the depths of urban New Jersey comes the debut of a mind full of mystic and wonder; an enigma. Unconventional and with depth, **Ralphie Graves** writes "with the magic and curiosity unseen in a generation." Also known as the Car Ghost, their works have been referred to as "refreshingly simple" and "delightfully twisted." They are "an artist, and the mind is the canvas" and are mastered in several different styles and genres. The impression left will linger beyond a lifetime. Facebook: theofficialcarghost*

The Lost City
by Daniel Purcell

The gods descended and laid siege to the island—a just punishment.

The Atlas King fled the scourging waters that flooded the ivory city and battlements and waded towards the beach.

His bloodied iron fists beat the grimy and crimson sand in despair. It was awash with his army: once arrogant, now bloated corpses.

A vast shiver made the island tremble tumultuously and thick plumes of ash closed in. The Atlas King fell to his knees and choked violently.

Those left on the island mourned silently as the waves washed over. It became but a memory beyond the Pillars of Heracles.

Daniel Purcell lives with his girlfriend in Glasgow, Scotland. He studied English at the University of Liverpool -- where he was born. He has upcoming short-fiction being or already published with Farther Stars Than These, four Black Hare Press anthologies, 101 Words, a Rogue Planet Press anthology (Halloween 2020 edition), Eerie River Publishing ('The Beast in the Black Isle' in It Calls From The Forest Volume 2), Iron Faerie Publishing (FAERIE, HEXED, FAMINE and PLAGUE Anthologies), Unity Volume 1: A Magical Realism Anthology, Tritely Challenged Volume 2, and AntipodeanSF (November).

Lost Rituals
by Stuart Conover

Chi sighed and slipped off her sandals.

She smiled as the sun beat down.

Many of her kind had tried to flourish in the North but America was a fickle mistress.

Still, she had done well for herself.

Gods were no longer worshipped but Chicomecōātl found salvation in humanity's love of food.

It surpassed gluttony.

Each new meal an offering to her.

The worship was missing but she thrived.

So much that she hadn't taken a life in years.

That was about to change.

The rituals may not return.

But the sacrifices would.

Or she would take their lives directly.

Stuart Conover is a father, husband, rescue dog owner, published author, blogger, journalist, horror enthusiast, comic book geek, science fiction junkie, and IT professional. With all of that to cram in daily, we have no idea if or when he sleeps or how he gets writing done! (We suspect it has to do with having evil clones.) Stuart is a Chicago native and runs the author resource Horror Tree.

Death of Odysseus
by Mark Kodama

When Odysseus saw the raiders taking his cattle, he strapped on his armour and baldric and ran to the beach. The white-haired adventurer was the only man strong enough to bend his bow.

Odysseus charged the leader of the thieves, a giant covered in bronze. The old warrior hurled his ash spear, his adversary ducking from its flight. The grey-eyed goddess Athena whispered to Odysseus, "It's time." The giant thrust his stingray-tipped spear through Odysseus' heart above his breastplate.

Odysseus lay on his back, his life ebbing away. "Who are you?" he asked.

"Your son, Telegonus," the giant replied.

Mark Kodama is a trial attorney and former newspaper reporter who lives in Washington, D.C. with his wife and two sons. He is currently working on Las Vegas Tales, a work of philosophy, sugar-coated with metre and rhyme and told through stories. His stories and poems appear in Apocalypse, Blaze, Cadence, Unravel, Dragon Bone Soup, Enigma, Hate, Tall Tales and Short Stories, Gleam, Fireburst, Latin Anthology, Maelstrom, Pride, Tempest, and What Sort of Fuckery Is This? "Land of the Pharaohs" won Story of the Month at World of Myths and "The Summer Camp" will appear in the Best of Potato Soup Journal.
Facebook: xkodama
Amazon: amazon.com/-/e/B07Z2HHKR6

Ammar's Shekel
by Drew Starling

Ammar found a shekel in the Arabian sand. A rough, old shekel that depicted a hideous beast with four horns, jagged teeth, and a face from hell. His father warned him, "Lose that coin. It bears the mark of the demon Asag." But Ammar placed it on his dresser and slept.

In the night, Ammar saw large, white, glowing eyes in the corner of his room. The living form of Asag appeared. It smiled at Ammar. All night it stood, grinning, watching the terrified boy.

When Ammar's father came to wake him, the shekel was gone.

And so was his son.

Drew Starling *is an author of horror and dark fiction. His short stories have been published in over a dozen anthologies and his collaborative novel "Storming Area 51: Horror at the Gate" spent time ranked as Amazon's #1 Sci-Fi Anthology. His only rule of writing is the dog never dies.*
Website: *www.drewstarling.com*
Twitter: *@ScaryStarling*

The Excavation
by Amber M. Simpson

They'd been digging for weeks—hoping to find remnants of an ancient civilisation—when Becca's crew found something interesting: a small wooden chest, strange markings engraved on the lid.

Excited, Becca removed her gloves and touched it. Zapped as if by electricity, she was thrown across the pit. Black smoke billowed from the box, descending on her crewmates.

As their screams died out one by one, the dark form loomed over her, blotting out the sun. There was nothing she could do as it streamed into her mouth.

Becca's old body stood and stretched, its new resident ravenous for blood.

Amber M. Simpson is a dark fiction writer from northern Kentucky with a penchant for horror and fantasy. Her work has been published in multiple anthologies, as well as online. She assists with editing for Fantasia Divinity Magazine, where she's gotten to work with many talented authors from all over the world. While she loves to create dark worlds and diverse characters, her greatest creations of all are her sons, Max and Liam, who keep her feet on the ground even while her head is in the clouds.
Website: ambermsimpson.com
Facebook: authorambermsimpson

Tying Up Loose Ends
by Laurence Sullivan

Clotho ceased her labour, raising up her hands to see how skeletal they had become. "I can take no more of this, Sisters. There is simply too much to weave…"

"Too many lives," murmured Lachesis, nodding in agreement. "Perhaps it is time to end this project?"

"An apocalypse…?" Atropos' eyes widened in wonder. "Yes, yes, they've brought it on themselves."

Lachesis gathered up the countless threads from around the room, as her two sisters watched on in silence.

"Sever them, Sister," whispered Lachesis, holding the great bundle of thread aloft. "End human life on Earth."

Atropos raised her shears. "Gladly."

*Runner-up in the Wicked Young Writer Awards: Gregory Maguire Award, **Laurence Sullivan**'s creative writing has appeared in such places as Londonist, The List, NHK-World-Japan, Literary Orphans and Crack the Spine. He became inspired to start writing during his studies at the universities of Kent, Utrecht and Birmingham—after being saturated in all forms of literature from across the globe and enjoying every moment of it. He is currently pursuing a PhD at Northumbria University in the Medical Humanities, exploring literary portrayals of women's domestic medicine during the eighteenth century.*
Website: www.laurencesullivan.co.uk
Twitter: @LozzySullivan

Hindsight
by Paul Carberry

Epimetheus knew that this day would arrive, Prometheus previously warned him. He refused to listen; Zeus had delivered him the most delicate tribute. Pandora arrived, carrying an intricately designed jar. One day she would free the lid, unleashing the Evil which it contained. That moment had finally come. Pestilence rose like a fine mist from Pandora's box. Tiny insects buzzed from the opening, spreading disease and plague to humanity. This was the high price of fire. As he watched the demonic entity escape from the jar, he realised he should have refused the present from Zeus. Judgement made in hindsight.

Paul Carberry is the author of the Zombies on the Rock series. His tales of the zombie apocalypse in Newfoundland are inspired by George A. Romero's Living Dead series. He has also published several short stories over three "from the Rock" anthologies including "Halloween Mummers", "The Light of Cabot Tower", "Into the Forrest", and "Harmon Field". His Zombies on the Rock series currently has three novels, "Outbreak", "The Viking Trail", and "The Republic of Newfound" and is currently working on the fourth novel "Extinction". Most recently Paul has been accepted in Black Hare Press' Oceans Anthology. Paul is from Newfoundland and is currently living in Shearwater, Nova Scotia.

The Face of Hym
by Brandi Hicks

I navigate the catacombs easily; I'm sent so often. They're scared of Hym. I don't know why; He's decrepit, but they say don't look at Hym's face.

I saunter in. "Here you go," I sneer as I slide Hym the tray with gauntlets of blood. Such foolishness.

Hym's voice booms off the walls, "YOU are the foolish one, boy. You don't believe what they say? Maybe you need to be an example."

He steps into the light. I see Hym's face for the first time and the last. My heart seizes. I collapse as His laugh echoes in my ears.

*Growing up in West Virginia, **Brandi Hicks** loved to have her nose in a book, her eyes towards the night sky and putting a pen to paper. Her imagination was always sparked by her grandfather and her mom taking her to new places and teaching her about the unusual. She loves fantasy, sci-fi, and learning about science and history. She has two beautiful children and hopes to instil creativity and a love of reading in them. Finding new crafts to try keeps her busy when not playing with her kids or working.*

The End of a Culture
by Galina Trefil

The ocean fiercely, suddenly withdrew. The Minoans watched, transfixed by the exposed, flopping fish, sea snails, and octopuses. Curious onlookers came forward to investigate…and then came the wave—one hundred feet tall and fast as a roaring bull. There was no chance of escape.

On higher ground, a massive serpent slithered through the opium poppies in its bare-breasted priestess' hair. The powerful snake, long-worshipped on this island as an earth deity, did not sense that the tsunami would end its reign… But the priestess grimly understood that, with this wave, came the domination of new gods and the end of culture.

Galina Trefil *is a novelist specialising in women's, minority, and disabled rights. Her favourite genres are horror, thriller, and historical fiction. Her short stories and articles have appeared in Neurology Now, UnBound Emagazine, The Guardian, Tikkun, Romea.CZ, Jewcy, Jewrotica, Telegram Magazine, Ink Drift Magazine, The Dissident Voice, Open Road Review, and the anthologies "Flock: The Journey," "First Love," "Sea of Secrets," "Coffins and Dragons," "Organic Ink volume One," "Winds of Despair," "Waters of Destruction," "Curses & Cauldrons," "Unravel," "Hate," "Love," "Oceans," "Forgotten Ones," "Dark Valentine Holiday Horror Collection," and "Suspense Unimagined."*
Website: galinatrefil.wordpress.com
Facebook: Rabbi-Galina-Trefil-535886443115467

Attila
by Stephen Herczeg

Quintus glanced around the dirt floored tent that served as audience chamber for the great Attila the Hun. He was unimpressed.

"The Senate has requested your presence for peace talks in Rome," he said.

Attila studied him before approaching. He stared deep into the Legionnaire's eyes.

"You think me a barbarian, as do your countrymen."

Quintus banished his disdain.

"Not at all. Rome respects your, ah, authority."

Attila breathed deep, anger percolating. His sword flashed. Quintus' head bounced away.

"Send that as my answer. We will come. In force. They will never forget us," he said.

The assembled chieftains cheered.

Stephen Herczeg *is an IT geek based in Canberra, Australia. He has been writing for over twenty years and has completed a couple of dodgy novels, sixteen feature length screenplays, and numerous short stories and scripts. His horror work has featured in Sproutlings, Hells Bells, Below the Stairs, Trickster's Treats #1 and #2, Shades of Santa, Behind the Mask, Beyond the Infinite, The Body Horror Book, Anemone Enemy, Petrified Punks, and Beginnings. He has also had numerous Sherlock Holmes stories published through the Belanger Books—Sherlock Holmes anthologies.*

Amazon: amazon.com/-/e/B07916SQQS
Facebook: stephenherczegauthor

Sabra's Will
by Wendy Roberts

The fires surround the stone slab that Sabra lays on. Staring at the night sky, she takes another deep breath as the snake venom slows her heart. The priest chants as they place the goddess of the night's jewellery on her hands and around her neck. The final piece is the crown that she will adorn once Nephthys returns after two thousand years. They need her if they're going to survive this war and Sabra's more than willing to be the sacrifice. With one more dragging breath, her heart nearly stops and something burns through her body to finally take over.

*Writing short stories and novels started as a past time for **Wendy Roberts** and has now become a full-fledged passion. She posts short stories on her website and can be found most days on Twitter.*
Website: flippinscribbler.com
Twitter: @_WARoberts

Battle Cry
by A.R. Johnston

She flew above the battleground. Little did those that were on the brink of death knew that the crow circling above was a goddess.

She spiralled down to land on a spear that is sticking up out of the ground.

"Stay away from him, crow!" A voice wailed and a stone sails past her wing.

With a shiver of magic, the bird disappears and, before them, a woman appeared.

Goddess of War and Fate, the Phantom Queen.

"I beg forgiveness, Queen Morrigan," he cried.

"You should listen to the calling of the crow. It spoke of your death." She smiled.

A.R. Johnston is a small-town girl from Nova Scotia, Canada. She is known to write mostly urban fantasy, though she goes where the muses lead her and you never know where that may be. She is a lover of coffee, good tv shows, and horror flicks and a reader of good books. She pretends to be a writer when real life doesn't get in the way. Pesky full-time job and adulting!
Facebook: arjohnstonauthor
Website: arjohnstonauthor.wordpress.com

Requiem for a Dead Queen
by D.J. Elton

Our queen has left.

Music plays continuously for thirteen days. The royal quarters, grounds, and gardens are embedded with gentle wind-like whistles of tin flutes. Stringed instruments send melodies invoking strong memories of this elder lady, her grace. Songs, soft high-pitched howls that clean the air, finish the corporeal identity.

Those listening know this is a celebration, not a mourning time. The queen's earthly representation of fertility and abundance now passed prepares ground for her daughter.

"Hai! Kalima!" The chant spins new energy. There is a wild dance, the body burns, and sandalwood fills the air as the soul passes over.

D.J. Elton is a writer living in Melbourne's west. As a child, she came from England to Australia, on the last boat down the Suez Canal, where she underwent a sacrificial dunking ritual in the court of King Neptune and has never looked back. She likes creating speculative microfiction and short stories, as well as random essays. Her work has been published in several anthologies, and she has written a historical fantasy novella, 'The Merlin Girl.' When not playing with a pen, she likes most of all to go to the green country.

Tribute to Ba'al
by Raven Corinn Carluk

The crowd roared with praise as High Priest Tinalous and the young sacrifice mounted the dais. Never before had a prince been offered.

Tinalous bowed his head, turned to the boy, and smiled. "Worry not, young prince," he whispered. "If your father paid the tithe, you'll roll safely through the fire. Life in exile is better than feeding the bull."

With a wordless nod, the prince stepped onto the statue's hands and waited to be tipped into the god's mouth.

Tinalous gestured for the sacrifice to be made; he'd only know the ransom was paid when there were no screams.

Raven Corinn Carluk *writes dark fantasy, paranormal romance, and anything else that catches her interest. She's authored five novels, where she explores themes of love and acceptance. Her shorter pieces, usually from her darker side, can be found in Black Hare Press anthologies, at Detritus Online, and through Alban Lake Publishers.*
Twitter: @ravencorinn
Website: www.ravencorinncarluk.com

The Lost Land of Lyonesse
by Stacey Jaine McIntosh

Lyonesse. The once grand home of Tristan, the immortalised lover of Isolde. Thought now to lie beneath the waves. Lost to the ravages of time, its beauty will never fade. The church bells still toll for the ones who perished and made their graves at the bottom of the ocean.

As the tides recede, some tell the story of a rider on a white horse coming out of a forest that once dwelt at the heart of the great city. Others take no stock in fairy stories, refusing to believe there ever was a land as grand as Lyonesse.

Stacey Jaine McIntosh *was born in Perth, Western Australia, where she still resides with her husband and their four children. Although her first love has always been writing, she once toyed with being a cartographer and subsequently holds a Diploma in Spatial Information Services. Since 2011, she has had a vast number of stories and a few poems published online as well as in various anthologies. Stacey is also the author of "Solstice", "Morrighan", "Lost", and "Le Fay" and is currently working on several other projects simultaneously. When not with her family or writing, she enjoys reading, photography, genealogy, history, Arthurian myths, and witchcraft.*
Website: www.staceyjainemcintosh.com

Molk

by Kathleen Halecki

Inside the Carthaginian temple dedicated to Ba'al-Hammon, the bronze god's extended hands seem welcoming, but beneath the altar, the furnace radiates from the heat. The high priest carries the child—purchased from the poor and raised from birth to be given over as molk.

Hamilcar cannot bear any more misfortune. He prays to Ba'al-Hammon for forgiveness for not giving over his future infant as he once promised, but he has no second son to give.

When it is over the priest places the human and animal bones together, inscribing on the urn: "The god heard my voice and blessed me."

Kathleen Halecki possesses a BA and MA in history and a doctoral degree in interdisciplinary studies. Although born in New York, she currently resides in a seventeenth century home in New England. Her work can be found in The Copperfield Review; Shadows in Salem: Wicked Tales from the Witch City; One Night in Salem; Midnight Rising: A Collection of Paranormal Tales; From a Cat's View Volume II; and Shadow of Pendle. She has also drabbled before in Curses and Cauldrons and Forest of Fear.

The Triad of Heaven
by Kimberly Rei

The Word whispered over the skin of believers. They were marked with brands behind the left ear, melted into their skin, nearly invisible.

Across time, fewer heard, fewer were marked. Those who listened never faltered, worshipping as they had been taught. They raised an altar and brought forth struggling sacrifices. Incantations, precious to Enki, were spoken over pleading sobs. A wild wind rose, and Enlil embraced each offering, lifting them high, dashing them to the rocks, and sending them to An.

And thus, believers returned to modern lives as bankers, lawyers, doctors, and scientists. And thus, the Triad was appeased.

Kimberly Rei has been writing for as long as she can remember. At five years old, her parents gifted her with a set of Children's Classics that she had no hope of reading yet. The potential alone sparked a love of words that has never wavered. Kim has taught writing workshops and edited novels for authors you may recognise. She has published several short stories and now can't stop chasing paper dragons. She currently lives in Tampa Bay, Florida, with her wife and an abundance of gorgeous beaches to explore.

An Example
by Radar DeBoard

Anthotepp had been taught the spells of his

people. The ancient chants that had been passed

down through the generations of his culture. The words

that made sure the tomb remained intact and sealed.

Anthotepp could recite the chants backwards

and forwards. He had participated in all the rituals

long ago. The problem was that the rituals required people

to perform them. His people were all but gone now.

Now it was just him and the tomb. Anthotepp had

noticed the cracks forming. He knew the beast

patiently waited inside. It knew that soon enough it would

finally be free.

Radar DeBoard is a horror movie and novel enthusiast who resides in the small town of Goddard, Kansas. He occasionally dabbles in writing and enjoys making dark tales for people to enjoy. He has had drabbles and short stories published in various electronic magazines and anthologies.
Facebook: WriterRadarDeBoard

Camazotz
by David A.F. Brown

The villagers had an ideal shelter for my warriors—a large cave, naturally camouflaged by the jungle's foliage.

We slaughtered them, clubbing heads and slicing flesh until a bloodbath of men, women, and children adorned the settlement.

Approaching the cave's mouth, we noticed a giant slab of rock surrounded by headless skeletons and animal carcasses. Suddenly, an enormous man-like beast with wings and the head of a bat emerged from the darkness. It roared, took flight, and began clawing through my men.

As my head was being ripped from my body, I realised: This isn't their home, it's an altar.

David A.F. Brown is a Canadian author whose fiction has appeared in various anthologies, magazines and podcasts, including Tales to Terrify, Tell-Tale Press, The Sirens Call, Deep Fried Horror, Forgotten Ones, Forest of Fear: Volume 1, Love: Dark Drabbles #7 and Oceans: Dark Drabbles #9. He was a finalist in the NYC Midnight Short Story Challenge 2019, an international competition of over 4,500 writers. He holds a BA (Hons) from Western University and resides in Caledon, Ontario, with his wife and son.
Facebook: browndavidaf

The Huodou
by Patrick Winters

Huang awoke to the sound of his mother yelling his name. She rushed into his room, scooped him to her bosom, and sped out of their house, repeating one word in her great panic: *Fire.*

The street was crazed with more shouting, and flames blazed across the roofs and homes around the area, the whole of the eastern side of town already a raging inferno.

Against the reds and yellows, Huang saw a great blackness.

It towered over all who fled, rearing up like a dog and belching out the all-consuming flames.

The Huodou raged on, and Huang knew fear.

Patrick Winters is a graduate of Illinois College in Jacksonville, IL, where he earned a Bachelor of Arts degree in English Literature and Creative Writing and achieved membership into Sigma Tau Delta, an international English honours society. Winters is now a proud member of the Horror Writers Association, and his work has been published in the likes of Sanitarium Magazine, Deadman's Tome, Trysts of Fate, and other such titles. A full list of his previous publications may be found at his author's site.
Website: wintersauthor.azurewebsites.net/Publications/List

Forever Hunting in Arnhem Land
by Monica Schultz

Min-na-wee has been hunting since the early days—when the world was still fresh from the dreaming. Yet in all that time men have not changed. They still hold the power, deliver the judgment.

But so can Min-na-wee.

They call her cursed. Still Min-na-wee treasures her scales and powerful jaws. Jaws that deliver justice.

Min-na-wee watches her prey fishing in the shallow water. She's followed him for weeks. Seen the bruises blossom across his children's faces. No more.

She lunges. Jaws latch onto his legs, dragging him under. He screams, but Min-na-wee is without mercy.

Min-na-wee rolls, tearing him apart.

Monica Schultz is a full-time Mathematics and History teacher from Ipswich, Australia, with a passion for writing fantasy. When she isn't busy finding "x" in the latest equation, you can find her curled up with a young adult book and a cat on her lap.
Website: https://monicaschultzauthor.weebly.com/
Instagram: @monicaschultzauthor

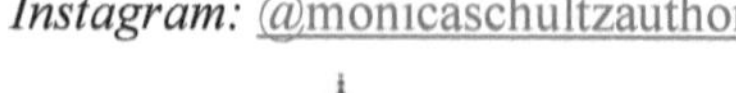

For Carthage
by David Green

Mago stood on the shores of Carthage, accompanied by his archers. Flaming braziers in front of each soldier.

Longboats approached. Men were returning, from battle in plague ridden lands. *No better place for a sickness to fester than a boat,* Mago thought grimly.

"In sixty seconds," he said to Gisgo, his second in command, "tell the archers to fire. Burn them all."

"But Sir," Gisgo replied, "those men fought for Carthage!"

"Now they'll die for her. Put any who make it to shore to the sword."

Mago walked away, unable to watch. He'd ordered his own son's death.

For Carthage.

David Green is a writer based in Co Galway, Ireland. Growing up between there and Manchester, UK meant David rarely saw sunlight in his childhood, which has no doubt had an effect on his dark writings. Published in places such as North West Words, The Devil Made Me Do It and Nymphs, David is aiming to release his debut novel in 2020.
Twitter: @David Green

Peerless
by Clint Foster

Green Dragon Crescent Blade swept through flesh and bones as though they were paper, and all who bravely stood before Guan Yu met the same end. Wielding the massive glaive with one hand and stroking his magnificent beard with the other, Liu Bei saw his brother ascend mortality upon the field of battle.

What his foes saw was something else entirely. Standing head and shoulders over each of them, his blows crushed their bodies and spirits alike. In the end, there were none left to fight, and the mewling cowards grovelled before the wrath of the God of War made flesh.

Clint Foster lives with his herd of four cats; beloved Basset, Zero; and wonderful wife, Nik. He loves to tell stories just as much as he loves to read them and is excited to share his work. A long-time consumer of media of all kinds, he enjoys giving back what he hopes everyone else thinks are good stories.
Facebook: ClintFosterAuthor

Knock on Wood
by G. Allen Wilbanks

Three women entered the woods to gather herbs and berries for the night's supper.

The first two women tapped their knuckles to the first tree they encountered and touched the silver Triquetra hanging at their throats, exclaiming, "We would ask thy protection, Esus."

When the third woman passed by the tree, one of her companions asked her, "Would ye not touch the tree?"

She shook her head. "Fairies and superstition. I have not the time for either. Nor should ye be so foolish."

The three walked on, unaware of the sprite in the branches above, claws extended, and teeth bared.

G. Allen Wilbanks *is a member of the Horror Writers Association (HWA) and has published over a hundred short stories in various magazines and online venues. He is the author of two short story collections and the novel "When Darkness Comes".*
Website: www.gallenwilbanks.com
Blog: DeepDarkThoughts.com

Xibalba
by Callum Pearce

A gust of hot, stale air rushed past the priest's face. Staggering back from the entrance to Hell, he wiped the moisture from his skin.

What decimated those Mayan cities didn't come from Hell itself. Instead it was the ancient parasites lifted by the earth's hot breath.

In the priest, they had found the perfect place to multiply and spread. So hungry were these monsters that had been trapped deep in the earth, they ate and multiplied then ate some more. The fluids that oozed from the disintegrating priest carried the parasite first to his flock and then farther abroad.

Callum Pearce is a Dutch storyteller, originally from Liverpool. He is a fiction writer published multiple times across variety of platforms. A Lover of the magical as well as the macabre. He lives in a foggy old fishing town in the Netherlands with his husband and a couple of cat shaped sprites. Popping up in lots of drabble collections and anthologies, he has also written factual articles. See the Amazon page for things that are available now.

Awaken the Kraken
by Wondra Vanian

He had slept since the children of Zeus abandoned mankind. All too soon, it seemed, shifting tectonic plates shook him awake again. He stretched groggily.

Thud.

A cylindrical object of honed metal struck one long tentacle. Tiny figures moved inside.

Humans?

Yes, humans had harmlessly taken to the seas in their silly wooden boats before but this…

Nap forgotten, he grabbed the cylinder and squeezed. Its destruction was rapid and satisfying—but the kraken wasn't finished. Shaking off millennia of sand, he pushed himself to the surface.

Humans had, it seemed, forgotten to fear the sea. He would remind them.

Wondra Vanian is an American living in the United Kingdom with her Welsh husband and their army of fur babies. A writer first, Wondra is also an avid gamer, photographer, cinephile, and blogger. She has music in her blood, sleeps with the lights on, and has been known to dance naked in the moonlight. Wondra was a multiple Top-Ten finisher in the 2017 and 2018 Preditors and Editors Reader's Poll, including the Best Author category. Her story, "Halloween Night," was named a Notable Contender for the Bristol Short Story Prize in 2015.
Website: www.wondravanian.com

A God's Choice
by Terri A. Arnold

I've roamed this earth for centuries. My name used to bring mere mortals to their knees in terror. In the twenty-first century, few remember my name, but they will.

The Fates no longer rule my life. They no longer tell me when time expires. I decide who deserves to come face to face with me. I choose who joins Hades in the underworld.

I've made my choice—I don't choose just one soul; I choose them all. It's time the gods take back what is ours; it's time we rule this planet again. My name is Thanatos; I choose annihilation.

Terri A. Arnold is an avid reader turned writer from a small town in Nova Scotia, who has spent her life reading and wishing she was writing. Although she has written a lot in those years, she has only recently begun to submit pieces for publication. With ongoing encouragement from family and writing challenges with friends, Terri felt the urge to try her hand at publishing.

In the Sky
by Eddie D. Moore

Mika rubbed his stained fingers together and laughed loudly as he admired his new cave painting. His closest friend, Tahoma, ran into the cave, slipped on the damp rock floor, and landed on his butt with an audible slap of skin against the stone. Mika doubled over holding his belly.

Tahoma pretended that he had intended to sit. "I came to see what is so funny." Still laughing, Mika pointed at the cave painting. "What did you paint in the sky above our hunt?"

"Can you imagine how long people will be asking that very question?" Mika's laughter grew maniacal.

Eddie D. Moore travels hundreds of hours a year, and he fills that time by listening to audiobooks. When he isn't playing with his grandchildren, he writes his own stories. You can find a list of his publications on his blog or by visiting his Amazon Author Page. While you're there, be sure to pick up a copy of his mini-anthology 'Misfits & Oddities'.
Website: eddiedmoore.wordpress.com
Amazon: amazon.com/author/eddiedmoore

Anasazi
by Joshua E. Borgmann

He had never noticed the pueblo on previous trips through the canyon, but he knew it immediately as a forgotten place of the enemy, Anasazi. His grandmother always said to avoid these places, but he often ignored his elders.

He found a rope leading up and climbed it. The place was grander than anything he'd ever seen before, a magnificent city carved out of the cliffside.

A whisper brought him into a dark room. Suddenly, countless dirty fingernails and sharp teeth were upon him. His screams fed these ancient enemies. They ate and then merely tossed aside his gnawed bones.

Joshua E. Borgmann holds degrees from Drake University, Iowa State University, and the University of South Carolina. He grew up on horror and science fiction and had long intended to become a great master of the art form before he was sucked into the bottomless pit of academia. He toils away his days as an English instructor at a small community college and dreams of being able to escape into a world of fantasy and terror where there are no student papers to grade. He and his wife reside in a nameless rural Iowa town surrounded by terrible cornfields where he is terrorised by several felines who have taken refuge in his home.

The Fomorians
by Stephen Herczeg

The Priestess consulted the three. They agreed; there was need for a sacrifice.

The ancient sea demons threatened us daily but were satiated by virginal blood. The clan chieftains drew together on midsummers eve every year. Ballots were drawn to decide which of the non-bled would be chosen.

I was named. My mother screamed.

Strong hands lashed me to the stone at the water's edge.

I was left alone. To wait.

In the darkening night, the bubbles appeared, followed by their slick skin and bulbous eyes.

It was their needle teeth that made me scream the loudest.

Stephen Herczeg is an IT geek based in Canberra, Australia. He has been writing for over twenty years and has completed a couple of dodgy novels, sixteen feature length screenplays, and numerous short stories and scripts. His horror work has featured in Sproutlings, Hells Bells, Below the Stairs, Trickster's Treats #1 and #2, Shades of Santa, Behind the Mask, Beyond the Infinite, The Body Horror Book, Anemone Enemy, Petrified Punks, and Beginnings. He has also had numerous Sherlock Holmes stories published through the Belanger Books—Sherlock Holmes anthologies.
Amazon: amazon.com/-/e/B07916SQQS
Facebook: stephenherczegauthor

The Writing on the Wall
by Jodi Jensen

"Takoda…"

Hearing her name whispered from deep inside the cave gave her a shudder. "Who's there?" She turned, shining her torch into the darkness. A single image wavered in the light.

Takoda stepped close and traced the ancient marks on the wall.

A severed head.

Gore dripping from the wound.

Weepy eyes.

A macabre jack-o-lantern grin.

She snatched her trembling fingers away. This particular drawing on a cave wall could only mean one thing…

Bodies buried here.

"Takoda…*friend to all*…help us."

She hesitated.

A creature lurched from the shadows, swallowing her screams as it carried her to the lower world.

Jodi Jensen, *author of time travel romances and speculative fiction short stories, grew up moving from California, to Massachusetts, and a few other places in between, before finally settling in Utah at the ripe old age of nine. The nomadic life fed her sense of adventure as a child and the wanderlust continues to this day. With a passion for old cemeteries, historical buildings, and sweeping sagas of days gone by, it was only natural she'd dream of time travelling to all the places that sparked her imagination.*
Twitter: @WritesJodi
Facebook: jodijensenwrites

Rites of Fire and Shadow
by Laila Amado

My face painted the colour of midnight, roots and herbs for the ritual in my basket, I step inside the circle of burning grass. Shadows dance across the disc of the Moon. Back at home, you lay in our bed—features pinched, hair plastered to the forehead, paler than the white linens—and the healer whispers that Mara, the merciful mistress of the dead, has laid her claim on you and there's nothing to be done. Wisps of fire singe the sky. I ask myself if I dare compete with the goddess, and the tarnished soil around me whispers, "Yes."

Laila Amado is currently marooned on a small island halfway between Africa and Europe. She writes dark fantasy and science fiction stories in her second language, lives in her fourth country, and cooks a decent paella. Her stories have appeared in 365 Tomorrows, 101 Fiction, Enchanted Conversation Magazine, Gyroscope Review, and other publications.
Twitter: @onbonbon7

Mistress of the Hearth
by Cecelia Hopkins-Drewer

Feni kissed her father goodbye. Cruel Hanish eyed her greedily, if he should succeed in bringing back the tusk of a mammoth, she would be given to him as wife.

She was a woman of the sea people, strong, brave and capable of managing her own yurt. Feni had no intention of being given to a man who would surely treat her badly.

The warriors used the product of a certain plant to poison their weapons. No one takes any notice of Feni foraging. She cooks a "welcome home" meal and kneels before Hanish, returning triumphant.

"My Lord, your food."

Cecelia Hopkins-Drewer *lives in Adelaide, South Australia. She has written a Masters paper on H.P. Lovecraft, and her weird poetry has been published in The Mentor (edited by Ron Clarke) and Spectral Realms (edited by S.T. Joshi). Her novels include a teenage vampire series commencing with Mystic Evermore. Short stories have been published in Worlds, Angels & Monsters, Beyond, Storming Area 51, and Unravel (Dark Drabbles anthologies edited by Dean Kershaw).*
Amazon: amazon.com/Cecelia-Hopkins-Drewer/e/B071G968NM
Website: chopkin39.wixsite.com/website

A Perfect Likeness
by Kelly Matsuura

"You're making the maiden figurines for Emperor Nintoku's tomb?" Koichi asked.

"Yes. I've finished several."

Koichi approved. "Excellent. Please make one of Priestess Chizue, too."

"Of course."

I began Chizue's haniwa figurine, starting with the usual cylindrical form. But I couldn't help infusing the artwork with my secret love for the pretty shamaness.

The final likeness was *too* perfect—when Chizue stood before it she cried out, reciting a frantic protection prayer.

Alas, her soul was pulled from her living body and into the funerary vessel. All I could do was use my tears to wipe the still-drying clay smooth.

Kelly Matsuura writes diverse YA, fantasy, and literary fiction. She is the Creator of The Insignia Series' anthologies (Asian fantasy themed) and has had stories published with Ink & Locket Press, A Murder of Storytellers, Crushing Hearts & Black Butterfly, and many more. Kelly lives in Nagoya, Japan, with her geeky husband. She loves travelling, knitting, cooking, and of course, reading.
Website: www.blackwingsandwhitepaper.com

Boating Lake
by Stephen Christie

"Fourth place!" hissed the coxswain of the dragon boat.

The crew sat in silence. Around them, the other teams prayed.

"How could you do this to me? You've made a fool of me…"

As Lake Baikal became unsettled, the other teams started rowing towards land.

"…I didn't come here for you to lose…"

The water parted as slick black scales emerged.

"…I came to win…"

"I am Ao Shun!" The dragon's voice boomed across the lake. "This contest is in my honour, human, not your glory."

Ao Shun returned to the depths, taking the lone dragon boat with him.

*A lifelong bookworm, cinephile, and wine connoisseur, **Stephen Christie** has decided to lay off the drink and try his hand at a little creative writing of his own. A fan of horror, science fiction, military fiction, and historical fiction, he hopes his years of enjoying a collection of great books will aid him in this new endeavour.*

God Agreed
by Eddie D. Moore

The giant Erzo hadn't planned on killing humans today. His human mother would've been disappointed. His angelic father, however, cheered him on in his mind as he smashed skulls and ripped off arms and legs. Humans were God's mistake. They all had to be exterminated.

With a defiant roar at the heavens, Erzo swung his sword and cut six of the puny creatures in half. Pride swelled in his chest when his kinsman answered his war cry with a deafening shout that shook the ground, but fear seized him when the ground cracked, and the waters came for them all.

Eddie D. Moore travels hundreds of hours a year, and he fills that time by listening to audiobooks. When he isn't playing with his grandchildren, he writes his own stories. You can find a list of his publications on his blog or by visiting his Amazon Author Page. While you're there, be sure to pick up a copy of his mini-anthology Misfits & Oddities.
Website: eddiedmoore.wordpress.com
Amazon: amazon.com/author/eddiedmoore

The Ocean Will Return
by Ximena Escobar

Strong as the 1960 tsunami, the irrepressible force of ancestral tradition failed to save the boy. But the men, acting at its behest, did so "without free will." Arms and legs removed, they'd stuck him like a stake in the sand, watching the tide take him to *Kai-Kai*.

Oesophagus of the sea, the serpent digested him.

Calmness returned to *Araucanía* but, still asleep in the far depths, *Kai-Kai* dreams of ancient battles against his rival. Echoes of the Earth Serpent's roar, and memories of her hot rock anatomy, stir his incontrollable urge for destruction.

The last of ever-sparser sacrifices, *Kai-Kai* wakes.

Ximena Escobar is writing stories and poetry. Originally from Chile, she is the author of a translation into Spanish of the Broadway Musical "The Wizard of Oz" and of an original adaptation of the same, "Navidad en Oz", both produced in her home country. Since 2018 she has published several short stories in various anthologies and online platforms and is now slowly working on her own collection. Ximena has a degree in Arts & Communication Science and lives in Nottingham with her family.
Facebook: Ximenautora
Twitter: @laximenin

The New Children of Ostara
by Joachim Heijndermans

The men of the faces stand on guard, their eye to the seas. The children await the coming of the white men on their great wooden ships. Our new mother, Ostara of flowers, sits on one of the men. She sings songs in her old tongue. This land, the land of our ancestors and the stone men of the faces, is now in her name and the day that carries it as well.

Of all the things the white men brought to us, she and her songs we love.

Although the rabbit with the coloured eggs is still strange though.

Joachim Heijndermans writes, draws, and paints nearly every waking hour. Originally from The Netherlands, he's been all over the world, boring people by spouting random trivia. His work has been featured in a number of anthologies and publications, such as Mad Scientist Journal, Asymmetry Fiction, Hinnom Magazine, Ahoy Comics' Edgar Allan Poe's Snifter of Terror, Metaphorosis, and The Gallery of Curiosities, and he's currently in the midst of completing his first children's book.
Website: www.joachimheijndermans.com
Twitter: @jheijndermans

The Carthaginian Package
by Alistair Crowe

The Carthaginian merchant pulled his cloak and meagre goods tight before departing the ship. His slow, limped gait let him watch Greek soldiers and irregulars pull the rich aside to search them before they entered Thessaloniki.

He shuffled away from the dock, pausing once to look back across Thermaikos Gulf at Mt Olympus. It would be a long, arduous walk.

As he sought food and shelter for the night, he touched the horns under his hood and smiled. The Gods of Greece assumed he would travel as a God. Ba'al had arrived undetected, but soon all would know his name.

Alistair Crowe, like all humans, was born from the darkness of the womb into the world. Unlike most, he returned to the darkness. As such he has written multiple articles credited as staff, acted on television (uncredited), and worked in radio where he was credited, but it was the overnight shift so no one listened to him. He decided to step from behind the scenes and publish, which allows him to write in solitude, yet remain behind the scenes. The aim of his writing is to enlighten, frighten, horrify and entertain in equal measure.
Facebook: CroweAlistair

Trial and Error
by K.B. Elijah

When Odysseus stepped onto the blood-stained sands of Troy, he felt a compelling sense of déjà vu.

When he watched Achilles die a torturous death, he knew how it would end.

When he smelt the burning bodies of city's people, he remembered that stench. Saw that child skewered by a sword, again and again.

He'd been here before. Many, many times.

The gods were playing with time, their immortal hands resetting history to find the timeline in which the great civilisation of Troy would fall. But the city was stubborn and proud. It took 190 attempts.

190 rivers of blood.

K.B. Elijah is a fantasy author living in Brisbane, Australia, with her husband and three cockatiels. A lawyer by day, and a writer by... also day, because she needs her solid nine hours of sleep per night (not that the cockatiels let her sleep past 6am). K.B. writes for various international anthologies, and her work features in dozens of collections about the mysterious, the magical, and the macabre. Her own books of short fantasy novellas with twists, *The Empty Sky* and *Out of the Nowhere,* are available on paperback and Kindle now.
Website: *www.kbelijah.com*
Instagram: *k.b.elijah*

The Moulded
by Thomas Sturgeon Jr.

I moulded mankind with my hands. I looked at the beauty of my creations with ease. Only to find out that my creations wanted to rebel against me. As I assaulted civilisations with my power, men trembled at hearing my name. For what is made can also be unmade. Bringing death along with it.

Along came war upon your lands. As the other Gods laughed at my dismay. There was a war being fought in Olympus for those which I had made. I stood by and watched as there are new rules.

For I am Prometheus. There are consequences now.

Thomas Sturgeon Jr. began writing at 13 years old. He loves to read and spend time with his family and friends. He loves horror movies and fiction. He currently lives in Chatsworth, Georgia, and wants more out of life. He's been published before in Weird Mask magazine and by Deadman's Tome. His short stories that were published were "The Dead City" and "Disturbed Valentine". He currently is at work on a horror short story collection and he is loved by his family and friends. Despite being told by his teachers that he would never be published, he has proved them wrong.

Ancients Reborn
by R.A. Goli

I can't remember when it started. They were supposed to be our protectors, but the grotesque statues betrayed us. Jagged teeth and claws like knives, they tore apart flesh and feasted on our meat. Nothing was off the menu.

The Gargoyles remained where they were resurrected. Perched and waiting. Smart people escaped the city early. It's what I should have done. There were no old Gothic buildings in small farming towns.

I looked at my cat, as starved as I was. Should I eat his puny body to help me live another day? Or should I let him eat mine?

R.A. Goli *is an Australian writer of horror, fantasy, and speculative short stories. In addition to writing, her interests include reading, gaming, the occasional walk, and annoying her dog, two cats, and husband. You can check out her numerous publications including her fantasy novella "The Eighth Dwarf" and her collection of short stories "Unfettered" on her website and sign up to her newsletter for free short stories, updates, and other fun stuff.*
Website: ragoliauthor.wordpress.com/
Facebook: RAGoliAuthor

Prophecy
by David Wright

Countless numbers vomit blood; tumours ravish their flesh. Mountains explode; fire and ash wound the sky. Hundreds of men crawl through mud, scythed like wheat, as beady-eyed rats gnaw on the abandoned bodies. Animals of metal rain destruction from open bellies. Creatures starved, beaten, barely recognisable as human, faces sunken, eyes bright, collapse clawing at their throats. Corpses in a mass grave. Cities burned in the blink of an eye. The oceans poisoned. The air toxic. So much death, like a shroud across the world.

The Oracle of Delphi claws out her eyes, screaming at the horrors yet to come…

__David Wright__ was once young and carefree. Once...

And Time Stood Still
by Rowanne S. Carberry

Chronus stepped onto the earth. Time stood still.

No tomorrow, no yesterday. Only now.

Gone is his seed that grew the land. Plastered over with concrete. The air polluted. Fumes seep out of every pour.

His offspring no longer interested in their community but glued to the devices in front of them.

"This will not do," Chronus cries.

"I made this Earth and I can remake it."

Stomping his feet, the ground shakes. Buildings crumble.

People decay.

Seconds pass for Chronus as a millennium passes on Earth.

He lays down a silver egg.

Time starts again, giving Earth another chance.

Rowanne S. Carberry *was born in England in 1990, where she stills lives now with her cat Wolverine. Rowanne has always loved writing, and her first poem was published at the age of 15, but her ambition has always been to help people. Rowanne studied at the University of Sunderland where she completed combined honours of Psychology with Drama. Rowanne writes to offer others an escape. Although Rowanne writes in varied genres, each story or poem she writes will often have a darkness to it, which helped coin her brand, Poisoned Quill Writing— Wicked words from a poisoned quill.*
Facebook: PoisonedQuillWriting
Instagram: @poisoned_quill_writing

By Tooth and Claw
by G. Allen Wilbanks

His people, his precious Aztecs, died by the thousands as the soldiers from Spain held siege upon their land. Xiuhtecuhtli could not save them. Hunger and disease cannot be defeated by tooth and claw. As his worshippers weakened, so too did the Fire God.

Xiuhtecuhtli roared his defiance, even as he retreated into the liquid rock. He would hide. He would sleep and wait. Wait for the soldiers to leave and allow his followers that survived to grow strong again.

When they were ready, he would awaken and rejoin them. He was confident, it would not take long.

G. Allen Wilbanks is a member of the Horror Writers Association (HWA) and has published over a hundred short stories in various magazines and online venues. He is the author of two short story collections and the novel "When Darkness Comes".
Website: www.gallenwilbanks.com
Blog: DeepDarkThoughts.com

Taller than the Linchpin
by Lynne Phillips

The defeated Tartar leader knew his fate, yet he returned cold face to Genghis Khan.

"Your people will be mine," Genghis gloated. His thin-bladed sword whipped through the air with little effort. The Tartar's severed head fell among the blood and guts in the dust and was trampled into the ground by the heavy carts as they rolled forward.

The defeated Tartars hid their fear and stood straight.

"You are too arrogant," Genghis told them. "Walk beside the carts. We will see who walks proudly." Those Tartars taller than the linchpin in the centre of the hub were instantly beheaded.

Lynne Phillips, a retired teacher, lives in the beautiful Northern Rivers Region of New South Wales, Australia. Her stories, across all genres, have been published in anthologies and various online magazines. Her priority is spending time with her family. Her passions are reading, writing, and keeping fit.

The Thirteenth Skull
by Sue Marie St. Lee

"Grandfather,"—Colel's concern pitched her voice higher than normal—"the people are trying to activate the knowledge. Legend says that at midnight the enlightenment begins."

"The legend will not be fulfilled tonight."

"But it is prophesied—December 21, 2012—all thirteen crystal skulls will create a global grid. Mankind will be spiritually transformed with knowledge from the ancients."

"Mankind has not evolved as expected. He cannot be trusted with such knowledge." Grandfather wrapped the thirteenth skull in a black cloth and placed it in the strongbox within the candle-lit cave.

"A new era of darkness begins at midnight. It is written."

*Born in Chicago, **Sue Marie St. Lee** currently lives in Oklahoma with her husband and Manx cat. A storyteller since learning to talk, her wild imagination caused reprimands from her mother. Her imagination persevered. Retired from Finance Management, Sue began ghostwriting until 2019, choosing to have works published internationally, in print and online, under her own name. Black Hare Press, Fantasia Divinity, and Spillwords Press are some of the publishers to feature Sue's work to date.*
Blog: suemariestlee.home.blog
Amazon: amazon.com/Sue-Marie-St.-Lee/e/B07WJFRF1L

The King of Sumer
by Cecelia Hopkins-Drewer

The collar chafed his neck. Forced to trudge along behind the chariot, King Lugal choked on dust and stumbled through horse droppings.

Until the battle, Lugal had been the statesman who brought the people of Sumer together and established a unified government. He fervently wished he had executed Sargon upon arrival in Uruk, as requested by his friend, the King of Kish.

Born of a forbidden liaison between gardener and priestess, the madman dreamed of the goddess. Sargon acknowledged no obligation, no loyalty, and now showed no mercy.

The chariot stopped. Lugal fell prostrate. The spiked club crushed his head.

Cecelia Hopkins-Drewer lives in Adelaide, South Australia. She has written a Masters paper on H.P. Lovecraft, and her weird poetry has been published in The Mentor (edited by Ron Clarke) and Spectral Realms (edited by S.T. Joshi). Her novels include a teenage vampire series commencing with Mystic Evermore. Short stories have been published in Worlds, Angels & Monsters, Beyond, Storming Area 51, and Unravel (Dark Drabbles anthologies edited by Dean Kershaw).
Amazon: amazon.com/Cecelia-Hopkins-Drewer/e/B071G968NM
Website: chopkin39.wixsite.com/website

Paradise
by Chris Bannor

They watched empires rise and fall, one after another. They watched civilisations form and reform and fall into darkness, only to light the way for future generations. Those generations belied the hope they spoke though. The Ancients knew they could no longer watch from afar.

Degradation and segregation, disease and despair. The world they hoped would follow in their wake had turned self-serving and cruel, driven by greed and politics.

The destruction humans wrought on the environment made the next flood easier than the last. This time the Ancients learned their lesson. They left no humans to taint their paradise.

Chris Bannor is a science fiction and fantasy writer who lives in Southern California. Chris learned her love of genre stories from her mother at an early age and has never veered far from that path. She also enjoys musical theatre and roadtrips with her family but is a general homebody otherwise.
Facebook: chrisbannorauthor
Website: ChrisBannor.com

A Job Well Done
by K.B. Elijah

Mama cheers with the rest when the torches are pressed to the statue's feet, but from my position I can see her wince. She spent weeks on this wicker man, threading and weaving sticks to make the giant monument incredibly lifelike, yet the fire will destroy it in minutes.

"Praise the gods," the Druid booms out beside Mama. She beams.

I'm proud of her. It's an impressive creation.

But I also wish she had slacked off for once, left a few gaps in the structure.

For as the flames consume the statue, they also devour those of us trapped inside.

K.B. Elijah *is a fantasy author living in Brisbane, Australia, with her husband and three cockatiels. A lawyer by day and a writer by... also day, because she needs her solid nine hours of sleep per night (not that the cockatiels let her sleep past 6am). K.B. writes for various international anthologies, and her work features in dozens of collections about the mysterious, the magical, and the macabre. Her own books of short fantasy novellas with twists, The Empty Sky and Out of the Nowhere, are available on paperback and Kindle now.*
Website: www.kbelijah.com
Instagram: k.b.elijah

Nightmarish Encounter
by Thomas Baker

Omar tossed and turned until horrific nightmares startled him awake. He awoke with an unbearable weight on him and the feeling that his hair was being twisted and pulled. He looked up in terror to find a mare sitting upon his chest. He struggled to move; he felt as though his entire body was pinned to the ground as fear consumed him. Omar trembled as a mixture of sweat and tears streamed down his cheeks. The creature stood with a snarling smile atop him. It began pressing down on his head until it collapsed under the intense pressure, killing him.

Thomas Baker is a lover of all things horror with a heavy emphasis on zombies, paranormal, and things of the slasher variety! He aims to keep his writing fast paced and fun. Thomas has several stories featured in different anthologies, but he is best known for his co-written "Outbreak Series" with his good friend and writing partner Robert Wagner. The series has reached trilogy status! You can follow him on his 6K Press page on both Facebook and Twitter to stay up to date on the latest shenanigans that are afoot! Be warned, some parental advisory required!

A Drop-Dead Winner
by Sue Marie St. Lee

Rufus secured leather reins tightly around Titus' chest ensuring the horses react to his body's tilt. After this twenty-fourth win, he would retire wealthy, the most famous charioteer in Roman history.

Sergius, consistent second-place winner, intended to thwart Titus' win.

First lap halfway complete, Sergius snapped his whip at Titus and his horses. Titus fell limp; his horses stampeded through the crowd until dropping dead.

Six laps later, Sergius walked to the winner's platform until tripping over his whip, the poison-laced popper gouged his leg. Sergius dropped dead holding the first prize, an olive oil flask—antidote for Lejasoutoxin.

*Born in Chicago, **Sue Marie St. Lee** currently lives in Oklahoma with her husband and Manx cat. A storyteller since learning to talk, her wild imagination caused reprimands from her mother. Her imagination persevered. Retired from Finance Management, Sue began ghostwriting until 2019, choosing to have works published internationally, in print and online, under her own name. Black Hare Press, Fantasia Divinity, and Spillwords Press are some of the publishers to feature Sue's work to date.*
Blog: suemariestlee.home.blog
Amazon: amazon.com/Sue-Marie-St.-Lee/e/B07WJFRF1L

That Petrifying Gaze
by Stephen Herczeg

Perseus.

I'd spit on him if I could.

I can see him standing there. Proud as punch with his mother Danae fussing over him.

He should be dead, or at least petrified stone.

That was the King's plan. Send the boy on a fool's quest to kill the gorgon Medusa, knowing that anyone on such a quest would surely die.

Damn it if he didn't succeed.

Returning to Seriphus, he confronted us all with Medusa's head.

I was too slow. That petrifying gaze turned me to stone.

I'm not dead. I can't move. I can't scream.

I can only see.

Stephen Herczeg *is an IT geek based in Canberra, Australia. He has been writing for over twenty years and has completed a couple of dodgy novels, sixteen feature length screenplays and numerous short stories and scripts. His horror work has featured in Sproutlings, Hells Bells, Below the Stairs, Trickster's Treats #1 and #2, Shades of Santa, Behind the Mask, Beyond the Infinite, The Body Horror Book, Anemone Enemy, Petrified Punks, and Beginnings. He has also had numerous Sherlock Holmes stories published through the Belanger Books—Sherlock Holmes anthologies.*
Amazon: amazon.com/-/e/B07916SQQS
Facebook: stephenherczegauthor

Drew Hid
by Steven Holding

Guitar gods stalk stages, deejays frenzied sets in tents; the assembled masses frantic thrashing resembles a more ancient gathering.

Wandering amongst revellers and ravers, hellbent upon a weekend bender, he marvels at the makeshift city erected for such festivities.

He knows his history, how the earth beneath his feet was sacred to the Druids. He can feel their energy still, tiny traces of magic that remain in the ley lines and stone circle.

Faces flicker, hollering and screaming, as the wicker man bursts into flames.

But only he seems to hear the anguished cry of the infant child he stashed inside.

Steven Holding lives with his family in the United Kingdom. His stories have appeared both online and in print. Most recently his work has featured in the collections 'TREMBLING WITH FEAR YEAR TWO', 'SPLASH OF INK', and the anthologies 'MONSTERS', 'BEYOND' and 'DARK MOMENTS - YEAR ONE' from Black Hare Press. He is currently working upon further short fiction and a novel. Website: www.stevenholding.co.uk

Osiris Lay Dying
by Umair Mirxa

Osiris coughed and leaned against his son Horus as they looked out the window. Alexandria burned before them in the wake of Roman legions marching through the ancient streets.

"They will pay for what they have wrought," growled Horus, helping Osiris back into bed. "This, I swear to you, father."

"No, son," said Isis, stepping into the room. "I fear Egypt's time is past. The Age of Rome begins now."

"We cannot—"

"Yet, we must."

Isis let escape a heavy sigh and watched, with tears in her eyes, the Great Library crumble even as Osiris lay dying behind her.

Umair Mirxa lives and writes in Karachi, Pakistan. His first published story "Awareness" appeared on Spillwords Press. He has since had stories accepted for publication in anthologies from Zombie Pirate Publishing, Blood Song Books, Black Hare Press, Iron Faerie Publishing, Clarendon House Publications, Fantasia Divinity Magazine & Publishing, and The ReAnimated Writers Press. He is a massive J.R.R. Tolkien fan, loves everything to do with mythology, fantasy, and history, and wishes with all his heart that dragons were real. When he's not writing, he enjoys reading novels and comic books, playing video games, listening to music, and watching movies, TV shows, and football as an Arsenal FC fan.
Website: umairmirxa.com

Before Punishment
by Joshua E. Borgmann

My brother was dead.

It was the outcast's fault.

I found him alone draining a horn of mead.

"Loki, you will pay."

He grinned. "Thor, what do I owe?"

My hammer was fast, but the weasel morphed into an iron statue absorbing my blow.

"You are upset about Balder?"

He was in Asgardian disguise again. I swung, connected, and he fell laughing.

"It's your fault."

I brought the hammer down again.

His face was covered in blood, yet he still grinned.

"Not me. The mistletoe."

"You lie," I said.

Barred from killing him, I left him bleeding on the floor.

Joshua E. Borgmann *holds degrees from Drake University, Iowa State University, and the University of South Carolina. He grew up on horror and science fiction and had long intended to become a great master of the art form before he was sucked into the bottomless pit of academia. He toils away his days as an English instructor at a small community college and dreams of being able to escape into a world of fantasy and terror where there are no student papers to grade. He and his wife reside in a nameless rural Iowa town surrounded by terrible cornfields where he is terrorised by several felines who have taken refuge in his home.*

The Homeless Goddess
by Galina Trefil

"You destroyed my city!" shrieked Venus Pompeiana, patron goddess of what was now only pitiful buried rubble. After eighteen hours of vomiting ash and pyroclastic surges, Vesuvius lay smug and sated. "Monster, you boiled the brains of my devotees!"

"Pipe down," Campi Flegrei, a larger volcano nearby, huffed. "Pompeii's loss is nothing. When I exploded 40,000 years ago, I made cavemen extinct all over Europe and Asia."

"No one remembers that ugly, ill-formed cavemen's disappearance," Vesuvius snapped defensively. "But everyone will remember this. I win!"

The now-homeless deity sobbed, beating her fists against them both. Their competition was her undoing.

Galina Trefil *is a novelist specialising in women's, minority, and disabled rights. Her favourite genres are horror, thriller, and historical fiction. Her short stories and articles have appeared in Neurology Now, UnBound Emagazine, The Guardian, Tikkun, Romea.CZ, Jewcy, Jewrotica, Telegram Magazine, Ink Drift Magazine, The Dissident Voice, Open Road Review, and the anthologies "Flock: The Journey," "First Love," "Sea of Secrets," "Coffins and Dragons," "Organic Ink volume One," "Winds of Despair," "Waters of Destruction," "Curses & Cauldrons," "Unravel," "Hate," "Love," "Oceans," "Forgotten Ones," "Dark Valentine Holiday Horror Collection," and "Suspense Unimagined."*
Website: galinatrefil.wordpress.com
Facebook: Rabbi-Galina-Trefil-535886443115467

Four Ahau, Three Kankin
by Paul Carberry

The explorer and his crew hung precariously over a towering mound of kindling. Suspended above the ground, hogtied by their arms and legs to a log by the Mayan savages. A diabolic chant enveloped the bluff. Foreign tongue demonically chanted *"Four Ahau, three Kankin"* as they prepared their sacrificial offering. An undertaking to appease the Gods and resolve the fifth cycle. Wood crackled and split as the fires spread. Intense heat rose, blistering his rear; anguished cries of terror drowned out by the sinister chant. Flames hungrily caressed his backside with greed. Doomsday would have to wait, the fire wouldn't.

Paul Carberry is the author of the Zombies on the Rock series. His tales of the zombie apocalypse in Newfoundland are inspired by George A. Romero's Living Dead series. He has also published several short stories over three "from the Rock" anthologies including "Halloween Mummers", "The Light of Cabot Tower", "Into the Forrest", and "Harmon Field". His Zombies on the Rock series currently has three novels, "Outbreak", "The Viking Trail", and "The Republic of Newfound" and is currently working on the fourth novel "Extinction". Most recently Paul has been accepted in Black Hare Press' Oceans Anthology. Paul is from Newfoundland and is currently living in Shearwater, Nova Scotia.

Asakku
by Kathleen Halecki

From the west, Asakku rolls over the earth like a storm. The waters have risen in the fields and the city is swirling in hot winds dampening the skin.

The buzzing of wings drives some to madness, and the people are weak as they burn with extreme fever. Holding their hands to their heads as they pray; their cracked lips move silently, begging Ninurta to defeat the Asakku demon who moves from house to house leaving those inside groaning in pain.

The priests have gathered in the temple while the king bemoans the evil fate that has befallen his empire.

Kathleen Halecki possesses a BA and MA in history and a doctoral degree in interdisciplinary studies. Although born in New York, she currently resides in a seventeenth century home in New England. Her work can be found in The Copperfield Review; Shadows in Salem: Wicked Tales from the Witch City; One Night in Salem; Midnight Rising: A Collection of Paranormal Tales; From a Cat's View Volume II; and Shadow of Pendle. She has also drabbled before in Curses and Cauldrons and Forest of Fear.

The Opening of the Mouth
by Matthew M. Montelione

City of Amun, Egypt. 595 BC.

At the rocky tomb's entrance, the priests raised the mummy of King Necho II in an upright position in the sand. The mummy's gold mask reflected the deep pink light of dusk over the hot desert.

Low-ranking priests cleansed the freshly wrapped mummy with water and incense, then slaughtered an ox and presented its severed foreleg to the dead king's face.

The *sem* priest, draped in leopard skin, spoke ancient words and touched an instrument to the *ka* statue and the mouth of the corpse.

The mummy suddenly exhaled, reaching for the horrified priests.

Matthew M. Montelione is a horror writer born and raised on Long Island in New York. His work has been published in many titles, including MONSTERS: A Horror Microfiction Anthology and Quoth the Raven: A Contemporary Reimagining of the Works of Edgar Allan Poe. Matthew lives with his wife in New York.
Website: maybeevils.com
Facebook: maybeevils

People of the Club and Spear
by Joshua E. Borgmann

Those few who survived the wrath of Tezcatlipoca buried themselves deep under the pyramids of Teotihuacan. Even after the city fell, they hibernated beneath the ruins, waiting. The world grew warm, the great ice melted, seas rose, and great fires spread.

Once again Teotihuacan fell; this time into the great fissures from which the Quinametzin arose. Resembling giant devils standing sixty feet tall, they shook the earth as they crossed burning forests to fall upon the human's cities.

They built thrones from the bones of slaughtered humanity, and now, we serve under the shadow of their clubs and onyx spears.

Joshua E. Borgmann *holds degrees from Drake University, Iowa State University, and the University of South Carolina. He grew up on horror and science fiction and had long intended to become a great master of the art form before he was sucked into the bottomless pit of academia. He toils away his days as an English instructor at a small community college and dreams of being able to escape into a world of fantasy and terror where there are no student papers to grade. He and his wife reside in a nameless rural Iowa town surrounded by terrible cornfields where he is terrorised by several felines who have taken refuge in his home.*

Seppuku in Shizuoka
by Umair Mirxa

Sayumi turned from the doorway, for she knew well her husband would never again walk through it. A tear drop rolled off her cheek and splashed onto the *kaiken* in her lap.

The rope binding her knees together now secure, she lifted the blade and wiped it dry with one delicate finger. No longer would it so caress her beloved's cheek.

Hoofbeats on the path.

Soon, they would arrive. The corrupt daimyo's men, murderers of her husband. Her sons. They would not take her alive.

"I love you, Ryōichi-san," whispered Sayumi and ran the *kaiken* gently across her neck.

Umair Mirxa lives and writes in Karachi, Pakistan. His first published story, 'Awareness', appeared on Spillwords Press. He has since had stories accepted for publication in anthologies from Zombie Pirate Publishing, Blood Song Books, Black Hare Press, Iron Faerie Publishing, Clarendon House Publications, Fantasia Divinity Magazine & Publishing, and The ReAnimated Writers Press. He is a massive J.R.R. Tolkien fan; loves everything to do with mythology, fantasy, and history; and wishes with all his heart that dragons were real. When he's not writing, he enjoys reading novels and comic books, playing video games, listening to music, and watching movies, TV shows, and football as an Arsenal FC fan. Website: umairmirxa.com

One Last Mead before the Show
by Stuart Conover

Walking in, he was the only patron at the bar.

With things what they were, no one was going out.

Politics, plagues, revolutions, the world was in chaos.

Everything was just so…mischievous.

"What'll it be?" the bartender absentmindedly asked, staring at the news.

The world was rife with chaos.

"A mead, my good sir."

He sipped it slowly.

It felt like centuries since he last tasted real mead.

This poor substitute would suffice.

He bursts into laughter.

"What's so funny?"

Loki continued to laugh.

The world burned and the show was about to begin.

Ragnarök was finally at hand.

Stuart Conover is a father, husband, rescue dog owner, published author, blogger, journalist, horror enthusiast, comic book geek, science fiction junkie, and IT professional. With all of that to cram in daily, we have no idea if or when he sleeps or how he gets writing done! (We suspect it has to do with having evil clones.) Stuart is a Chicago native and runs the author resource Horror Tree.

Muttagisu
by Kathleen Halecki

Vagrant, wandering ghosts, muttaggišu. Their bodies are left to rot without a grave and they find no rest in the House of Darkness. With no one to perform the rituals of remembrance, and no food and water, they have only dust to eat.

Their thirst drives their jealousy on, and they seek to exact revenge on the living. They lurk in empty spaces; the ruins of yesterday become their haunt. Roaming the mountains and the deserts waiting in the shadows, they know it is only a matter of time.

The young and foolish never heed the warning of their elders.

Kathleen Halecki possesses a BA and MA in history and a doctoral degree in interdisciplinary studies. Although born in New York, she currently resides in a seventeenth century home in New England. Her work can be found in The Copperfield Review; Shadows in Salem: Wicked Tales from the Witch City; One Night in Salem; Midnight Rising: A Collection of Paranormal Tales; From a Cat's View Volume II; and Shadow of Pendle. She has also drabbled before in Curses and Cauldrons and Forest of Fear.

Strength
by Brian Rosenberger

Strength was celebrated in the village. None stronger than Uva. He pulled nets of fish that required five of the villagers.

Uva held his own at the tavern. Strong pours from the barkeep. Afterwards, three wenches were needed to make Uva sweat. Pity the wenches.

Enter the Giant. 20 oxen tall.

So began the drinking contest. Giant and Uva.

Stein after stein consumed. A village record.

The Giant and Uva, both staggered to stay erect.

Uva succumbed first. The Giant the victor.

Uva, first to rise to congratulate the victor. Axe in hand.

Uva's axe, a cure for hangovers.

Next.

Brian Rosenberger lives in a cellar in Marietta, Georgia, USA, and writes by the light of captured fireflies. He is the author of "As the Worms Turns" and three poetry collections. He is also a featured contributor to the pro-wrestling literary collection "Three-Way Dance", available from Gimmick Press. Facebook: HeWhoSuffers

When It Rises
by Cindar Harrell

The ruins were revealed during the drought. No one knew anything about them—there was no record of anyone having ever settled in that area—and yet there it stood, unveiled from its watery prison.

I entered the main building, looking at the dripping architecture. Moving deeper inside, a sudden chill made me apprehensive. In the farthest room, there was a sarcophagus displayed on a dais at the centre.

Without looking at the markings, I opened the lid.

They will never find me. But I'll be here, waiting for the next person to stumble in when the ruins rise again.

Cindar Harrell loves fairy tales, especially ones with a dark twist. Her writing is often fairy tale inspired, but she also loves mystery and horror. Her stories can be found in various publications. Travelling is a passion for her as it inspires her imagination to run wild, especially in places that have a mystic presence in the air. She regularly moonlights as another human, but no matter who she is, she is always writing. Her novella inspired by "The Snow Queen" is set for release in 2020 as well as her debut novel "Lithium" and short story collection "Perchance to Dream".
Facebook: CindarHarrell

What All Men Desire
by Johann van der Walt

"What brings you to this fine establishment?"

The barkeep didn't look up.

"My dying wish," answered the cowboy.

"Such as all others." The barkeep nodded to the stone statues throughout the joint.

"Love took a bite out of you."

"She did." The cowboy's legs now almost solid stone.

"Last wishes ain't cheap you know?"

The cowboy produced a dead snake.

"Give me man's true desire."

The barkeep poured a tall glass of bourbon.

The cowboy took a sip, his throat dry.

"Who would have known?"

The barkeep grinned.

"Love kills but only liquor paves the way. Medusa knows that."

Johann van der Walt lives in Johannesburg, South Africa and works in the television industry. he has written two children's books and has debuted with poetry collections in both South Africa and in the States in 2020.

Bad Dog
by Patrick J. Gallagher

The pup was driving him crazy. Under his feet all the time, snatching food, chewing shoes. He was at his wits' end.

But what could he do? The pup was part of the family. His own flesh and blood.

He reached towards the side table, for the slice of cake he'd placed there not a moment before.

Gone.

That was it, the final straw.

Loki rose from his comfortable chair by the fire and stretched. Crossing to the heavy front door, he swung it open, allowing the harsh wind to enter.

"Alright Fenrir, it's time for you to go out."

Patrick J. Gallagher is a television cameraman and photographer, working in Canberra for the Australian Parliament. He has a lifelong fascination with mysteries, the paranormal, and things generally horrific and unknown. He has self-published several books on various topics related to those interests, including the Loch Ness Monster, and an almost-forgotten serial killer operating in London at the same time as the infamous Ripper. All this folklore and history becomes grist for the mill of his imagination.
Facebook: PatJGallagher

The Wrath of Atum
by Matthew M. Montelione

Atum was disgusted with humankind. Born of his tears, he gave them sunshine and seasons of plenty. Despite his generosity, humans plotted against him numerous times. Their treachery was unforgivable. They had to be punished.

Atum arose from his stone throne, the hairs on his golden skin bristled with rage. "Now, daughter!"

Sekhmet, the ferocious lioness goddess, dropped from her perch in the heavens and descended on mankind in a fury. She feasted on their guts, devouring, punishing, drinking rivers of blood.

His pride satisfied, Atum restrained her.

Humankind never recovered, living in fear of the wrath of the gods.

Matthew M. Montelione is a horror writer born and raised on Long Island in New York. His work has been published in many titles, including MONSTERS: A Horror Microfiction Anthology and Quoth the Raven: A Contemporary Reimagining of the Works of Edgar Allan Poe. Matthew lives with his wife in New York.
Website: maybeevils.com
Facebook: maybeevils

Mummified
by Brianna Witte

How does one know when you're truly dead?

Do they see your soul enter the Underworld? Is it when your last breath escapes your lips?

All these thoughts came to me now as I laid on the stone slab, awaiting my final approach to the afterlife. I could see the priest hovering over me. He pushed the sharp hook up my slender nose ready to pull out my delicate brain. My body suddenly came alive and filled with pain, thrashing uncontrollably. The priest jumped back in shock unable to believe it was true.

I guess I wasn't dead after all.

*As a writer from Ontario, Canada, **Brianna Witte** has a passion for spinning tales of adventure and fantasy. She enjoys taking readers on a ride through the realm of fiction by weaving magical and mystical stories that materialise from her wildly creative dreams and vivid imagination. Brianna has received a commendation for her short story, The Hunt, in the 2019 Author of Tomorrow Award by the Wilbur and Niso Smith Foundation and has many short stories published in various anthologies. She has also released her first book, Witches and Vampires, in December 2019.*
Facebook: BriannaWitteAuthor
Instagram: briannawitteauthor

Babylonian God
by Owen Morgan

A man outlined in shadow, shielded his eyes against the setting sun; his vision fixed on a red dot in the heavens. A lion sat, curling and uncurling its forepaws and yawned. The man jumped back, eyes wide.

"Oh, don't mind me."

The man gasped, "You can talk?"

"Yes, all gods can talk whether in animal form or not. Ah, you were looking at the red dot. Mars is so, so close now."

"Who are you?"

"Nergal, God of Disease and War.

He stammered, "What do you want?"

"Oh, I've spread enough disease, for now; how about a good, old, bloody war?"

Owen Morgan writes science fiction, fantasy, and alternate history and lives in the fishing port of Steveston, British Columbia.
Website: httpwwwkingauthor.wordpress.com
Twitter: @owen_morgan1066

The Shaman
by Simon Clarke

When the weather turns brutal and food is scarce, new-borns are abandoned.

The shaman is always sad, but what must be, must be. He stays with them as the cold leaches out their life and smiles as the people praise him for his kindness. He is not kind. He is fearful. The drumming ritual needs to be carried out to protect the village. One year he was away and returned too late. They still talk of the haunted winter when whole families became mad and killed each other.

The lost spirit of a discarded baby is a wild, destructive thing.

Simon Clarke *lives and writes in Norfolk, United Kingdom. His first published microfiction story "Loss" appeared on Black Hare Press. His first short story was published in "What If?" on Black Hare Press. He enjoys writing fiction and poetry. He regularly submits to UK and international publications and enjoys reading short pieces and poetry at open mic events. He is currently working on his first novel. His main influences reflect authors he read as a teenager: J.R.R. Tolkien, Ian Fleming, Peter O'Donnell, H.P. Lovecraft, Raymond Chandler, and Sir Arthur Conan Doyle. He loves Gothic literature and all things mystical and mysterious.*

Emperor Father
by Shawn M. Klimek

The endless rain was putting Emperor Tezoztli in a foul mood. His wives complained that the scarcity of dry wood made cooking impossible, and proliferating mould had already ruined his favourite jaguar pelt. How must his subjects not sheltered by a stone palace be suffering?

He scowled at the kowtowing high priest.

"It seems 100 slaves did not appease the gods, Patli."

"I fear the gods prefer a more personal sacrifice, Lord."

"One of my children, perhaps?"

Patli lifted his face, gone pale. "No, Lord…however…"

"Careful, Patli."

"The people refer to you as Emperor Father. That makes them your children."

Shawn M. Klimek is the internationally published author of more than 170 poems and stories, in several genres. He is the author of Hungry Thing, an illustrated fantasy tale told in five poems. He lives in Illinois, USA, with his wife and their Maltese.
Website: blog.jotinthedark.com
Facebook: shawnmklimekauthor

Lord of Annwn
by Stacey Jaine McIntosh

Three ravens circle overhead, cawing loudly. Arawn sat on his throne made of milk white bones, presiding over Annwn. Two large white hounds, ears red as blood, lounged at his feet, guarding the entrance to the underworld.

In his hands he held a sword. The tip rested on the ground, waiting to be picked up, again.

The bones of the dead lay scattered around him. It had been a long time since Arawn had to harvest a soul. Longer still since anyone living had ventured down here.

But there she stood. So, he grabbed his blade and went to work.

Stacey Jaine McIntosh was born in Perth, Western Australia, where she still resides with her husband and their four children. Although her first love has always been writing, she once toyed with being a Cartographer and subsequently holds a Diploma in Spatial Information Services. Since 2011, she has had a vast number of stories and a few poems published online as well as in various anthologies. Stacey is also the author of Solstice, Morrighan, Lost, and Le Fay and she is currently working on several other projects simultaneously. When not with her family or writing she enjoys reading, photography, genealogy, history, Arthurian myths, and witchcraft.
Website:

Spirit of the Dead
by Paula R.C. Readman

The bones of your body lay bare for all to see as I peer through the glass; your vacant eye sockets stare back at me. You left your sunny Mediterranean life far behind and rode on chariots across Roman London a millennium or so ago. Only twenty summers passed when death took you so young. In this foreign land, your loved ones showed us your worth. They decorated your lead coffin with scallop shells, a symbol of the soul's journey to an afterlife. I guess they didn't see your afterlife ending here, behind the glass of a museum display case.

Paula R.C. Readman *learnt 'How to Write' from books which her husband purchased from eBay. After 250 purchases, he finally told her 'just to get on with the writing'. Since 2010, she's had 34 stories published.*
Blog: paulareadman1.wordpress.com

Cabinet of Curiosities
by Patrick J. Gallagher

It had been his pride and joy. His own private museum filled with artefacts of ages past.

Beads from a mummy's shroud, a Mayan figurine, pottery from the Anasazi tribe. Dozens of relics representing the power of myriad ancient cultures.

All in the same small space at the same time.

As he placed the final piece, an exquisite carving of a crystal skull, at the centre of the cabinet, the floor shook, and fiery clouds billowed into the room.

Torn apart by the competing demons of a dozen cultures, his only thought was…

It had been his pride and joy.

Patrick J. Gallagher *is a television cameraman and photographer, working in Canberra for the Australian Parliament. He has a lifelong fascination with mysteries, the paranormal, and things generally horrific and unknown. He has self-published several books on various topics related to those interests, including the Loch Ness Monster, and an almost-forgotten serial killer operating in London at the same time as the infamous Ripper. All this folklore and history becomes grist for the mill of his imagination.*
Facebook: PatJGallagher

Erra
by G. Allen Wilbanks

Erra opened his eyes and gazed towards the sky. He did not know what had awakened him, but he could feel the world had moved on while he was asleep.

He reached out with his thoughts, feeling for any traces of civilisation nearby. What he found made him smile.

It had been 1500 years since his precious Mesopotamia had been overrun by those zealous Christians, and he had been forced into this extended hibernation. But that was over now.

The God of Plague and Discord would rise to walk the Earth again, and his timing could not be more perfect.

G. Allen Wilbanks is a member of the Horror Writers Association (HWA) and has published over a hundred short stories in various magazines and online venues. He is the author of two short story collections and the novel "When Darkness Comes".
Website: www.gallenwilbanks.com
Blog: DeepDarkThoughts.com

Halloween
by Jo Mularczyk

She laid the last pieces of kindling and glanced around the harvested fields. Stacks were erected haphazardly, some with flames licking their edges, others with smoky tendrils rising into the night sky.

"Can I light it, Mama? Like Papa used to?"

"Yes love," Saoirse answered. "But…" She was about to regale her son with the significance of Samhain but she was young enough to remember her own fascination with the bonfires. "…take care."

Saoirse felt an unearthly touch upon her shoulder, and she knew her husband had passed through the thin veil to join them this All Hallows' Eve.

Jo Mularczyk's stories and poems appear in magazines and anthologies including - The School Magazine's Blast Off and Touchdown; One Surviving Story; fourW thirty; Wonderment; Zinewest; Short and Twisted; several Storm Cloud Publishing anthologies; Daily Science Fiction; the US magazine Cricket; an upcoming UK collection; other Black Hare Press publications and several upcoming anthologies. Jo mentors a gifted and talented students' writing group, runs writing workshops and is a co-author with the student literacy program, Littlescribe, providing writing tips and story starters for students to complete. Jo lives in Australia with her husband and three children.
Website: www.jomularczyk.com
Facebook: jo.mularczyk.author

Ancient Origin
by Ximena Escobar

Before diving into the frigid waters, the young fisherman smeared her body with seal blubber. Born near a tangle of trees and underbrush, she always was an unusual native of *Chiloé* Island, not only for the odd scar on her forearm but also for her imaginings, eerily real like old memories, of whale songs and the icy flow of receding waters.

The ocean opened like a firmament as she submerged, stars and light spinning throughout her. Struck by the illusion of claws as she pulled herself back up, she looked at her patch of amphibious-like skin and, finally, understood something.

Ximena Escobar is writing stories and poetry. Originally from Chile, she is the author of a translation into Spanish of the Broadway Musical "The Wizard of Oz" and of an original adaptation of the same, "Navidad en Oz", both produced in her home country. Since 2018 she has published several short stories in various anthologies and online platforms and is now slowly working on her own collection. Ximena has a degree in Arts & Communication Science and lives in Nottingham with her family.
Facebook: Ximenautora
Twitter: @laximenin

City's End
by Charles Reis

The wind ruffled the feathers in his headdress as Gueybana stood on the ledge of the palace. The skies darkened as thousands of birds flee; the screams of hundreds of people pounded his ears.

Yesterday in a dream, the gods revealed that the city would be submerged. Today, a tidal wave stretched to the clouds; its rumbling grew louder. The waters devoured the three pyramids with flat tops that towered over the land.

A glint of tears formed in his eyes. He failed to honour the gods, now he suffered in witnessing the fall of a city his ancestors built.

Charles Reis was born and raised in Coventry, Rhode Island, but currently lives in neighboring West Warwick. He graduated from the University of Rhode Island with a BA in English Literature in 2012 and currently works as a museum tour guide. Additional works of his have appeared in "One Night in Salem", "Trembling with Fear: Year 1", "13 Postcards from Hell", and "Coffins & Dragons".
Facebook: charles.reis.35
Instagram: cthulhudawn1979

Order of the Rose
by Raven Corinn Carluk

The Elder cleared his throat. The Thirteen grew quiet and waited for him to speak. "After nine millennia, the time has finally arrived."

A sigh filled the darkened room. Expectant. Relieved.

"We have only this final push. The humans have willingly bred for stupidity and docility—"

"Though far slower than expected," hissed a woman. Others clicked, expressing agreement and frustration.

"Do not falter now," the Elder chided softly. "Setia will be avenged. We need only 'raise' them up with technology and knowledge—"

"Then tear everything away, as they did us!"

He nodded his reptilian head, ready for the next millennia.

Raven Corinn Carluk writes dark fantasy, paranormal romance, and anything else that catches her interest. She's authored five novels, where she explores themes of love and acceptance. Her shorter pieces, usually from her darker side, can be found in Black Hare Press anthologies, at Detritus Online, and through Alban Lake Publishers.
Twitter: @ravencorinn
Website: www.ravencorinncarluk.com

The Oak
by Simon Clarke

Worshipped by Druids, I ruled the grove; now my soul lives inside this ship. I enjoy the freedom, listening to the whisper of wind singing my shape as the world turns beneath me across the receding sea; seasons rotate around me, infinite night circles round and down.

I can absorb the world, my skin seeing, smelling, tasting, all at once. I hear sirens beckon as winds force me hard into billowing waves.

Suddenly, I long to give in, be with the sea forever. The worst that can happen is also the best; I surrender to the exquisite pleasure of destruction.

Simon Clarke lives and writes in Norfolk, United Kingdom. His first published microfiction story "Loss" appeared on Black Hare Press. His first short story was published in "What If?" on Black Hare Press. He enjoys writing fiction and poetry. He regularly submits to UK and international publications and enjoys reading short pieces and poetry at open mic events. He is currently working on his first novel. His main influences reflect authors he read as a teenager: J.R.R. Tolkien, Ian Fleming, Peter O'Donnell, H.P. Lovecraft, Raymond Chandler, and Sir Arthur Conan Doyle. He loves Gothic literature and all things mystical and mysterious.

A Centurion's Lament
by Gary Rubidge

I must consult with the ancient Seers on the mount to ask for the protection of my Regina.

Aurelius watched as the mysteriously cloaked figures surrounded the fire in a trance, chanting for Jupiter, their god.

I need to know she will be safe because pillaging is the way of those Gothic barbarians and if they take her as their slave, I fear that would be a fate worse than death for my beloved.

I have seen these beasts at work on the battlefield, its deathly veil having already shrouded me, my broken corpse can do no more for her.

Gary Rubidge currently resides in Western Australia and is a newcomer to writing, having reached the age of 50 without consideration to authoring anything other than work reports. Encouraged by friends to put his ideas to paper, he has finally taken the plunge and this is his first effort. There are many more ideas begging to be released and they are lining up to be put to paper.

The Dead God
by Owen Morgan

A slender, young woman shivered in the torch-lit stone corridor. Footsteps echoed in the distance, approaching her. She swallowed hard to clear her throat and summon her courage. A tall, gaunt man with greenish skin swathed in linen strode to her.

She licked her cracked lips. "Who are you?"

"I am Osiris, Judge of the Dead. Your life was cut short, but I am tempted to send you back to the land of the living."

"Why would you do such a kind thing?"

"To give your life full meaning. Come with me, and I shall show you your complete path."

Owen Morgan *writes science fiction, fantasy, and alternate history and lives in the fishing port of Steveston, British Columbia.*
Website: httpwwwkingauthor.wordpress.com
Twitter: @owen_morgan1066

Ordinary Sacrifice
by Kim Jackways

Mine is a mundane sort of magic: slipping blades between joints, dragging skin from flesh, plucking the fur from goats.

Hordes from around the kingdom climb the hill, panting. They scratch themselves. They stink of sweat and desperation.

Here, pelts hang like clouds against the blue. And the line inches forward, trembling for her voice. I etch the fates of the rich into these skins, scratching the fall of forces in potent verse.

Last moon, I combed knots from her hair as she spoke of her brother. We held hands, slurped from the sacred spring.

But oracles have no past.

Kim Jackways is a freelance writer and blogger from New Zealand. She has had fiction published in Flash Frontier and The Best Small Fictions and uses her background in Psychology and Linguistics to inspire her work.
Facebook: facebook.com/kimwriter
Website: www.writersideoflife.com

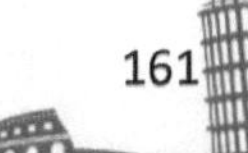

The Wrath of Zeus
by Dawn Knox

Prometheus woke at dawn, hopeless and desperate, shackled to the great rock.

He knew today's attack was imminent. It would be like every other morning.

First the eagle's shadow would caress Prometheus' body as the bird circled above, slowly descending. Then its claws would pierce his skin as it landed and gripped tightly, steadying itself for the assault. The creature would pause before its razor-sharp beak ripped into his flesh, exposing and tearing out his liver.

Then, blood-stained and sated, the eagle would rise into the air, leaving Prometheus in agony and despair, knowing Zeus' punishment would last for eternity.

Dawn Knox enjoys writing in different genres and has had romances, speculative fiction, sci-fi, humorous, and women's fiction published in magazines, anthologies, and books. She's also had two plays about World War I performed internationally. Her current work in progress is a story set in Bletchley Park during World War II.
Website: dawnknox.com
Twitter: SunriseCalls

Blood Bath
by Nerisha Kemraj

Eztli watched the rains pour over Tenochtitlan—the first in over a year. They were saved.

Tlaloc was appeased. But at what cost?

He cried remembering the children's screams before the cruel blade silenced them. Their severed heads rolled across the concrete slabs, decorating the floor in death.

"The tears of a child could produce rain…" they said.

Now, the Rain God had accepted their blood.

The showers of blessing would wash away the crimson around the sacrificial pit… Their suffering forgotten.

But now, as Eztli looked up to the heavens, he saw blood, not water, bathing the earth.

Nerisha Kemraj resides in Durban, South Africa, with her husband and two mischievous daughters. Writing since 2017, she has had over 100 short stories and poems published in various publications, both print and online. She has also received an Honourable Mention Award for her tanka in the Fujisan Taisho 2019 Tanka Contest. She holds a Bachelor's degree in Communication Science, and a Post Graduate Certificate in Education from the University of South Africa.
Amazon: amazon.com/author/nerisha_kemraj
Facebook: Nerishakemrajwriter

My Name is Hafez of Shiraz
by D.J. Elton

I am Sufi, a mystic and a poet of Persia.

I wrote of courtship, love, wine and nightingales.

My birth city, Shiraz, rivalled Baghdad in its greatness—the home of poets, artists, and scholars. A traveller described the people of Shiraz as the most subtle, ingenious, and vivacious amongst all Persians.

And he was right.

Even the wild rampaging Mongols did not destroy Shiraz.

Our wisdom and ancient sophistication ensured that the place stayed solid and become one of the greatest cities ever.

I died here; my grave is proudly visited by many who have love for poetry and God.

__D.J. Elton__ is a writer living in Melbourne's west. As a child, she came from England to Australia, on the last boat down the Suez Canal, where she underwent a sacrificial dunking ritual in the court of King Neptune and has never looked back. She likes creating speculative microfiction and short stories, as well as random essays. Her work has been published in several anthologies, and she has written a historical fantasy novella, 'The Merlin Girl.' When not playing with a pen, she likes most of all to go to the green country.

Night Visitor
by Kevin Hopson

Asgall ascended the spiral staircase. The beacon of light atop the tower, which warned of impending danger, hadn't been used in years. But it filled the sky this very night. Asgall noticed a familiar face as he reached the top.

"Derwen?" Asgall said.

"Do I know you?"

"No, but you were Commander of the Guard when I was just a boy. I thought you died during the siege."

"Up until tonight, I was enslaved by the Romans. I see you wear the same pin. You're Commander now?"

Asgall nodded. "Who's coming? The Romans?"

"No. Those approaching aren't of this world."

*Prior to hitting the fiction scene in 2009, **Kevin Hopson** was a freelance writer for several years, covering everything from finance to sports. Since then, he has released over a dozen books with MuseItUp Publishing, and he has also been published in various magazines and anthology books. Kevin has dabbled in many genres over the years, but crime fiction and fantasy are his true loves. His novelette, Pursuing the Dead, was a 2019 Author Shout Reader Ready Awards winner. It was a "Top Pick" in the mystery and thriller category. And for readers of light fantasy, check out The Emperor's Guard series. You can learn more about Kevin by visiting his website at http://www.kmhopson.com.*

Watch My Work
by Charles Reis

From his fishing boat, Rishaan watched billows of smoke rise in the distance. He never thought that Lanka, the island fortress with golden walls, towers, and a citadel, would burn.

As he wiped ash off his Koli loin cloth, the boat jolted. He swung his arms. After he regained his balance, Rishaan gasped when he saw a man with light blue skin and a monkey face standing at the bow of the boat. The man smiled while looking at the destruction.

"Hanuman!" Rishaan dropped to his knees.

"Namaste." Hanuman held out his hand. "Come join me and watch my work."

Charles Reis *was born and raised in Coventry, Rhode Island, but currently lives in neighboring West Warwick. He graduated from the University of Rhode Island with a BA in English Literature in 2012 and currently works as a museum tour guide. Additional works of his have appeared in "One Night in Salem", "Trembling with Fear: Year 1", "13 Postcards from Hell", and "Coffins & Dragons".*
Facebook: charles.reis.35
Instagram: cthulhudawn1979

Babylon Falls
by David Green

"My king, we are ready."

"There are so many," Nabonidus whispered, staring through the tower's window. Beyond the city walls, a mass of flame. Their chants and cries a haunting wind. Cyrus of Persia had amassed his armies. By dawn, Babylon would fall.

"Give the order," Nabonidus said, dismissing his general. The Persians were animals; he would not let his people suffer.

The Babylonian army would move quietly through the night, granting Babylon a silent, painless death.

At least as my final act, Nabonidus thought, taking a deep breath before climbing up to the window, *I can give them that.*

David Green *is a writer based in Co Galway, Ireland. Growing up between there and Manchester, UK meant David rarely saw sunlight in his childhood, which has no doubt had an effect on his dark writings. Published in places such as North West Words, The Devil Made Me Do It and Nymphs, David is aiming to release his debut novel in 2020.*
Twitter: *@David Green*

The Curse of the Pharaohs
by Wondra Vanian

Scientists have, they believe, categorically disproven the ancient belief that curses guard the tombs of the pharaohs. Nothing more than mould, they insist. Superstitions, bad luck, and toxins.

Fools.

It isn't their fault. It's not as though they were there when the pyramids were sealed.

Not like I was.

If you ask me, those filthy graverobbers disguised as scholars don't deserve what they get. Why should they be allowed to die while I live forever in the service of my god-king?

Am I bitter?

A little.

But, above all else, I am dutiful. Enter a pyramid and I'll be waiting.

Wondra Vanian *is an American living in the United Kingdom with her Welsh husband and their army of fur babies. A writer first, Wondra is also an avid gamer, photographer, cinephile, and blogger. She has music in her blood, sleeps with the lights on, and has been known to dance naked in the moonlight. Wondra was a multiple Top-Ten finisher in the 2017 and 2018 Preditors and Editors Reader's Poll, including the Best Author category. Her story "Halloween Night" was named a Notable Contender for the Bristol Short Story Prize in 2015.*
Website: www.wondravanian.com

The Bone Flute
by Nicola Currie

I've completed digs all over North America but found nothing so spectacular. The mouthpiece is carved into a ferocious bear. The barrel is engraved with ancient writing that I expertly decipher.

It tells the story of a wandering tribesman who fought with a bear, his victory hard won, and his arm sacrificed. Despite his loss, he carved the flute from his own severed bone, vowing to play it for sacrificial ceremonies in the mighty bear's honour.

I should treat it preciously but cannot resist, place it to my lips, blow.

I scream as my arm snaps, vanishes. The bone flute grows.

Nicola Currie *is from Cambridge, UK, where she works in educational publishing. She has published poetry in literary magazines, including Mslexia and Sarasvati, and short stories in various anthologies. She has also completed her first novel, which was longlisted for the Bath Children's Novel Award.*
Website: *writeitandweep.home.blog*

With Your Shield, or on It
by Paul Carberry

A young Spartan warrior settled amongst his brethren, a sea of crimson enveloping him. The very earth he stood upon quivered beneath his feet as the Persian army advanced. White knuckles clutched the hilt of his shield; his spear lay unbalanced in his fist. Before he felt the warmth of a woman's embrace, he would experience the bitter clutches of death. Blotted out by arrows, the sunlight vanished, concealed under a veil of wooden bolts. The first arrow tore through the tender flesh of his shoulder. His King had ordered him "to come home with your shield, or on it."

Paul Carberry is the author of the Zombies on the Rock series. His tales of the zombie apocalypse in Newfoundland are inspired by George A. Romero's Living Dead series. He has also published several short stories over three "from the Rock" anthologies including "Halloween Mummers", "The Light of Cabot Tower", "Into the Forrest", and "Harmon Field". His Zombies on the Rock series currently has three novels, "Outbreak", "The Viking Trail", and "The Republic of Newfound" and is currently working on the fourth novel "Extinction". Most recently Paul has been accepted in Black Hare Press' Oceans Anthology. Paul is from Newfoundland and is currently living in Shearwater, Nova Scotia.

The Oracle
by David Green

Arcadias had plotted carefully. The pieces were almost in place. Before making his final move, his last act for the throne of Sparta, he journeyed to see Pythia, the Oracle of Apollo. The warrior left nothing to chance.

The temple was silent as the Oracle knelt before Arcadias.

"Ask," she whispered.

"Will I be king?" he demanded without hesitation.

Pythia, blind eyes bound, cocked her head.

"No."

Arcadias unsheathed his sword, swinging it in a mighty arc. The Oracle's head fell to the floor.

What does the witch know? he thought, wiping his blade clean, *she didn't see that coming.*

David Green *is a writer based in Co Galway, Ireland. Growing up between there and Manchester, UK meant David rarely saw sunlight in his childhood, which has no doubt had an effect on his dark writings. Published in places such as North West Words, The Devil Made Me Do It and Nymphs, David is aiming to release his debut novel in 2020.*
Twitter: @David Green

The Anubis Autopsy
by Jasmine Jarvis

The open corpse lays on the autopsy table behind me. I place the heart on the scales and watch the needle move back and forth waiting for final judgement. When it stops, I record the details on the chart.

"This heart has been judged against the feather, and it is no good. You will not ascend to Heaven," I say, as I take up the heart and walk over to the incinerator my assistant had nicknamed Ammut. A disembodied scream tears through the autopsy room as I toss the heart into Ammut's open mouth, her flames feasting on the sins.

Jasmine Jarvis is a teller of tales and scribbler of scribbles. She lives in Brisbane, Australia, with her husband, Michael; their two children, Tilly and Mish; their German Shepherd, Ripley; and indoor fat cat, Dwight K. Shrute.

Last Act of Grace
by Chris Bannor

Fog rolled over the ground of the ancient site, but the dawn would soon come. The ceremonies had been completed the day before. The jhator was a man's last act of grace, giving his very flesh with his death.

The sun came and with it, the flapping wings of the Himalayan griffin vultures. They were hungry today, and he spotted the oldest of them as he flew down to rest on the rocks and wait. His plumage was impressive and his wings strong. He bowed his head slightly, and the noble birds accepted the last gift of a dead man.

Chris Bannor is a science fiction and fantasy writer who lives in Southern California. Chris learned her love of genre stories from her mother at an early age and has never veered far from that path. She also enjoys musical theatre and roadtrips with her family but is a general homebody otherwise.
Facebook: chrisbannorauthor
Website: ChrisBannor.com

Galatea and Pygmalion
by McKenzie Richardson

Galatea was thankful to Aphrodite for giving life to her stone form, though she didn't much care for being stuck with Pygmalion. True, he had carved her into existence, but she was merely his concept of perfect beauty personified.

From the table, she snatched the chisel that had shaped her and crept into the bedroom where her husband slept soundly.

A woman is not a thing to be made, forced into the form of one's own desires. A woman has a mind of her own. And this one had made up hers.

This chisel could create. It could also destroy.

***McKenzie Richardson** lives in Milwaukee, WI. Her horror stories have been featured in various anthologies including Evil Lurks, Pandemic, and After: Undead Wars. She has also published a variety of poems and flash fiction pieces.*
Facebook: mckenzielrichardson
Blog: www.craft-cycle.com

A New Beginning
by Tracy Davidson

While all else crumbled, one pyramid remained. Only those faithful to Anubis stayed safe within its protective walls. Immune to the pestilence that spread across the world, for them thousands of years passed in mere months.

One day, they emerged from their long hibernation. Slaves led the way, followed by priests, then the concubines, all bearing the jackal God's progeny. Finally, Anubis himself stepped out into his new domain. Whatever remained of humanity was now his.

His satisfaction faded as the earth shook. Anubis looked up. The prophets never prophesised this.

Even a God was no match for an asteroid.

Tracy Davidson lives in Warwickshire, England, and writes poetry and flash fiction. Her work has appeared in various publications and anthologies, including Poet's Market, Mslexia, Atlas Poetica, Writing Magazine, Modern Haiku, The Binnacle, A Hundred Gourds, Shooter, Journey to Crone, The Great Gatsby Anthology, WAR, and In Protest: 150 Poems for Human Rights.

Fundinn
by Kimberly Rei

I leaned over the man strapped to my work bench, brushing his hair away from his eyes tenderly. Politeness mattered.

"I know you can't remember. But I saw the ravens. *I* know you. Soon, you will, too. I can free you!"

His eyes widened in terror, but I ignored that. I moved quickly, slashing across one orb. He howled as the blade swiped and disappointment filled my heart. He should have howled in glory and release, not anguish.

"I'm so sorry. You're not him."

With a quick plunge into the socket, I ended his fear.

"I'll have to keep looking."

Kimberly Rei has been writing for as long as she can remember. At five years old, her parents gifted her with a set of Children's Classics that she had no hope of reading yet. The potential alone sparked a love of words that has never wavered. Kim has taught writing workshops and edited novels for authors you may recognise. She has published several short stories and now can't stop chasing paper dragons. She currently lives in Tampa Bay, Florida, with her wife and an abundance of gorgeous beaches to explore.

Aliens in the Louvre
by Ximena Escobar

Stardust spun through the Persian Gulf, slipping between two oyster shells. Like a secret locked in a dead princess' lips, it grew into a unique gem, such as, in life, said princess dreamed she possessed. She ordered its retrieval, but none delivered other than common pearls.

Millenia later, she attained it. As newfound jewels arrived in *Gallerie D'Apollon*, eyes opened in the darkness of her sarcophagus. The gem on *Eleanor of Aquitane's* long lost sceptre gleamed with starlight, but visitors escaped as cracks extended and walls crumbled.

Bone gripped gold—the distant firmament exploded with incoming stars.

"I'm here, Mother!"

Ximena Escobar is writing stories and poetry. Originally from Chile, she is the author of a translation into Spanish of the Broadway Musical "The Wizard of Oz" and of an original adaptation of the same, "Navidad en Oz", both produced in her home country. Since 2018 she has published several short stories in various anthologies and online platforms and is now slowly working on her own collection. Ximena has a degree in Arts & Communication Science and lives in Nottingham with her family.
Facebook: Ximenautora
Twitter: @laximenin

The Return
by Maxine Churchman

Troy had fallen; we returned at last. My only wish: to hold my wife in my arms again. For years, her beautiful face, etched in my memory, was all that kept me alive.

Familiar sights lifted my spirits as I approached home. I ran up behind Melissa and wrapped my arms around her waist.

She screamed and I recoiled from her swollen belly. A blow to my head sent me crashing to the ground. A man held Melissa; a child peeked from behind her skirts. I welcomed the darkness creeping into my vision. I had nothing left to live for.

Maxine Churchman lives in Essex, UK, and has recently started writing poetry and short stories to share. Her interests include learning to improve her writing, reading, knitting, walking, and teaching yoga. She is also planning a novel.

Diablo
by Jim Bates

Even though they were small in number, Cortes' soldiers fought with fierce skill and determination. The cavalry was led by Pedro Sanchez and his horse, Diablo, a big, dabbled grey Arabian with a flowing white mane. During the last battle with the Aztec warriors, the fearless Diablo nearly died from an arrow wound to the heart. His spirit was strong, however, and he lived out his days with Pedro and his family on a farm in Cuba, beloved for his gentle nature and kind disposition, especially with the sick and infirm. A warrior of a different kind to the end.

Jim Bates lives in a small town twenty miles west of Minneapolis, Minnesota. His stories have appeared online in CafeLit, The Writers' Cafe Magazine, Cabinet of Heed, Paragraph Planet, Nailpolish Stories, Ariel Chart, Potato Soup Journal, Literary Yard, Spillwords (December 2019, Author of the Month), The Drabble, The Academy of the Heart and Mind, and World of Myth Magazine. In print publications: A Million Ways, Mused Literary Journal, Gleam Flash Fiction Anthology #2, the Portal Anthology and the Glamour Anthology by Clarendon House Publishing, The Best of CafeLit 8 by Chapeltown Publishing, the Nativity Anthology by Bridge House Publishing, and Gold Dust Magazine.
Website: www.theviewfromlonglake.wordpress.com

Forgotten
by G. Allen Wilbanks

Herostratus danced in the light of the flames, reveling as the mighty temple of Artemis came to ruin at his hands. "This is my doing," he cried to any who would listen.

He danced a second time on the rack, his bones breaking under the strain, as the people of Ephesus demanded he explain his actions.

"I have done what none other would dare," Herostratus said with triumph. "I have done the unthinkable and now all shall remember my name."

His body was buried where it could never be found, and his name forbidden to ever be spoken aloud again.

G. Allen Wilbanks *is a member of the Horror Writers Association (HWA) and has published over a hundred short stories in various magazines and online venues. He is the author of two short story collections and the novel "When Darkness Comes".*
Website: www.gallenwilbanks.com
Blog: DeepDarkThoughts.com

Lamashtu
by Patrick Winters

Enlil sat looking at Ningal, pacing the hut, child at her breast for the first time.

Both had been overjoyed that the birthing went well and that their prayers warded off what they should. They had been blessed.

Enlil smiled at Ningal as she passed into their bedroom. He sat there a moment more, savouring the night.

When a shadow entered their hut, knocking him to the ground, contentedness went away.

When Ningal screamed, he knew Lamashtu had come after all.

He got to his feet in time to see demon and child fly out their window, into the night.

Patrick Winters is a graduate of Illinois College in Jacksonville, IL, where he earned a Bachelor of Arts degree in English Literature and Creative Writing and achieved membership into Sigma Tau Delta, an international English honours society. Winters is now a proud member of the Horror Writers Association, and his work has been published in the likes of Sanitarium Magazine, Deadman's Tome, Trysts of Fate, and other such titles. A full list of his previous publications may be found at his author's site.
Website: wintersauthor.azurewebsites.net/Publications/List

Fallen Land of Rivers
by C.L. Williams

A beautiful utopia, it is even known as the first civilisation of humans. *The Land Between Rivers* was what they called it. Now, this beautiful land is a battleground with its people unable to do anything about it.

The Romans came in with their plans to "rule the world" with their expansion going across continents. The people were ready to stand their ground against the vast army of Romans; the Persians also arrived, wanting the land between rivers.

The war resulted with only one loss—the natives themselves. A once beautiful land now torn in two and ruled by tyrants.

C.L. Williams is an international best-selling author currently living in central Virginia. He has written eight poetry books, four novellas, one novel, and a contributor to a multitude of anthologies and magazines. His most recent anthology appearance ANGELS: Dark Drabbles #2 from Black Hare Press became a number one in hot new releases. C.L. Williams is currently working on his second novel and a new poetry book.
Facebook: writer434
Twitter: @writer_434

Rise of Videsta
by Jo Seysener

"Put the box down, Videsta. You never know what will come out."

"You've been a horseman for eternity. I just want my turn." It was whingeing and she hated it. "It's not fair."

"I said, put it down." Con Pestilene shook his head. "You're 1900 years old. Not even old enough to have seen the man on the tree, for Hoove's sake. Now look what you've done."

The lid shifted. Videsta peered inside.

"Nothing's coming out."

Con covered his face. Sobs echoed around them.

"Brilliant. The humans will think up some stupid name for this. Probably call it Co-Vid19."

Jo Seysener is a mum of three crazies, a scatter of chickens, a decrepit kelpie, and a rambunctious GSD. She lives with her husband near Brisbane, Australia. When she is not exposing her kids to cult storybooks from her childhood, she can be found in the kitchen experimenting with new flavours and pairings. She adores alpacas.
Facebook: joseysener
Website: www.joseysener.com

Waiting
by Melissa Elborn

Some places are never meant to be seen. Even the creatures that slither within are eyeless.

A mouth opens in a centuries-old yawn. New life ventures in, seeking sanctuary while forgotten life stirs.

The brave and intrepid try to conquer its depths, to pull out its secrets into the salt-washed air.

Others understand it—carving their warnings into its walls. But the cave outlives their ancient alphabets. And the dead they buried deep inside, cannot resist the penetration of water. Bones sink into rock. Dreams and fears are imprinted into stone.

Waiting to be felt.

Waiting to be heard.

Waiting.

Melissa Elborn is a writer of dark fiction and her work has previously appeared in Horla Horror, Siren's Call, and Spelk Fiction. She has recently completed an MA in Creative Writing specialising in horror. She haunts deepest Bedfordshire, England, with her husband, daughter, and two cats.

Recluse
by Crmetheus Christopher

Achen was well aware of the world above her. She'd been lying beneath it for over a thousand years.

She was a goddess. Second generation of her bloodline, dark, vile, and ravenous.

Achen placed the last piece of dark rotted meat under her tongue and began to hum.

"The heart of Rah." The light of a god she'd extinguished herself.

They would hear her call as she could taste their fear. They would come to Zoser, to Saqqara.

Achen traced the engravings on the artefact. The curse.

They would come in search of history. She would greet them with death.

Crmetheus Christopher *is an author from Boston, Massachusetts. He is an eclectic artist who writes with a unique passion and flair for storytelling, he is the author of two books. When The Lions Came (Fantasy) and Mayhaps Tomorrow (Psychological Thriller). He is also the creator of The Authors Embers Podcast.*

Mistake
by Eleanor Whitworth

I beam in, keen for the take, and see six whale bones immediately: worthwhile trip. They stand two-by-two, bleached, porous, monumental—once entrances to Thule homes. I kneel between the nearest pair and push my lever into the earth trying to lift one out. A woman's grinding voice reverberates rhythmically around me. I flinch and look up. There is only the bone. A response issues from the other bone, catching and shaking the centres of my cells. A warm hearth, coarse comforting fur, the thick smell of whale. The now-awoken women play. Katajjaq.

And it is me who is taken.

Eleanor Whitworth lives in Sydney with her husband, young child and many story ideas. She has been published in Meanjin, SQ Magazine, Not One of Us, and the Stories of Hope anthology (Deadset Press). Her story, 'A Thousand Million Small Things,' was included in Tangent's 'Best Online 2017 Recommended Reading List.' She's a graduate of the 2018 HardCopy program. In her nonfiction world, Eleanor works as a copywriter for artists, universities, and Arup's foresight and innovation team. You can find her on Twitter as @elewhitworth or more backstory at eleanorwhitworth.com.

The Lost Art
by Dawn DeBraal

Pulling the brain through the nose, the embalmer prepared the Pharaoh's body. Aharon's selection was an honour, a testament to his expertise. He was chosen above all the others in his trade—those who knew the old ways.

He wrapped the corpse with cloths soaked in herbs and oils, lovingly prepared, winding the fabric strips around the dead body, layer upon layer, to preserve his master for the afterlife.

The knowledge of preservation was lost over time. Once his job is completed, he would be sealed in the tomb with his creation—with all his mummification knowledge buried with his beloved king.

Dawn DeBraal lives in rural Wisconsin with her husband Red, two rat terriers, and a cat. She has discovered that her love of telling a good story can be written. Published her stories with Palm-sized Press, Spillwords, Mercurial Stories, Potato Soup Journal, Edify Fiction, Zimbell House Publishing, Clarendon House Publishing, Blood Song Books, Black Hare Press, Fantasia Divinity, Cafelit, Reanimated Writers, Guilty Pleasures, Unholy Trinity, The World of Myth, Dastaan World, Vamp Cat, Runcible Spoon, Dark Christmas, Siren's Call, and Iron Horse Publishing, also appearing as a Falling Star Magazine 2019 Pushcart Nominee.
Amazon: amazon.com/Dawn-DeBraal/e/B07STL8DLX

The Black Annis
by Jasmine Jarvis

Shhh! Can you hear that? She is grinding her teeth. Hide, my child! Don't make a sound, for the Black Annis is here.

Oh, if only you had not stolen the acorns from her oak tree!

She will take you to her cave and cleave you into pieces with her iron claws.

Oh, if only you had not stolen the acorns from her oak tree!

She will wear your skin.

Click!

The door! It wasn't locked!

Oh, if only you had not stolen the acorns from her oak tree!

Shhh child! Don't make a sound!

Oh, if only you had...

Jasmine Jarvis is a teller of tales and scribbler of scribbles. She lives in Brisbane, Australia, with her husband, Michael; their two children, Tilly and Mish; their German Shepherd, Ripley; and indoor fat cat, Dwight K. Shrute.

Tyr and the Wolf
by J.B. Wocoski

Tyr, the Norse sky god, rushed maddeningly into battle with the giant wolf, for what seemed like an eternity. Late in the day, the wolf shattered Tyr's shield, trying to swallow his arm whole. However, before the wolf could bite off his arm, Tyr sliced through its neck, killing it.

As the wolf's head hit the ground, Tyr saw his bloody hand fall from the wolf's throat. Dropping to his knees, he bled to death.

In the morning, Heimdall sounded the horn restarting Ragnarök, raising Tyr and the wolf to battle for eternity, forever repeating daily Tyr's death blow.

J.B. Wocoski is the author and narrator of the shortstorypodcast.com with three flash fiction short storybooks published in the last three years. He is currently working on book 4 "Short Story Podcast 2019." He writes mostly science fiction, fantasy, and horror stories. He won the 2016 Little Tokyo Short Story Writing Contest with his short story "The Last Master of Go."
Website: shortstorypodcast.com

Ancient Power
by T.W. Garland

"To heal you," Isis said, "I need to know your true name."

"Saying my name," Ra said, "will reveal my ancient power." The venom of the snake bite burned into his neck, its poison plunging him closer to annihilation.

"It is the cost of your life."

Ra leant forward and whispered his true name.

Restoring life to a God is no easy task. Even with the true name of Ra, the healing ritual pushed Isis to the very brink of destruction, but the poison receded.

Life returned to Ra, and Isis smiled as her snake hid itself amongst her robes.

T.W. Garland has a stack of Victorian novels that taunt him with their unbroken spines. He has published stories containing monster hunters, supernatural creatures, steampunk adventurers, aberrations of nature, crazed criminals, and psychic detectives. He buys more books than he could hope to read and is glad not to have been born in the nineteenth century or in a novel by Dickens. One day he hopes to live in the real world.
Website: twgarland.wordpress.com

Foreshadowed
by Paula R.C. Readman

Genius stood in a forgotten realm, foreshadowing a spoiled child. She kept one step in either front to protect it or behind to catch it when it fell. As the child grew into adulthood, they became more arrogant and selfish.

"What of my life?" Genius asked, "Do I have no value?"

"Your job is to protect the child from the cradle to the grave. Nothing more, or less.

"But what if they're not worthy of their life?"

"It's not our place to question, or ours to let them die."

Genius nodded, turned her back on her ward, and closed her eyes.

Paula R.C. Readman *learnt 'How to Write' from books which her husband purchased from eBay. After 250 purchases, he finally told her 'just to get on with the writing'. Since 2010, she's had 34 stories published.*
Blog: paulareadman1.wordpress.com

Hell's Baker
by Kimberly Rei

I told her. This wasn't the place for her, but she wouldn't listen. Now she's taken over the Lake of Inimitable Flames. Last I heard, she was knitting caps for everyone in the Ninth Circle. "That ice looks nasty," she said. Of course, it does! It's Hell!

She's asking questions about the other Circles. No doubt she'll soon be making tea and cookies for the gluttons on Three. She already baked treats for Cerberus. He wags when she visits. My terrifying, slavering hellhound. Wagging.

I sent to St Peter for help. The messenger returned. Said Pete just walked away. Laughing.

Kimberly Rei has been writing for as long as she can remember. At five years old, her parents gifted her with a set of Children's Classics that she had no hope of reading yet. The potential alone sparked a love of words that has never wavered. Kim has taught writing workshops and edited novels for authors you may recognise. She has published several short stories and now can't stop chasing paper dragons. She currently lives in Tampa Bay, Florida, with her wife and an abundance of gorgeous beaches to explore.

Let the Children Cry
by Zoey Xolton

The dutiful mother wept silently as she ascended the *Templo Mayor*, the Great Temple. The walk felt like an eternity, each step like a knife to the heart. At the top, the dual shrines of her people awaited. With an aching soul, she approached the shrine of Tlaloc, the Aztec God of Rain and Storms.

Crushing the child to her chest one last time, she placed the wailing infant on the altar and turned away. The priests advanced with their incense and ceremonial blades.

The tears of children were sacred to Tlaloc and would ensure rain and prosperity for all.

Zoey Xolton *is an Australian speculative fiction writer, primarily of dark fantasy, paranormal romance, and horror. She is also a proud mother of two and is married to her soulmate. Outside of her family, writing is her greatest passion. She is especially fond of short fiction and is working on releasing her own themed collections in the future.*
Website: www.zoeyxolton.com

Mother Medea
by Joshua E. Borgmann

It wasn't just the divorce. Jason leaving me after I saved him from fertilising my father's garden stung. However, the children brought it on themselves. They kept telling me that now they'd have a real mother not some "foreign whore." My eldest called me a witch and an abomination to motherhood. He said the gods spat on me. I am the daughter of a demigod, a priestess, a princess. Yet my children mocked me. Jason suffers rightfully, but those wretched children were sacrifices. I am a woman with the blood of Titans in her veins, and I am never sorry.

Joshua E. Borgmann holds degrees from Drake University, Iowa State University, and the University of South Carolina. He grew up on horror and science fiction and had long intended to become a great master of the art form before he was sucked into the bottomless pit of academia. He toils away his days as an English instructor at a small community college and dreams of being able to escape into a world of fantasy and terror where there are no student papers to grade. He and his wife reside in a nameless rural Iowa town surrounded by terrible cornfields where he is terrorised by several felines who have taken refuge in his home.

Condor
by Beth W. Patterson

I first saw Condor as I headed towards the Temple of the Sun. The wind was his chariot. I saw him next in the streets of Cuenca, disguised as a man. The wind was his voice through the melodic bamboo rondador.

The third time I saw Condor was in dreamtime. The wind was his servant, blowing leaves to the ground into a celestial mandala. He said, "If you step into the circle, you can never return."

The Incan Sun or the Cañari Moon? I made my choice as black wings engulfed me. The talons through my heart brought exquisite agony.

Beth W. Patterson *was a full-time musician for over two decades before diving into the world of writing, a process she describes as "fleeing the circus to join the zoo". She is the author of the books* Mongrels and Misfits, *and* The Wild Harmonic, *and a contributing writer to over forty anthologies. Patterson has performed in nineteen countries, expanding her perspective as she goes. Her playing appears on over a hundred and ninety albums, soundtracks, videos, commercials, and voice-overs (including seven solo albums of her own).*
She lives in New Orleans, Louisiana with her husband Josh Paxton, jazz pianist extraordinaire.
Website: www.bethpattersonmusic.com
Facebook: bethodist

Save Me
by Ximena Escobar

A fingertip on his palm before the tip of a rusty nail sets. He keeps his eyes open, as if the colour blue can ease the pain, but he feels it all the same, cotton anguish opening inside him. He sees the dreadful swing in the periphery and feels the terrible wind, the clink reverberating as iron crosses skin, flesh, and cartilage.

Bound to the wood he screams, yet still hears the crisp steps on the gravel, senses the looming shadow above the other hand.

The blue light flickers in the daytime sky, but he only sees its trail abandon him.

Ximena Escobar is writing stories and poetry. Originally from Chile, she is the author of a translation into Spanish of the Broadway Musical "The Wizard of Oz" and of an original adaptation of the same, "Navidad en Oz", both produced in her home country. Since 2018 she has published several short stories in various anthologies and online platforms and is now slowly working on her own collection. Ximena has a degree in Arts & Communication Science and lives in Nottingham with her family.
Facebook: Ximenautora
Twitter: @laximenin

The Labyrinth
by R.S. Nevil

Aetius ran, sprinting through the corridor.

He needed to hide, needed to find a way out.

It was no use though. There was no place to hide. And there was no escape. Not from the maze.

A roar echoed through the hallway, the sound spinning him back the way he had come.

He could hear footsteps now, the clashing of hooves against stone.

His body began to shake, his mind racing.

There was no way out, not as the creature rounded the corner.

Half-man. Half-bull. It was enormous. It was the largest being he had ever seen.

It was the Minotaur.

R.S. Nevil is an avid reader and author. He mainly writes science fiction, while also dabbling in different types of short stories. From a small town in rural Georgia, R.S. has a Bachelors in Civil Engineering from Georgia Southern. Writing has always been a passion of his, and he hopes to one day be published. While also working his primary job at the local Nuclear Plant, R.S. spends most of his free time reading, writing, and trying to perfect his craft.

Sons and Daughters
by Lyndsey Ellis-Holloway

The Sons of Anubis threw back their jackal-like heads and howled at the darkening sky.

Ra took the sun in his fist, robbing the desert of its light.

The Daughters of Bastet had betrayed them—had killed a Son, stabbed him in the back, and sent him into the Abyss.

Once the eclipse was at its peak, they would attack, these warrior Sons would have their revenge.

They would pay for this betrayal, the Sons would ensure their brother was avenged, that his former Mate found him in the Abyss herself, for retribution.

Her blood would stain the sands.

Lyndsey Ellis-Holloway is a writer from Knaresborough, UK. She writes fantasy, sci-fi, horror, and dystopian stories, focussing on compelling characters and layering in myth and legend at every opportunity. Her mind is somewhat dark and twisted, and she lives in perpetual hope of owning her own dragon someday; but for now, she writes about them to fill the void...and to stop her from murdering people who annoy her. When she's not writing, she spends time with her husband, her dogs, and her friends enjoying activities such as walking, movies, conventions, and of course writing for fun as well!
Website: theprose.com/LyndseyEH

Stallo
by J.M. Meyer

Stallo, a troll in the Far North, slept very late one morning and woke up ravenous. Unable to control his hunger, he ate all his wives and children. Five minutes after the last scream signalled his feast's end, the loneliness started. He decided to abduct several Sami children and their mothers to start another family. Stallo, who was tall as the highest evergreen, walked many miles to the humans' small cabins. The shaking earth alerted the humans to pray to Horagalles, god of lightning, to scare this evil monster. But Horagalles also slept late. The god did not hear their prayers.

J.M. Meyer is a writer, artist, and small business owner living in New York, where she received her Master's degree from Teachers College, Columbia University. Jacqueline enjoys writing speculative fiction and mysteries. Her favourite author is Alice Munro and her favourite film…is…anything horror related. Jacqueline also enjoys hiking with her dog Molly and the company of her husband Bruce and daughters Julia, Emma, and Lauren. Jacqueline's mantra lately: there's no such thing as failing, it's called learning.
Website: jmoranmeyer.net
Amazon: www.amazon.com/author/jacquelinemoranmeyer

The Usurper
by Zoey Xolton

The Great King of the Underworld and Judge of the Dead, Osiris, sat slumbering upon his golden throne. By the flickering torchlight, through the tangible silence of the crypt kingdom, crept his brother, Set.

As swift as lightning he struck—cleaving Osiris' head from his shoulders with a glinting scythe. Then, like a maddened butcher, he hacked his sibling into twenty-six pieces before setting out and delivering the remains to all those whom he desired to implicate in his brother's murder.

While the ancient gods clamoured and fought amongst themselves, he would seize the throne of the Underworld for himself.

Zoey Xolton *is an Australian speculative fiction writer, primarily of dark fantasy, paranormal romance, and horror. She is also a proud mother of two and is married to her soulmate. Outside of her family, writing is her greatest passion. She is especially fond of short fiction and is working on releasing her own themed collections in the future.*
Website: *www.zoeyxolton.com*

Lord of Smoking Mirrors
by A.R. Johnston

The jungle was hot and oppressive, even at night. He didn't care. He walked through it like the shadow he was. Tezcatlipoca, the Lord of Smoking Mirrors. He was a supreme ruler, a god above all others. He was vengeance personified, for he could see evil behaviour anywhere in the world and he could strike it down.

Jaguars snarled and howled out in the nights to him. He smiled. The cats were letting him know that there was something not quite right going on within his domain. He would set things right.

Death and destruction were on the menu tonight.

A.R. Johnston is a small-town girl from Nova Scotia, Canada. She is known to write mostly urban fantasy, though she goes where the muses lead her and you never know where that may be. She is a lover of coffee, good tv shows, and horror flicks and a reader of good books. She pretends to be a writer when real life doesn't get in the way. Pesky full-time job and adulting!
Facebook: arjohnstonauthor
Website: arjohnstonauthor.wordpress.com

The Golden One
by Simon Clarke

El Dorado stands waiting high above.

You are the greatest of all offerings. So you freely give yourself to imagined horror. You have been kept deep in the temple and moved from level to level through dark passages. At each stage you wait and recite the golden words. All offerings made before you increase in significance, until it is time to move into the heat and light of the highest platform at the House of the Chosen Woman.

"Cuxi, know the walls of your womb are lined with light and life, promising everything."

"With such understanding you can now accept death."

Simon Clarke *lives and writes in Norfolk, United Kingdom. His first published microfiction story, 'Loss', appeared on Black Hare Press. His first short story appeared in What If? on Black Hare Press. He enjoys writing fiction and poetry. He regularly submits to UK and international publications and enjoys reading short pieces and poetry at open mic events. He is currently working on his first novel. His main influences reflect authors he read as a teenager: J.R.R. Tolkien, Ian Fleming, Peter O'Donnell, H.P. Lovecraft, Raymond Chandler, and Sir Arthur Conan Doyle. He loves Gothic literature and all things mystical and mysterious.*

Queen of Connaught
by Stacey Jaine McIntosh

Darkness rose in Ulster, Her Majesty's cattle raid progressed during a cloudless night.

Full of ire, the Queen of Connaught rode out with her army of men; her heart set on regaining her prized bull.

The sounds of men and cattle could be heard long into the night.

At last dawn rose and blood turned the muddied ground to rust. Maeve emerged, victorious; her face and chest drenched with the blood of Ailill mac Mata's men.

She roared, triumphant. As mighty and proud as her bull. Then she raised Ailill's head upon her spear for her men to look upon.

Stacey Jaine McIntosh *was born in Perth, Western Australia, where she still resides with her husband and their four children. Although her first love has always been writing, she once toyed with being a Cartographer and subsequently holds a Diploma in Spatial Information Services. Since 2011, she has had a vast number of stories and a few poems published online as well as in various anthologies. Stacey is also the author of Solstice, Morrighan, Lost, and Le Fay and she is currently working on several other projects simultaneously. When not with her family or writing she enjoys reading, photography, genealogy, history, Arthurian myths, and witchcraft.* *Website:* www.staceyjainemcintosh.com

VIII.XXIV
by Ralphie Graves

Constricted and choking, your eyes dance to the sky. Is it snow?

I warned you not to come a-knocking past midnight; yet here you sit, gasping for breath and pleading silently for life.

Perhaps you misunderstood my wrath the first time. Perhaps you're as lost in your pleasures as they were. Pompeii.

The shadows flicker from the corners, from the earth, from the sky. Pure darkness takes you—the black of closed and unlighted rooms.

I am smiling at your misfortune, my first amusement since 079. *I am Vulcan.* My voice shakes the mountainsides.

You—buried and forgotten—alone.

—Consum—

*From within the depths of urban New Jersey comes the debut of a mind full of mystic and wonder; an enigma. Unconventional and with depth, **Ralphie Graves** writes "with the magic and curiosity unseen in a generation." Also known as the Car Ghost, their works have been referred to as "refreshingly simple" and "delightfully twisted." They are "an artist, and the mind is the canvas" and are mastered in several different styles and genres. The impression left will linger beyond a lifetime. Facebook: theofficialcarghost*

Hunger
by Abi Marie Palmer

Ravenously, they cast their torches around my home. Gold, gleaming gemstones, and ornamental glass wink back at them, immaculate. The balding one prods a gold collar, inset with blood-red carnelian. I wore it to the grand procession of Ptolemy Philadelphus, during my human years.

"This piece alone will be worth millions—*hundreds of millions*—John!"

I lick what's left of my lips, enjoying their obliviousness. As they explore, they theorise idly about my life. They suspect I chose to be buried with this treasure out of greed. They are right, in a way.

But the treasure is merely the bait.

Abi Marie Palmer is a freelance proofreader and editor with an English Literature degree from Cardiff University. She is training to become an English teacher and enjoys writing in her spare time.
Instagram: abimariepalmer

The Rise and Fall
by Dawn DeBraal

Ancient Rome was amazing in its inventions. Newspapers, grid-based cities, aqueducts, sanitation, sewer systems, roads, surgical tools, techniques, Julian calendar, arches, Roman numerals (go figure), all attributed to Roman ingenuity and the spread of their empire.

Somewhere along the line, the Roman empire fell. After years of research and several offered theories, one theory still holds.

Lead in the pipes that fed the water to their houses and fountains—Romans drank it, bathed in it. Memory problems, sterility, abdominal cramps, tingling hands, and feet. How ironic that the toxicity of metal would bring down the most powerful of all empires.

Dawn DeBraal lives in rural Wisconsin with her husband Red, two rat terriers, and a cat. She has discovered that her love of telling a good story can be written. Published stories with Palm-sized press, Spillwords, Mercurial Stories, Potato Soup Journal, Edify Fiction, Zimbell House Publishing, Clarendon House Publishing, Blood Song Books, Black Hare Press, Fantasia Divinity, Cafelit, Reanimated Writers, Guilty Pleasures, Unholy Trinity, The World of Myth, Dastaan World, Vamp Cat, Runcible Spoon, Dark Christmas, Siren's Call, Iron Horse Publishing, Falling Star Magazine 2019 Pushcart Nominee.
Amazon: amazon.com/Dawn-DeBraal/e/B07STL8DLX

The Final Curtain
by J.W. Garrett

Today would go down in history as a win for the people—if their band of assassins was successful. The Theatre of Pompey was quiet, its own silent omen before the planned carnage to come. His comrades trusted him with this role. His job as actor provided perfect cover for the daggers hidden just off stage where he could dole out the weapons to the killers lying in wait.

If discovered prematurely his life ended.

Today.

But if successful…

An accomplice circled his cue.

Waiting…

Knives brandished, sinking repeatedly into the Emperor's flesh, dripped red.

Blood slicked, his body fell.

__J.W. Garrett__ has been writing in one form or another since she was a teenager. She currently lives in Florida with her family but loves the mountains of Virginia where she was born. Her writings include YA fantasy as well as short stories. Since completing Remeon's Quest-Earth Year 1930, the prequel in her YA fantasy series, Realms of Chaos, she has been hard at work on the next in the series, scheduled to release August 2020. When she's not hanging out with her characters, her favourite activities are reading, running, and spending time with family.

Website: www.jwgarrett.com

BHC Press: www.bhcpress.com/Author_JW_Garrett.html

Life on the Great Wall
by Gary Rubidge

"Build and move on." Guang kept repeating angrily to himself. "Zhen, China's first Emperor, has unified the warring states, yet he's still building this great wall across the northern borders to keep the terrifyingly vicious nomadic invaders out. Well, I've never seen any of them in these parts ever!"

Then, to his surprise, an arrow suddenly appeared in his chest where his heart should be.

Screaming Xiongnu tribesman charged over the hill on horseback waving swords, scattering the defenceless peasants.

Even those who'd already died building the wall were fleeing and Guang joined them, scared for a life already lost.

Gary Rubidge currently resides in Western Australia and is a newcomer to writing, having reached the age of 50 without consideration to authoring anything other than work reports. Encouraged by friends to put his ideas to paper, he has finally taken the plunge and this is his first effort. There are many more ideas begging to be released and they are lining up to be put to paper.

Sumerian Burial
by McKenzie Richardson

When a loved one dies in this land between the Tigris and Euphrates rivers, we bury them under our homes. It is easy to tend to the graves when they are nearby. If the rituals are not done properly, the dead return as ghosts.

Recently, there have been many unhappy spirits, but their ghosts are not all that rise. This room fills with the sound of my father's fingernails clawing beneath the mud bricks of the floor. He died last week; I buried him myself. Still he stirs.

Something is coming. And I do not think it is merely ghosts.

McKenzie Richardson lives in Milwaukee, WI. Her horror stories have been featured in various anthologies including Evil Lurks, Pandemic, and After: Undead Wars. She has also published a variety of poems and flash fiction pieces.
Facebook: mckenzielrichardson
Blog: www.craft-cycle.com

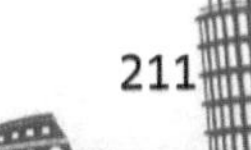

Oya
by Rowanne S. Carberry

The Santera leads the worship. Chanting a mashup of words, the meaning lost over years of bastardisation.

The women dance.

Oya stares in disgust as the dance leads to an altar with a chicken. She leads its spirit away as the body dances without a head.

They want rain? I'll give them rain.

Oya raises her hands, wishing they could see the real chants.

Cheers below as skies open.

It quickly floods; they try to flee.

With a flash of her hand, Oya brings down her sword, mirrored by lightning on Earth.

She walks away, leaving their souls to wander.

Rowanne S. Carberry *was born in England in 1990, where she stills lives now with her cat Wolverine. Rowanne has always loved writing, and her first poem was published at the age of 15, but her ambition has always been to help people. Rowanne studied at the University of Sunderland where she completed combined honours of Psychology with Drama. Rowanne writes to offer others an escape. Although Rowanne writes in varied genres, each story or poem she writes will often have a darkness to it, which helped coin her brand, Poisoned Quill Writing—Wicked words from a poisoned quill.*
Facebook: PoisonedQuillWriting
Instagram: @poisoned_quill_writing

Caesar's Vengeance
by Jasmine Jarvis

It was my first session into past life regression, and I was sceptical as I let his voice guide me back in time.

"What do you see?" he asks.

"An…emperor…I'm holding a dagger… I stab him… We all stab him."

"Yes, what else?"

"Cheering. We are all cheering. I have his blood on me."

A blow strikes my chest and my eyes shoot open. The very dagger I had seen in my past life now protrudes from my chest.

He watches me as I bleed out.

"One down, twenty-two to go." I hear him say as I lose consciousness.

Jasmine Jarvis is a teller of tales and scribbler of scribbles. She lives in Brisbane, Australia, with her husband, Michael; their two children, Tilly and Mish; their German Shepherd, Ripley; and indoor fat cat, Dwight K. Shrute.

Back in Church, Come Sunday
by Galina Trefil

My effigy is adorned in ribbons and herbs; then paraded through town, amidst dancing and singing. Inevitably, someone pulls out a lighter. Suddenly flames are hastily licking the straw doll's limbs like a lover's overeager caress. As it burns, my devotees celebrate their victory over the destruction that I, Morana, goddess of winter and death, can bring.

Usually, these Slavs are Christians, but on March 21, that imported religion is ignored and I am as feared in my ancient lands as I was 2000 years ago.

I laugh.

They'll be back in Church, come Sunday, pretending they aren't still Pagans.

Galina Trefil is a novelist specialising in women's, minority, and disabled rights. Her favourite genres are horror, thriller, and historical fiction. Her short stories and articles have appeared in Neurology Now, UnBound Emagazine, The Guardian, Tikkun, Romea.CZ, Jewcy, Jewrotica, Telegram Magazine, Ink Drift Magazine, The Dissident Voice, Open Road Review, and the anthologies "Flock: The Journey," "First Love," "Sea of Secrets," "Coffins and Dragons," "Organic Ink volume One," "Winds of Despair," "Waters of Destruction," "Curses & Cauldrons," "Unravel," "Hate," "Love," "Oceans," "Forgotten Ones," "Dark Valentine Holiday Horror Collection," and "Suspense Unimagined."
Website: galinatrefil.wordpress.com
Facebook: Rabbi-Galina-Trefil-535886443115467

Curse of the Cartographer
by Daniel Bagley

Those who find the fabled vault of the enigmatic Cartographer will yield no such reward, save for the curse embedded inside the crystalline metal alloy.

For the foolish, it is not death that awaits them, but something far more…consequential.

As with every myth and legend, the lure of treasure is too great for the minds of dim-witted adventurers, ignoring all perils.

Hasty actions require eternal punishment; with a single touch, the crystal siphons the raw essence of a human soul, using it to power the enchantment.

Let this be a lesson for all who dare to wander.

Daniel Bagley has spent the last three years finding his way through the world of literacy, to understand different styles and its various audiences. Dark fiction, for him, is a rarity among genres, because not many will explore its crevices. Of course, he sees it as a reflection of one's life, the journeys we have to take to seek redemption. Through the power of words, he finds it easier to unleash his emotions to convey my point. Despite its name, it's a genre worth exploring.

A Stirring of Fire in the Soul
by Jo Seysener

Bronzed skin coated the muscles of a mortal man, arched upwards, his supplication, beneath the heavenly body burning a scar towards the horizon.

His cries came in the tongue of his race, a backward, newborn species who called the gods their own. Her malcontent rippled across the sky in brilliant colours, lighting half their globe, so small, in the vastness of nothing.

Tiny echoed their awe, multitudes bowing before the muscled man on his golden pedestal. His pride spread, and they believed. His arms outstretched, promising a god his heart. Small, but perhaps worthy.

She reached out and took it.

Jo Seysener is a mum of three crazies, a scatter of chickens, a decrepit kelpie, and a rambunctious GSD. She lives with her husband near Brisbane, Australia. When she is not exposing her kids to cult storybooks from her childhood, she can be found in the kitchen experimenting with new flavours and pairings. She adores alpacas.
Facebook: joseysener
Website: www.joseysener.com

A Cat's Life
by Eddie D. Moore

Bahiti licked her leg and watched the priests pray over the former pharaoh. She wondered how much longer they'd poke, prod, and wrap his body. The man was dead; he wasn't coming back. She slow blinked and sighed at the human's death rituals.

Surely, a new pharaoh would be selected soon and then everything could go back to normal. Life was great in the palace. There was plenty of fresh fish to eat and mice to hunt. Bahiti began to purr at the thought of fresh food. She stopped purring when the priest holding a leather cord picked her up.

Eddie D. Moore *travels hundreds of hours a year, and he fills that time by listening to audiobooks. When he isn't playing with his grandchildren, he writes his own stories. You can find a list of his publications on his blog or by visiting his Amazon Author Page. While you're there, be sure to pick up a copy of his mini-anthology 'Misfits & Oddities'.*
Website: eddiedmoore.wordpress.com
Amazon: amazon.com/author/eddiedmoore

The Quipu
by Chris Hewitt

Carl loved ancient history. He scoured the globe, deciphering the written records of countless long-dead civilisations. He'd studied them all, bar one. The one that would make his name. Finally, high in the Andes he found his holy grail, a legendary quipu. Running his hand over its multi-coloured tangle of knotted strings, he knew the elder would demand a high price. As he pulled out his wallet, an agonising stabbing pain floored him. "Why?" he pleaded. The elder held a finger to Carl's bloodstained lips and turning to the quipu tied a red knot. Another offering to the old gods.

Chris Hewitt *resides in the beautiful garden of England, Kent UK and in the odd moments that he isn't dog walking, he pursues his passion for all things horror, fantasy and science-fiction.*
Blog:mused.blog
Twitter: @i_mused_blog

Bast's Last Priestess
by Alanna Robertson-Webb

I'm the last priestess of the goddess Bast.

You laughed when I said this, and you broke my fingers as punishment for worshipping a long-dead deity. What you didn't know was that I've gathered everything I need to put her back together, and it's you that she'll feast upon first.

The moon will be full soon, then I'll pull the pieces of Bast's Ka into my flesh. When I grow fangs and claws, you'd better run or attempt to grovel for forgiveness.

She's a kind goddess, but she enjoys ripping the flesh off those who willfully harm innocent people.

Alanna Robertson-Webb is a New York author who enjoys long weekends of LARPing, is terrified of sharks, and finds immense fun in being the chief editor at Eerie River Publishing. She lives with a fiancée and two cats, all of whom like to take over her favourite cosy blanket when they think they can get away with it. She is currently an MRO support member by day and an editor and author by candlelight. While she has been published before, which is wonderful, she one day aspires to run her own nerd-themed restaurant.
Website: arwauthor.wixsite.com/arwauthor
Amazon: amazon.com/Alanna-Robertson-Webb/e/B07LFYJYS5

The Blank Book
by Maura Yzmore

James hurls profanities towards the crypt and throws his hat on the ground. "It's gone! The gold is all gone!"

I sigh, "Graverobbers."

"At least your book's here." James cracks open the leather cover, flips a few pages, then hands it to me. "It's blank."

I smile and close my eyes. My fingertips fly across the pages and I read the embossed script in an ancient language, a chant floating off my lips.

James' face contorts with mounting terror, the sand whirling around us.

The one I awoke emerges from the crypt, glorious, the last sight before our blanching eyes.

Maura Yzmore is a writer and science professor based in the American Midwest. Some of her darker fare can be found in The Molotov Cocktail, Aphotic Realm, Coffin Bell, and elsewhere.
Website: maurayzmore.com
Twitter: @MauraYzmore

Beware Anubis
by J.B. Wocoski

In a fit of jealous rage, Osiris stole the Underworld from Anubis, forcing him into a granite sarcophagus next to the Sphinx. As Osiris sealed the lid, Anubis swore, "I will get revenge!"

Slowly, the Pharaohs and his minions vanished from the Nile Valley. Osiris faded from this world, as fewer and fewer followers entered the Underworld. Recently, an archaeologist unwittingly opened the sarcophagus and died of fright from the whirlwind howl of Anubis.

Beware Anubis, howling in the whirlwinds, collecting souls to rebuild his minions, demanding revenge on all those he encounters. Beware Anubis, the dog who swallowed millions.

J.B. Wocoski is the author and narrator of the shortstorypodcast.com with three flash fiction short storybooks published in the last three years. He is currently working on book 4 "Short Story Podcast 2019." He writes mostly science fiction, fantasy, and horror stories. He won the 2016 Little Tokyo Short Story Writing Contest with his short story "The Last Master of Go."
Website: shortstorypodcast.com

The Fourth Matsabi
by Sue Marie St. Lee

A golden orb hovered in front of Foreman Abasi's eye. Turning translucent, it measured alignment and level of the granite monoliths laid for Khufu's Great Pyramid. Satisfied, Abasi signalled for placement of the next slab.

Uadjit and the other winged-serpent riders descended to set the next block. One of the ropes broke, workers scrambled, Abasi tripped, and the slab crushed him.

Architect Thabit ran to the fallen granite. "What happened?"

"Nothing," Uadjit answered, "We laid the slab for the fourth mastaba."

Thabit measured the alignment and level with the golden orb. "Good job. Where is Abasi?"

*Born in Chicago, **Sue Marie St. Lee** currently lives in Oklahoma with her husband and Manx cat. A storyteller since learning to talk, her wild imagination caused reprimands from her mother. Her imagination persevered. Retired from Finance Management, Sue began ghostwriting until 2019, choosing to have works published internationally, in print and online, under her own name. Black Hare Press, Fantasia Divinity, and Spillwords Press are some of the publishers to feature Sue's work to date.*
Blog: suemariestlee.home.blog
Amazon: amazon.com/Sue-Marie-St.-Lee/e/B07WJFRF1L

An Unfortunate Birth
by Shawn M. Klimek

Visibly drunk and anxious, Han Chunhui leaned against his brother, Zimu. "Yuexin cries out nonstop," he said. "I fear for her life and for that of the baby."

"Have courage, brother," said Zimu. "Li cried the same way during labour with your nephews. It is an auspicious sign. It means the baby is vigorous and eager!"

Both men froze to listen as the birthing cries suddenly paused, soon followed by a baby's angry squall. When womanly wails of sorrow joined the noise, Chunhui fell despairing to his knees.

Both men realised instantly what the wailing meant.

It was a girl.

Shawn M. Klimek is the internationally published author of more than 170 poems and stories, in several genres. He is the author of Hungry Thing, an illustrated fantasy tale told in five poems. He lives in Illinois, USA, with his wife and their Maltese.
Website: blog.jotinthedark.com
Facebook: shawnmklimekauthor

Our Goddess Rides from the East
by Shelly Jarvis

We dip the head in the ochre, then the long bones, and the fingers. Some do not bury the fingerbones as we do, but those hands did so many things.

The fire is high and hot, ready for the rest of him. It burns him up, filling our noses with the scent of flesh, so thick I can taste it on the back of my tongue. I breathe deep, filling my lungs with the fragrance of my friend.

We bury the head facing east, so he can see the goddess when she rides out to meet him, taking him home.

Shelly Jarvis is a speculative fiction author from West Virginia, US. She found a lifelong love of sci-fi and fantasy in the third grade when she found Madeleine L'Engle's "A Wrinkle in Time." Shelly is an avid reader, a Whovian, the ideal viewer of dog rescue videos, and undoubtedly Ravenclaw. She currently has three YA sci-fi books available for purchase on Amazon.
Website: www.ShellyJarvis.com

In the Tombs
by Radar DeBoard

Far under the great European cities, there are catacombs that run for miles. These long stretches of tunnel lead deep underground and end in the great tombs.

These graves are home to the ancient kings of long ago. Without their leadership and courage, the world of man wouldn't exist. They were the ones who brought man out of servitude and gave them their current place as rulers of the world.

But there is something else in the tombs.

The ones who came before man. These immortal creatures have been trapped for too long. That is why I set them free.

Radar DeBoard *is a horror movie and novel enthusiast who resides in the small town of Goddard, Kansas. He occasionally dabbles in writing and enjoys making dark tales for people to enjoy. He has had drabbles and short stories published in various electronic magazines and anthologies.*
Facebook: WriterRadarDeBoard

Chthonic
by T.M. Brown

The old man looked at his son with grave seriousness. "There are many who believe that a god dies when they are no longer worshipped. This is not true. Though defeated and driven into the earth by the Children of Chronos, the Titans are not dead. They cannot die. They cannot even sleep. They no longer hope to reclaim their status."

"In the abyssal depths of Tartarus, they can only imagine the terrible vengeance they will exact when they re-emerge. Wrath metastasizes in their dark hearts. No son… When a god is no longer worshipped, a terrible monster is born."

Captain T.M. Brown is a Space Operations Officer in the United States Army. He currently lives with his wife, Anna, and their two dogs, Fry and Zapp, in Colorado Springs. Although he has long held a passion for dark fantasy, cosmic horror, and speculative fiction, he has only recently taken up writing for publication.

Trial & Error
by Peter J. Foote

The stone locks into place with a thud. Reed torches highlight sand leaking from the shaft's roof.

"Vizier Nebankh, the trap is ready."

Nebankh brushes sand from his linen robes. "Proceed. Tombs belong to the dead."

Guards bring the convict forward.

"Reach the end of the shaft and you shall have your freedom," Nebankh says.

The convict runs, springing the trap with his target in sight.

Screams ring out. They discover the stone has pinned the convict rather than slay him.

Using his blade to kill the convict, Nebankh speaks, "Reset the trap, we must try again; Pharaoh demands it."

Peter J. Foote is a bestselling speculative fiction writer from Nova Scotia. Outside of writing, he runs a used bookstore specialising in fantasy & sci-fi, cosplays, and alternates between red wine and coffee as the mood demands. His short stories can be found in both print and ebook form, with his story "Sea Monkeys" winning the inaugural "Engen Books/Kit Sora, Flash Fiction/Flash Photography" contest in March of 2018. As the founder of the group "Genre Writers of Atlantic Canada", Peter believes that the writing community is stronger when it works together.
Twitter: @PeterJFoote1
Website: peterjfooteauthor.wordpress.com

The Kukeri
by Koji A. Dae

The clanging of brass bells makes me drop my spoon into my soup. The windows are black as pitch. No moon on the longest night of the year.

"Get your cloak," Mama commands.

The creatures pass our house wrapped in stinking goat pelts and roaring through vicious masks. I tremble as Mama pays them a sack of flour. Two weeks' bread.

We follow with the villagers. I cling to Mama. For warmth. For courage.

The Kukeri stomp their feet and bellow. Mama says their dance frightens evil spirits.

I try to hide my shaking. Mama can't know what I am.

Koji A. Dae is an American writer living in Bulgaria. She has work published with Tales from the Moonlit Path and ParABnormal Magazine, and forthcoming with Daily Science Fiction. When not writing, she can be found dancing the blues. Website: kojiadae.ink

Passion
by Kerri Jesmer

Aodh followed Varik out upon the moors, the sun setting and his sword at his side. He glanced behind to ensure no others saw them. His anger stirred. When distance seemed enough and night had fallen, Aodh quietly approached and called Varik's name. As Varik turned, he felt only the sword's initial strike before the light of life vanished in his eyes. At the water's edge, Aodh washed his hands and sword of blood. Varik would be found; his body made ash and his urn buried in the field beyond the village. And Varik would never look upon Ove again.

*Born in Germany, **Kerri Jesmer** was raised on the Eastern Plains of Colorado and currently lives in Utah with her husband and adult daughter, two dogs, and three cats, one of which is a fur grandbaby. She is an author and mentor. She has been published in Dastaan World Magazine, Fifty-word Stories, Spillwords.com, Inner Circle Writers' Magazine, Dark X-mas Holiday Drabbles (100 Word Holiday Horror Stories) Anthology, and Portal, The Inner Circle Writers' Group Children's Anthology. She spent several years mentoring her daughter's middle and high school writing groups. She has three blogs, the newest on writing, and has been blogging since 2004.*

Medea
by Paul Benkendorfer

What does a man love most in the world?

He betrayed me. After everything I have done for him. After I saved his life repeatedly during my father's trials for the Golden Fleece. I loved him unconditionally, gave myself to him, abandoned my home, and bore his children.

Now I discover Jason, to whom I devoted my life, has forsaken me for another.

Tears gushing, I look at our sleeping children—his children. Knife in hand.

What does a man love most in the world?

I will destroy him the way he destroyed me. I will take that which he loves most.

Paul Benkendorfer is an English and history teacher from Scottsdale, Arizona, who mainly writes historical fiction, poetry, and non-fiction. He is currently working on his novel A Bridge Outside of Limerick based on the events of his great-grandfather who fought in the Irish Revolution of 1916. Paul has nearly 15 years' experience working with at-risk youth and children with special needs and continues to primarily work with them to this day. In 2014 Paul received a Bachelors in Creative Writing from the University of Arizona and is currently process of obtaining his Masters in Teaching Writing from Johns Hopkins University.
Twitter: @PBenkendorfer

Revenge
by Brian Rosenberger

His priests bind me. The linens suffocate and constrict my nose, mouth, and throat. Making breathing and curses difficult.

My grave mistake. I was caught. The Pharaoh's Bride, my queen, was not a temptation I could deny. Her will was my will and her will demanded satisfaction. I could not deny my queen.

She writhed beneath me in the sand, in the Royal Hall, and in the Pharaoh's chambers.

Anubis smiles, a mirror of the Pharaoh's.

I smile too as his priests wrap my death shroud tighter.

My queen is pregnant.

My child will satisfy my vengeance.

Anubis salivates, more death.

Brian Rosenberger lives in a cellar in Marietta, Georgia, USA, and writes by the light of captured fireflies. He is the author of "As the Worms Turns" and three poetry collections. He is also a featured contributor to the pro-wrestling literary collection "Three-Way Dance", available from Gimmick Press.
Facebook: HeWhoSuffers

Ra-Horakhty
by Matthew M. Montelione

The morning sun quickly climbed across the sky in a bright red blur, revealing a terrifying yet tantalising vision.

Ra-Horakhty, god of the rising sun, sat on a giant sandstone throne high above me. The sun disc above the towering falcon-headed deity obscured the features of his beaked face, but I knew what he desired: the sounds of my harp, which lay beside me, as it had in life.

I tried playing, but my heart, laden with sin, turned my fingers to dust.

Ra-Horakhty stood up angrily.

I finally saw the details of his face as he lunged towards me.

Matthew M. Montelione is a horror writer born and raised on Long Island in New York. His work has been published in many titles, including MONSTERS: A Horror Microfiction Anthology and Quoth the Raven: A Contemporary Reimagining of the Works of Edgar Allan Poe. Matthew lives with his wife in New York.
Website: maybeevils.com
Facebook: maybeevils

The Gifts We Bear
by James S. Austin

It was by divine right. Our divine right. How could one not see it so?

She, the great weaver, comes to us with hope. Her blessings to fill us, to make this world whole and true.

We were bestowed this gift, this night, on the rooftops of Eridu. Lying here, looking to the stars.

Our people, the mighty Sumerians, lords of the great rivers, hold all that matters. To think the savages could lay claim to our lands. A midnight pilferer.

My stomach rumbles now. Uttu's children will burst forth to bring ruin to the people of the sands.

I was born and raised near St. Petersburg, Florida. My early years were spent in the US Army and receiving BAs in Anthropology and History. I have edited three anthologies, 'It's a Grimm Life', 'Haunted by the Past', and 'Shattered Space' and have a few published short stories here and there, spanning from fantasy to horror, to science fiction. I also actively publish fantasy gaming products, building stories in another fashion. When not writing or editing, I spend my time as a traditional and digital artist.

Brazen
by S.N. Graves

Phalaris had enraged the bull and let its haunting bellows wash over Acragas more times than memory. He'd filled its burning belly with thieves and liars, politicians and rivals, old friends and new enemies alike. Even the bull's father, Perillos, who'd sculpted its beautiful, horrible face and gave it the voice of its victims through clever engineering, had been swallowed up.

Was perhaps fitting then, as Acragas mutinied, that Phalaris should find himself locked within its gut, fire roaring beneath, baking in his own juices and marinating in his own desperate pleas.

And how the bull did bellow that day.

S.N. Graves earned her MFA in Popular Fiction from Seton Hill University in 2014 and was a senior editor at Loose Id LLC until it closed its doors. She is now a professor at Southern New Hampshire University, teaching genre fiction with a concentration in horror. Graves also freelance edits and creates art, including book covers.
Website: www.sngraves.com
Facebook: Shannon.N.Graves

Queen of Denial
by Frances Tate

"It ends in flame and fangs, my princess." The diviner's head bowed. "The empire that founded Alexandria, the library that educated you, lost. Your family tradition of parental and sibling rivalry survives… Roman generals come…go, leaving scandal and offspring. Empires—and houses—fall."

"What of my legacy?" The young girl persisted. "Tell me I leave one that endures."

"Across centuries and continents." The diviner revealed. "The fascination you hold over men makes you immortal. Your strategy and cunning, iconic."

"And worth every drop of blood that I, and others, will pay for it."

"So, you'd change—"

"Nothing." Smiled Cleopatra.

Frances Tate is a British self-published writer of vampires and drabbles who lives in the north west of England. She enjoys gardening, exploring historical sites, cinema, reading, and travelling. She's taken pleasure in flight planning a cabbage white butterfly approach to careers, preferring to generalise rather than specialise. She trained as an Economics high school teacher and has a private pilot's licence amongst other things. Currently she writes (very restrained) overhaul instructions for an engineering company.

Honour of a Fallen Samurai
by Gary Rubidge

Minamoto glanced at the decapitated assassins beside him. "I am ashamed for I have brought great dishonour upon myself," he cried out with remorse to the soldiers and nobles nearby.

"I knew about this assassination attempt of my lord but did nothing. It is now my duty to repay my error in judgement. I am a Samurai, and harakiri is the only option left for me to restore my honour."

Minamoto swiftly dropped to his knees and commenced the ritual ceremony that started with him drinking his saké and will end with his suicide by disembowelment with his tantō.

Gary Rubidge currently resides in Western Australia and is a newcomer to writing, having reached the age of 50 without consideration to authoring anything other than work reports. Encouraged by friends to put his ideas to paper, he has finally taken the plunge and this is his first effort. There are many more ideas begging to be released and they are lining up to be put to paper.

Tebwem
by Stephen Herczeg

The elders warned us.

"Stay away from the deep waterhole. The Tebwem, the eater of flesh, lives there."

I believed them. Why would they lie to us?

Iluka didn't.

The day was hot. We'd been picking berries on the edge of the forest.

As we headed back, Iluka spied the deep waterhole. She dropped her load, ran, and dived in.

I saw its wake. I screamed. Iluka disappeared beneath the water.

It rose, with Iluka, dead in its jaws. I ran.

I've never seen anything like it, I never will again, and I'll never go near the deep waterhole.

Stephen Herczeg *is an IT geek based in Canberra, Australia. He has been writing for over twenty years and has completed a couple of dodgy novels, sixteen feature length screenplays, and numerous short stories and scripts. His horror work has featured in Sproutlings, Hells Bells, Below the Stairs, Trickster's Treats #1 and #2, Shades of Santa, Behind the Mask, Beyond the Infinite, The Body Horror Book, Anemone Enemy, Petrified Punks, and Beginnings. He has also had numerous Sherlock Holmes stories published through the Belanger Books—Sherlock Holmes anthologies.*

Amazon: amazon.com/-/e/B07916SQQS
Facebook: stephenherczegauthor

Charnel Beach
by Simon Clarke

People say that after a storm you must never venture onto the beach at old Dunwich, especially at twilight. There are no shadows at twilight so the shades roam unseen.

Below the waves, in haunted cloisters, the monks' chants merge with the rushing and shushing sea. They tried prayers, ancient magic. Still the dark waters rose and consumed the town. But sacred duty continues even after death. Forced to emerge once more to collect bones washed from old graves high on Dunwich cliff, robed wraiths noiselessly cross the beach to take all lost souls back beneath the waves.

Simon Clarke *lives and writes in Norfolk, United Kingdom. His first published microfiction story, 'Loss', appeared on Black Hare Press. His first short story appeared in What If? on Black Hare Press. He enjoys writing fiction and poetry. He regularly submits to UK and international publications and enjoys reading short pieces and poetry at open mic events. He is currently working on his first novel. His main influences reflect authors he read as a teenager: J.R.R. Tolkien, Ian Fleming, Peter O'Donnell, H.P. Lovecraft, Raymond Chandler, and Sir Arthur Conan Doyle. He loves Gothic literature and all things mystical and mysterious.*

Our Billy
by Hannah Retallick

Our Billy loves the Ancient Romans. He had the Best Project Award telling the school about crucifixion. Facts, techniques, fancy diagrams…he had them squirming.

He's proper into his practical research, like a scientist historian, spreading it out across the kitchen—glue, wood, string, and the like. The wriggling mice screech on their crosses, dripping blood on the worktop. He always clears up after though, so as I can get on with dinner. Such a hard worker he is.

Best Project Award, no less. His father and I never did well at school. We couldn't be prouder of our Billy.

Hannah Retallick *is a twenty-six-year-old from Anglesey, North Wales. She was home educated and then studied with the Open University, graduating with a First-class honours degree, BA in Humanities with Creative Writing and Music, before passing her Creative Writing MA with a Distinction. She was shortlisted in the Writing Awards at the Scottish Mental Health Arts Festival 2019, the Cambridge Short Story Prize, the Henshaw Short Story Competition June 2019, and the Bedford International Writing Competition 2019.*
Website: ihaveanideablog.wordpress.com

Ys

by Stacey Jaine McIntosh

The king slept. Princess Dahut stole the key to the kingdom gate, to give to the Red Knight with whom she was besotted. And chaos ensued when the Red Knight revealed himself to be the Devil. Delighted by the screams of all who drowned.

As the king now awakened, saddled his horse Morvac'h, to whisk his daughter away to higher ground, struggled and nearly drowned himself. It was only when he cast his child into the sea, he was freed. She however didn't drown. Instead, Dahut is turned into a mermaid as punishment. Forced to lure sailors to their deaths.

Stacey Jaine McIntosh *was born in Perth, Western Australia, where she still resides with her husband and their four children. Although her first love has always been writing, she once toyed with being a Cartographer and subsequently holds a Diploma in Spatial Information Services. Since 2011, she has had a vast number of stories and a few poems published online as well as in various anthologies. Stacey is also the author of Solstice, Morrighan, Lost, and Le Fay and she is currently working on several other projects simultaneously. When not with her family or writing she enjoys reading, photography, genealogy, history, Arthurian myths, and witchcraft.*
Website: www.staceyjainemcintosh.com

Mother of Harappa
by Monica Schultz

Everyone in the Indus Valley adores their Mother, but it isn't enough. They do not worship her as they should. There are no temples to withstand the ages, nor blood sacrifices to strengthen her. All her children offer are idols and open prayer spaces.

The neighbouring Goddesses laugh.

They titter as Mother's once fertile soil burns under dancing demons.

They snicker as the howling wind steals Mother's precious monsoon rain.

They cackle as Mother dwindles to a flickering flame, easily snuffed, while they become raging wildfires.

Now, forsaken by her children, the earth reclaims Mother, until a worthy generation rises.

Monica Schultz is a full-time Mathematics and History teacher from Ipswich, Australia, with a passion for writing fantasy. When she isn't busy finding "x" in the latest equation, you can find her curled up with a young adult book and a cat on her lap.
Website: https://monicaschultzauthor.weebly.com/
Instagram: @monicaschultzauthor

The Watcher, the Walker
by Liam Hogan

I walk the Earth for years without number.

I watch ancient civilisations rise and fall, leaving behind only myths of their passing. I walk scorched fields below which lie city walls I can still trace, in memory, at least. Kerma, Nobatia, Carthage, Benin… The bones of those I meet will crumble to dust ere I pass this way again.

Each mighty empire, no more nor less than this one, felt certain it would last forever, their future as hazy and distant as their past.

I would tell them, if only they would listen.

This too shall pass.

I walk on.

Liam Hogan *is a London based short story writer, the host of Liars' League, and a Ministry of Stories mentor. His story "Ana", appears in Best of British Science Fiction 2016 (NewCon Press) and his twisted fantasy collection, "Happy Ending Not Guaranteed", is published by Arachne Press.*

Corona Borealis
by Rachel Miller

The hemp-clothed peasants pound her pristine wooden temple walls. Escalating shouts of "Bù zài" reverberate through the inner sanctuary. They owe her blood. Without their annual tribute, she has only hours before fading.

A wall cracks. Only one option now.

Corona forces her last bits of invulnerability into the transformation. Sickly yellow emanates from her. She's on fire. Screeching, she shoots through the ceiling to the northern sky and splits into seven fireballs as she ascends.

Corona would endure. She'd wait there. One day, she'd demand the blood of millions. The world would fear her by her new name: virus.

Rachel Miller graduated with degrees in English and Theology this May. She enjoys biting off more than she can chew and getting involved in every project that interests her. Currently, she's interested in drabble writing and would like to thank her writing professor for all his support and feedback. Gloriam Deo.

Timeless
by Stuart Conover

The old man bowed.

"For decades, I searched for you."

The woman studied him.

The most successful businessman on the planet.

A man who believed himself superior to all.

Especially women.

His vast wealth was worthless in the face of death.

Only a divine being could alter the course of destiny.

"Sit, there is no need for pretence."

Joints aching, he lifted himself to the seat.

"Magu. I don't want to die."

"What would you give to live eternally?"

"Anything!"

Smiling, she granted his wish.

Now, the old man was a young woman.

Penniless.

Nameless.

Her latest servant.

For eternity.

Stuart Conover *is a father, husband, rescue dog owner, published author, blogger, journalist, horror enthusiast, comic book geek, science fiction junkie, and IT professional. With all of that to cram in daily, we have no idea if or when he sleeps or how he gets writing done! (We suspect it has to do with having evil clones.) Stuart is a Chicago native and runs the author resource Horror Tree.*

Feathers
by Brian Rosenberger

The elders exchanged stories.

Her favourite was the blackbird born as a man.

Long ago, the coughing sickness killed many villagers. Neither prayer nor roots gathered from the forest saved the dying.

One villager sought the Hag for her knowledge. She cackled when he described the sickness, eyes turning blood red. She agreed for a price. He nodded. Her cure worked. A debt needed paid.

Skin exchanged for feathers. Teeth now a strong beak. Talons for tearing.

Sometimes a blackbird visited his wife's dreams. She asks, "Do you miss me?"

"Like I would miss the wind."

Beneath her pillow, a black feather.

***Brian Rosenberger** lives in a cellar in Marietta, Georgia, USA, and writes by the light of captured fireflies. He is the author of "As the Worms Turns" and three poetry collections. He is also a featured contributor to the pro-wrestling literary collection "Three-Way Dance", available from Gimmick Press. Facebook: HeWhoSuffers*

Sing His Song as I Find Rest
by Shelly Jarvis

I step into the enclosure to the thunder of a thousand voices raised in supplication. The words pulse with the beat of my heart, faster with each step. Inside my body betrays my fear; outside I move with steadiness.

I am here to serve, to sacrifice.

The elders chose me for this honoured task. My eyes wander to the other nine men approaching and I smile, grateful I will not pass to the Undying Lands alone.

The priests approach with blessed blades. As blood pours from me, I listen to the chants and prepare to worship at the Creator's feet.

Shelly Jarvis is a speculative fiction author from West Virginia, USA. She found a lifelong love of sci-fi and fantasy in the third grade when she discovered Madeleine L'Engle's "A Wrinkle in Time". Shelly is an avid reader, a Whovian, the ideal viewer of dog rescue videos, and undoubtedly Ravenclaw. She currently has three YA sci-fi books available for purchase on Amazon. Website: www.ShellyJarvis.com

The Neikea
by Gabriella Balcom

One man spoke to his neighbour, who shook his head, and their voices rose, steadily growing louder. A few others began arguing, and soon everyone was.

The invisible Neikea, immortal Greek spirits of quarrels and grievances, watched. As one, they gestured towards the people.

Within minutes, the villagers were striking one another with their fists, weapons, anything available. Despite typically being a peaceful, loving people, they now thirsted for each other's blood; it flowed right and left from injuries.

The battle only stopped when no one remained alive to fight, dead bodies lying everywhere motionless.

Eyes glowing, the Neikea smiled.

Gabriella Balcom *lives in Texas with her family, loves reading and writing, and thinks she was born with a book in her hands. She works in a mental health field and writes fantasy, horror/thriller, romance, children's stories, and sci-fi. She likes travelling, music, good shows, photography, history, interesting tales, and animals. Gabriella says she's a sucker for a great story and loves forests, mountains, and back roads which might lead to who knows where. She has a weakness for lasagne, garlic bread, tacos, cheese, and chocolate, but not necessarily in that order.*
Facebook: GabriellaBalcom.lonestarauthor

What Was Once Lost
by Kimberly Rei

Fourteen years of research. Five years arguing with governments. Two years searching, promising his team the next turn would bring success. It was all worth it.

Aemon watched his students clear away sand, painstakingly uncovering bits of Yam, once lost to time and wind.

The first scream made him smile. In moments, they were all clawing at their throats, desperate for air. As blood poured from eyes and mouths, soaking into the desert, Aemon's beloved city rose. He drank in the sight, the souls, and the heat and shed the last illusion of mortality. It was good to be home.

Kimberly Rei has been writing for as long as she can remember. At five years old, her parents gifted her with a set of Children's Classics that she had no hope of reading yet. The potential alone sparked a love of words that has never wavered. Kim has taught writing workshops and edited novels for authors you may recognise. She has published several short stories and now can't stop chasing paper dragons. She currently lives in Tampa Bay, Florida, with her wife and an abundance of gorgeous beaches to explore.

The Ball Game
by Dawn DeBraal

The Mayans believed that the winner takes all. The game was vicious; the wounds were real. The kicks were meant to break the bones of their competitor's arms or legs. It was not a game of friends. It was fighting to the death.

For the winner, the honour of the victory. The loser beheaded and thrown into a cenote, deep in the jungle. The blood of the losing team members still stains the rocks and the water years after the custom was stopped. The dead would not remain hidden; their souls trapped in the dirty waters of death, crying out.

Dawn DeBraal *lives in rural Wisconsin with her husband Red, two rat terriers, and a cat. She has discovered that her love of telling a good story can be written. Published her stories with Palm-sized Press, Spillwords, Mercurial Stories, Potato Soup Journal, Edify Fiction, Zimbell House Publishing, Clarendon House Publishing, Blood Song Books, Black Hare Press, Fantasia Divinity, Cafelit, Reanimated Writers, Guilty Pleasures, Unholy Trinity, The World of Myth, Dastaan World, Vamp Cat, Runcible Spoon, Dark Christmas, Siren's Call, and Iron Horse Publishing, also appearing as a Falling Star Magazine 2019 Pushcart Nominee.*
Amazon: amazon.com/Dawn-DeBraal/e/B07STL8DLX

The Doom of Fate
by Olivia Arieti

The streaks of smoke marked the skyline ominously, and Aeneas kept pacing the deck without lowering his glance. The warmth of Dido's body was still in his arms, the lust of their embrace in his senses. Why did he leave?

"You have a duty, man; fate has made you his own," Mercury whispered one night, "Delays are not allowed."

At once, the Trojan's heart hardened; no pity was spared, his sword only was left behind…

While Lavinia was in his timeline, the dying queen's curse had signed his descendants' doom and the shadow of Hannibal was already preparing the elephants.

Olivia Arieti has a degree from the University of Pisa and lives in Torre del Lago Puccini, Italy, with her family. Besides being a published playwright, she loves writing retellings of fairy tales and, at the same time, is intrigued by supernatural and horror themes. Her stories appeared in several magazines and anthologies like Enchanted Conversations, Enchanted Tales Literary Magazine, Fantasia Divinity Magazine, Cliterature, Medieval Nightmares, Static Movement, 100 Doors To Madness Forgotten Tomb Press, Black Cats Horrified Press, Bloody Ghost Stories Full Moon Books, Death And Decorations Thirteen O'Clock Press, Infective Ink, Pandemonium Press, and Pussy Magic Magazine.

Pierce My Heart
by Lynne Phillips

The clock struck midnight. The hooves of his noble white steed clattered against the uneven cobblestones. People hid in their houses, trembling with fear. Doomed to repeat this ritual every night for eternity, the Templar Knight cradled his head in his lap. A red cross on his chest flashed in the moonlight.

"Please some brave soul, grab my sword and pierce my heart. Only such a fearless deed will release me from this endless torment and allow me to leave the streets of Prague," he pleaded. "Only then will I be forgiven for my sins; my beheading was not enough."

Lynne Phillips, a retired teacher, lives in the beautiful Northern Rivers Region of New South Wales, Australia. Her stories, across all genres, have been published in anthologies and various online magazines. Her priority is spending time with her family. Her passions are reading, writing, and keeping fit.

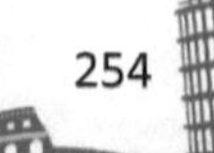

All in a Day's Work
by J.W. Garrett

Aharon climbed the quarry wall, turned, lifted the limestone to his neighbour, Fadil, farther up the cliff. The sun set. Aharon, sighed, relieved to meet his quota to finish the pyramid tomorrow. High on the cliff someone screamed, careening to his death, chased by the totality of their work for the afternoon, dumped when he fell. Dust and rock clouded Aharon's vision; he shifted his path, the roar of the rock getting closer. The team scurried, adding more limestone to the avalanche. Aharon prayed to Isis, calling on magic for safety as the falling rock buried the two men alive.

J.W. Garrett has been writing in one form or another since she was a teenager. She currently lives in Florida with her family but loves the mountains of Virginia where she was born. Her writings include YA fantasy as well as short stories. Since completing Remeon's Quest-Earth Year 1930, the prequel in her YA fantasy series, Realms of Chaos, she has been hard at work on the next in the series, scheduled to release August 2020. When she's not hanging out with her characters, her favourite activities are reading, running, and spending time with family.
Website: www.jwgarrett.com
BHC Press: www.bhcpress.com/Author_JW_Garrett.html

Bhoot Bangla, the House of Ghosts

by Lynne Phillips

The sun lit the tall stone walls of Bhangath Fortress, casting a shadow across the surrounding land, once again eclipsing Baba Balnath's retreat.

"I curse the Singh family. Your word is not worth the dust beneath my feet," the ancient ascetic roared. "There will be dark shadows on your fortress for eternity."

"Our crops have failed for five years, and sickness and death are everywhere," the people lamented. "It's the curse we are doomed forever."

The ghosts of their dead wandered the streets at night and even today no one dares stay after dark lest they remain trapped with them forever.

Lynne Phillips, a retired teacher, lives in the beautiful Northern Rivers Region of New South Wales, Australia. Her stories, across all genres, have been published in anthologies and various online magazines. Her priority is spending time with her family. Her passions are reading, writing, and keeping fit.

Ant Soldiers
by J.B. Wocoski

Professor Anderson, the archaeologist, remarked, "Ant inscriptions! This must be the Myrmidon Tomb; inside is the proof this site is Troy of the Iliad."

Breaking the Tomb seals, the workers tried to pry open the massive stone doors but to no avail. "Professor, the doors are too heavy to move, we need to bring down heavy equipment."

"All right, stop the excavation, everyone back to the…"

Beginning to move, the heavy stone doors shuddered.

"Wait, what's going on here?" were the last words Anderson muttered as the Myrmidon charged out of their unsealed hive, killing all in their path.

J.B. Wocoski *is the author and narrator of the shortstorypodcast.com with three flash fiction short storybooks published in the last three years. He is currently working on book 4 "Short Story Podcast 2019." He writes mostly science fiction, fantasy, and horror stories. He won the 2016 Little Tokyo Short Story Writing Contest with his short story "The Last Master of Go."*
Website: shortstorypodcast.com

Patagonia
by Ximena Escobar

Hard palms stretched on the dark bank of Lake Yelcho, Wentru stares silently at the water… Still as his contemplation, like the cleanest mirror to double the all-surrounding beauty: the star-pricked firmament, the black silhouette of the forest on the far side, and, ever imposing, the snow-covered mountain peaks, fluorescently luminous—an overwhelming monument of his privilege. *I am sky contained within this body… I am the absolute, within the minimum.* Nails digging into the stony sand, his fists close till blood warms him. *We won't build grand pyramids nor cities. But this…this…is what I'll die defending.*

Ximena Escobar *is writing stories and poetry. Originally from Chile, she is the author of a translation into Spanish of the Broadway Musical "The Wizard of Oz" and of an original adaptation of the same, "Navidad en Oz", both produced in her home country. Since 2018 she has published several short stories in various anthologies and online platforms and is now slowly working on her own collection. Ximena has a degree in Arts & Communication Science and lives in Nottingham with her family.*
Facebook: Ximenautora
Twitter: @laximenin

Fall of Osiris and His Children
by C.L. Williams

They were smart and intelligent, and followed Osiris loyally. Their infrastructure was believed to withstand any magnetic quake that could come their way. However, Mother Nature made a different plan.

The great flood came in and destroyed the land. Many cried and yelled for their god Osiris to save them; alas, he did not answer their calls.

The civilisation that once worshipped the god Osiris is beginning to fall below the world and into the waters; people are dying as they call for their god.

As for Osiris, it's believed he was in Egypt, being killed for his inhumane actions.

C.L. Williams is an international best-selling author currently living in central Virginia. He has written eight poetry books, four novellas, one novel, and a contributor to a multitude of anthologies and magazines. His most recent anthology appearance ANGELS: Dark Drabbles #2 from Black Hare Press became a number one in hot new releases. C.L. Williams is currently working on his second novel and a new poetry book.
Facebook: writer434
Twitter: @writer_434

Pieces of the Hoax
by T.W. Garland

"Take home a piece of the hoax," the advertisement read.

Hundreds of humanoid lizard figurines waited in the Museum. Their numbers failed to decrease as they were given away. Carried home to mantelpieces. Displayed in cabinets and on the iron shelves of hipster cafes. Lost in toy boxes.

The lizard figurines became a commonplace addition to every home. The discredited artefacts, initially considered the 7,000 year old remains of a dead civilisation, were forgotten in their abundance. Forgotten, until the whispers started. Whispers echoing through the darkness.

When the plaster cracked and horrors emerged, the whispers were replaced with screams.

T.W. Garland has a stack of Victorian novels that taunt him with their unbroken spines. He has published stories containing monster hunters, supernatural creatures, steampunk adventurers, aberrations of nature, crazed criminals, and psychic detectives. He buys more books than he could hope to read and is glad not to have been born in the nineteenth century or in a novel by Dickens. One day he hopes to live in the real world.
Website: twgarland.wordpress.com

The Darkness Looms
by J.W. Garrett

Khaba's scowl shifted to terror as the daylight turned dark in an instant. Pharaoh had explained away these strange happenings due to volcanic eruption…the Gods' anger unleashed. The blood water, insects, boils, hail, locusts. He was losing count but had the scars and endured sickness from each. Khaba just needed the strength to see it through.

His uncle, the Pharaoh, had answers. Khaba stumbled through the inky blackness, filled with hidden hazards that didn't exist in the light. Screams numbed his mind. He fell.

"Who's there?"

The hiss of a blade sounded. A flash tore the air.

"Your end."

J.W. Garrett has been writing in one form or another since she was a teenager. She currently lives in Florida with her family but loves the mountains of Virginia where she was born. Her writings include YA fantasy as well as short stories. Since completing "Remeon's Quest-Earth Year 1930", the prequel in her YA fantasy series "Realms of Chaos", she has been hard at work on the next in the series, scheduled to release August 2020. When she's not hanging out with her characters, her favourite activities are reading, running, and spending time with family.
Website: www.jwgarrett.com
BHC Press: www.bhcpress.com/Author_JW_Garrett.html

In the Water
by Warren Benedetto

"He's there," Yoasi whispered. "In the water." He crept towards the riverbank.

Davi suppressed a cruel smile. *Fool,* he thought. The hallucinations from the *ebene* he gave Yoasi were starting. Davi decided to play along to scare him.

"Is it Oko?" Davi asked. He knew Yoasi was terrified of the River God.

Yoasi nodded, his eyes on the water.

"What does he want?"

Yoasi looked at Davi, then smiled.

"You."

Something seized Davi's ankle. His fingers carved trenches in the mud as he was dragged into the piranha-filled river.

Yoasi spit the unchewed *ebene* into his hand.

Fool, he thought.

Warren Benedetto has a Master's degree in Film/TV Writing from USC. He writes short fiction about horrible people doing horrible things, to distract himself from the present political reality of horrible people doing horrible things. He is also the developer of StayFocusd, the world's most popular anti-procrastination app. He built it while procrastinating.
Website: www.warrenbenedetto.com

Shtorka
by J.M. Meyer

Mojica keeps her children obedient with threats of my name and stories of harsh punishments.

"Ivan, eat. Shtorka hates waste."

"Anya, stoke the fire. Shtorka doesn't like disobedient children."

The children respect me but Mojica, I believe, has forgotten that I am real, lurking in the dark places of this fortunate woman's home. Then foolish Mojica leaves the washing outside all night. I follow her to the well before dawn. She recognises me and remembers too late. I enjoy the taste of her flesh and the music of her screams as we crash through the earth and enter eternal hell.

J.M. Meyer is a writer, artist, and small business owner living in New York, where she received her Master's degree from Teachers College, Columbia University. Jacqueline enjoys writing speculative fiction and mysteries. Her favourite author is Alice Munro and her favourite film…is…anything horror related. Jacqueline also enjoys hiking with her dog Molly and the company of her husband Bruce and daughters Julia, Emma, and Lauren. Jacqueline's mantra lately: there's no such thing as failing, it's called learning.
Website: jmoranmeyer.net
Amazon: www.amazon.com/author/jacquelinemoranmeyer

Let Sleeping Giants Lie
by Peter J. Foote

Tires gouge into the hillside, spewing gravel as the jeep fishtails upwards.

"Give'r Chad!", "Gun it", the watching crowd yelling down encouragement.

The abused hillside drops away and a gigantic eye blinks, eyelashes big as tree roots fling dirt into the sky. A house-sized fist explodes from the hill and seizes the jeep, tossing it away. The rest of the hill collapses as the giant emerges, fragile humans tumble, and land unmoving, the ground stained in blood.

Hrungnir stretches from his millennia-long nap and peers at the crushed humans. "Anyone knows where a giant can get a drink around here?"

Peter J. Foote is a bestselling speculative fiction writer from Nova Scotia. Outside of writing, he runs a used bookstore specialising in fantasy and sci-fi cosplays and alternates between red wine and coffee as the mood demands. His short stories can be found in both print and ebook form, with his story "Sea Monkeys" winning the inaugural "Engen Books/Kit Sora, Flash Fiction/Flash Photography" contest in March of 2018. As the founder of the group "Genre Writers of Atlantic Canada", Peter believes that the writing community is stronger when it works together.
Twitter: @PeterJFoote1
Website: peterjfooteauthor.wordpress.com

Shedding Skin
by Rich Rurshell

"I don't trust you," said the archaeologist. "Talking snakes have a reputation."

"Yet you trust old books written centuries ago," laughed the snake. "After eating the apple of knowledge, I pitied your kind, so I gave you understanding. I ate the plant of eternal youth, preventing Gilgamesh from a reign of eternal tyranny. You know of my power and influence on mankind, and still you trespass here and insult me."

The ancient ruin shook as the chamber doors rumbled shut.

"What's happening?"

"I opened your eyes, yet you fail to see," replied the snake. "I eat…and since you're here…"

Rich Rurshell is a short story writer from Suffolk, England. Rich writes horror, sci-fi, and fantasy, and his stories can be found in various short story anthologies and magazines. Most recently, his story "Subject: Galilee" was published in World War Four from Zombie Pirate Publishing, and "Life Choices" was published in Salty Tales from Stormy Island Publishing. When Rich is not writing stories, he likes to write and perform music.
Facebook: richrurshellauthor

Hyakume
by Jacek Wilkos

He climbed and leaped over the gate. His goal was the old temple in the necropolis centre. Easily picking the lock, he got inside in a flash. He opened his backpack, looking for precious things.

A shuffling sound disturbed the silence enveloping the temple. A shadow separated from the dark corner, barely outlined by the faint moonlight. The flashlight illuminated a pink lump of flesh covered with yellow eyes.

The thief dropped his backpack and flee. He stopped petrified just outside the doorstep. Dozens of silhouettes stood on the stairs. Bodies with empty eye sockets.

They started walking towards him.

Jacek Wilkos is an engineer from Poland. He lives with his wife and daughter in the beautiful city of Cracow. He is addicted to buying books, and he loves coffee, dark ambient music, and riding his bike. He writes mostly horror drabbles. His fiction in Polish can be read on Szortal, Niedobre literki, Horror Online. In English, his work was published in Drablr, Rune Bear, Sirens Call eZine, and Trembling with Fear.
Facebook: Jacek.W.Wilkos

Hecatomb
by Nicola Currie

"But you have gathered only ninety-nine cattle," the high priest chastises.

It takes me a second longer than my fellow acolyte, who gathered the bulls with me, to realise how the count must be made. His hands grip my shoulders before I have a chance to move.

I do not make it easy and struggle, trying to shift the balance but it is to no avail. He thrusts me into the sacrificial pit below.

The priest lights the sanctified oil and I am trapped amongst the flaming, bellowing beasts.

"Feed his great appetite, honoured boy. You wanted to serve Apollo."

Nicola Currie is from Cambridge, UK, where she works in educational publishing. She has published poetry in literary magazines, including Mslexia and Sarasvati, and short stories in various anthologies. She has also completed her first novel, which was longlisted for the Bath Children's Novel Award.
Website: *writeitandweep.home.blog*

Delicate but Deadly
by A.R. Johnston

What a tangled web, my own being the most tangled and deceptive.

Am I still angry? Indeed. Was it Athena's fault? Not entirely. I never truly appreciated my gift of weaving. I bragged that my talents were greater than the goddess who granted them.

Athena granted mercy when I tried to take my life after my defeat. Who was I to think I could beat a goddess?

Here I sit, spinning my beautiful web to trap and dispose of those that would disrespect the gods. I am the warning that something delicate and beautiful can be deadly, I am Arachne.

A.R. Johnston is a small-town girl from Nova Scotia, Canada. She is known to write mostly urban fantasy, though she goes where the muses lead her and you never know where that may be. She is a lover of coffee, good tv shows, and horror flicks and a reader of good books. She pretends to be a writer when real life doesn't get in the way. Pesky full-time job and adulting!
Facebook: arjohnstonauthor
Website: arjohnstonauthor.wordpress.com

The Archaeologist's Wish
by Christopher T. Dabrowski
Translation Julia Mraczny

Andrew found a real treasure during the excavations—a ritually sealed jug.

Finally! Three wishes!

He dug it up and opened it.

There was smoke coming and then it turned into a man.

"You released me! I'll fulfil your three wishes!"

"I want to be rich."

"Fulfilled!"

"I want the most beautiful woman."

"Done!"

"Third wish?"

He wanted to ask what awaited him in five years, but he misspoken:

"What will happen to me in five weeks?"

"You don't want to know."

"I do!"

"All right then."

Andrew saw himself dead. Terrified, he suffered from a heart attack and died.

Christopher T. Dabrowski *was born in Poland in 1978. He has stories published in "Anomaly", "Escape", "Anomalia", "La fuga" (Royal Hawaiian Press, 2019), "Deathbirth" (Armoryka, 2008), "Anima Vilis" (Initium, 2010), "Grobbing" (Novae Res, 2012), "Deathbirth and Other Stories" (Agharta & Armoryka, 2012 & 2017), "Z życia Dr Abble" (Agharta, 2013), "Orgazmokalipsa" (Alternatywne, 2016), "Anomalia" (Forma, 2016), "Ucieczka" (Dom Horroru, 2017), and "Nie w inność" (Waspos, 2019), as well as in Playboy.*
Facebook: _Krzysztof-T-Dąbrowski-166581686751600_

Norte Chico Shaman
by Kerri Jesmer

The bones fall. The clattering brings silence to the crowd around me. The spirits tell me what they mean. Darkness, blood, death. I see their frightened faces that plead for answers. I cannot tell them this, so I speak of difficulty. Perhaps war. I advise strengthening strongholds and prayer to their gods. A sacrifice must be given—a rare occurrence. A child, I say, looking at her eyes aglow in the fire. She is evil and knows I have discovered it. She seeks my death, too. But I do not tell them our people will come to an end soon.

*Born in Germany, **Kerri Jesmer** was raised on the Eastern Plains of Colorado and currently lives in Utah with her husband and adult daughter, two dogs, and three cats, one of which is a fur grandbaby. She is an author and mentor. She has been published in Dastaan World Magazine, Fifty-word Stories, Spillwords.com, Inner Circle Writers' Magazine, Dark X-mas Holiday Drabbles (100 Word Holiday Horror Stories) Anthology, and Portal, The Inner Circle Writers' Group Children's Anthology. She spent several years mentoring her daughter's middle and high school writing groups. She has three blogs, the newest on writing, and has been blogging since 2004.*

Great Zimbabwe
by Vonnie Winslow Crist

While herding cattle, Davu walked the grasslands between the Limpopo and Zambezi Rivers. Lest herdsmen or beasts become a big cat's dinner, at day's end, they returned to the cluster of stone buildings that was home.

One afternoon as Davu approached the city, he studied the Great Enclosure which dwarfed the *zimbabwe* beside its granite towers and walls.

The Shona are mighty indeed, Davu thought.

He squinted. Circling over the highest tower was a golden bird. It shrieked, then flew towards the north.

"It is an omen," whispered Davu. Frightened, he watched as a dark, leopard-shaped cloud swallowed the sun.

Vonnie Winslow Crist is author of The Enchanted Dagger, Owl Light, The Greener Forest, Murder on Marawa Prime, and other award-winning books. Her fiction is included in "Amazing Stories," "Cast of Wonders," "Outposts of Beyond," Killing It Softly 2, Defending the Future—Dogs of War, Midnight Masquerade, Chaos of Hard Clay, and elsewhere. A clover hand who has found so many four-leafed clovers, she keeps them in jars, Vonnie strives to celebrate the power of myth in her writing.
Website: www.vonniewinslowcrist.com

The Mayans Were Right
by Michelle Anderson

Ben woke to the sounds of his Grandfather yelling. He glanced at the clock—11:50 pm.

He found his Grandfather, as always, in his study with its piles of books and pictures and graphs of the Mayan calendar plastered upon every inch of the wall. Understanding that calendar had been his life's obsession.

"We got the date wrong!" he said triumphantly to Ben. "The world didn't end on December 21st, 2012. No, it's June 20th, 2021!"

"That's today!" Ben exclaimed.

As the mantle clock struck midnight, the room started to shake, and a ghastly red glow appeared in the windows.

Michelle Anderson is an author of personal essays, poetry, and fiction. She has had a drabble published in the Apocalypse anthology by Black Hare Press.
Medium: https://medium.com/@michelleanderson_27221.

Wrath of Ostara
by C.L. Williams

I wake up to greet the spring equinox as I can begin my time of harvest. Only, I was not greeted with warmth and fresh land to harvest. Today, I walk outside and am greeted with coldness and a dead meadow.

"What is going on here?" I wail as I look to the sky.

"You can call this my revenge!" a woman says as she reveals herself.

"Who are you?" I ask.

"I am Ostara; as a harvester you should know who I am, and you don't! Consider us even!" She disappears as I stare at my dead, bleak land.

C.L. Williams is an international best-selling author currently living in central Virginia. He has written eight poetry books, four novellas, one novel, and a contributor to a multitude of anthologies and magazines. His most recent anthology appearance ANGELS: Dark Drabbles #2 from Black Hare Press became a number one in hot new releases. C.L. Williams is currently working on his second novel and a new poetry book.
Facebook: writer434
Twitter: @writer_434

Spectator
by Jo Mularczyk

She couldn't tear her eyes away from the spectacle before her. The colours wove a vivid tapestry, swathes of scarlet most stark among them. The physicality of the performance left her breathless, her own adrenaline keeping apace. Sounds enveloped her—grunts of exertion from the competitors punctuated by the metallic symphony of battle and the roar of the crowd. She was surprised to hear her own savage screams among the throng as the conquest ended. The victor stood astride the fallen, ringed by rivulets of red. She would bet on him in the next round she decided, this reigning gladiator.

Jo Mularczyk's stories and poems appear in magazines and anthologies including - The School Magazine's Blast Off and Touchdown; One Surviving Story; fourW thirty; Wonderment; Zinewest; Short and Twisted; several Storm Cloud Publishing anthologies; Daily Science Fiction; the US magazine Cricket; an upcoming UK collection; other Black Hare Press publications and several upcoming anthologies. Jo mentors a gifted and talented students' writing group, runs writing workshops and is a co-author with the student literacy program, Littlescribe, providing writing tips and story starters for students to complete. Jo lives in Australia with her husband and three children.
Website: www.jomularczyk.com
Facebook: jo.mularczyk.author

House of Dust
by David Green

Sargon of Akkad, king of all Mesopotamia, stared down at the newborn child in its crib.

"Are you sure this is the one?" he murmured.

"Yes," Inanna whispered, the High Priestess' face hidden behind her purple veil, and laid her hand on his bicep. "You must stop this child from becoming the usurper. Without this threat, you'll be the next Gilgamesh. Greater!"

"Leave me," Sargon breathed.

Hefting his mace, he held the weapon above his head.

"Gods forgive me," he cried, swinging a killing blow.

Sargon fell to his knees and wept. His rule safe but his soul damned for eternity.

__David Green__ is a writer based in Co Galway, Ireland. Growing up between there and Manchester, UK meant David rarely saw sunlight in his childhood, which has no doubt had an effect on his dark writings. Published in places such as North West Words, The Devil Made Me Do It and Nymphs, David is aiming to release his debut novel in 2020.
Twitter: @David Green

Beltane
by L.P. Hernandez

All hearths are extinguished, and now the tribe gathers 'round the Beltane fire. 'Neath a blanket of wolf-grey clouds they dance and sing.

False smiles.

False merriment.

Their eyes are wild; skin pulled drum-tight over bulbous bones. No decent harvest in years, cattle mauled in the fields, bones picked clean.

This season will be different.

Her eyes are milk white, hair the same colour but for a few streaks of red. Led by the elbow, she smiles, until the heat from the fire caresses her naked skin. The constellations of freckles on her cheeks twitch.

Yes, this season will be different.

*L.P. Hernandez is an author of horror and speculative fiction. His stories are featured in many collections, including Tavistock Galleria, Black Rainbow, and Monstronomicon. His work has also been adapted as audio productions on the NoSleep Podcast. He is an NYC Midnight Short Story Challenge Finalist and was awarded second place in the 2019 Writer's Digest Annual Writing Competition.
Website: www.lphernandez.com*

Words for One and All
by Shelly Jarvis

I am the Queen of Sheba. He cannot command me. And yet, he does.

His words slither into my ears, coating them like honey, sickly sweet. I am powerless to resist. So, I fashion wax to fill my ears, to block his words. He may speak, may command, but I will not obey. I will not be weak in front of my people this day.

The temple is full as I bow before the grey god from the stars. I smile as his lips move, until I realise he isn't talking to me, and every worshipper has drawn a blade.

Shelly Jarvis is a speculative fiction author from West Virginia, USA. She found a lifelong love of sci-fi and fantasy in the third grade when she found Madeleine L'Engle's "A Wrinkle in Time." Shelly is an avid reader, a Whovian, the ideal viewer of dog rescue videos, and undoubtedly Ravenclaw. She currently has three YA sci-fi books available for purchase on Amazon.
Website: www.ShellyJarvis.com

The Moon-Eyed People
by Raven Corinn Carluk

Stalking Wolf gripped his tomahawk, waiting with the other Creek warriors. The full moon would be overhead soon.

Movement between the trees caught his attention. Fair skin and pale hair glowed in the minimal light as half-sized people attempted to remain in the darkness. Berries still had to be harvested, and crops had to be tended even with a blinding moon riding the sky.

Chief Fighting Deer gave the signal, and the warriors passed it along the line. Bursting from the shadows, they descended upon the tiny people, driving them back into their caves.

The valley would be theirs forevermore!

Raven Corinn Carluk *writes dark fantasy, paranormal romance, and anything else that catches her interest. She's authored five novels, where she explores themes of love and acceptance. Her shorter pieces, usually from her darker side, can be found in Black Hare Press anthologies, at Detritus Online, and through Alban Lake Publishers.*
Twitter: @ravencorinn
Website: www.ravencorinncarluk.com

Daughter of Ra
by Nicola Currie

I pray as I run through the gloaming forest, searching for the sky, for the last crepuscular light.

Help me, Father. Do not leave me to darkness.

I do not glance back at the man chasing me through the trees, his breathing heavy and excited. I look only towards the diminishing halo of the sun's departure, its torrid shade like fire between the branches.

At last, the woods part above steep sea cliffs, my father only a tear of flame across the horizon now.

It is enough. My pursuer is blinded, does not see the drop, falls.

Thank you, Father.

Nicola Currie is from Cambridge, UK, where she works in educational publishing. She has published poetry in literary magazines, including Mslexia and Sarasvati, and short stories in various anthologies. She has also completed her first novel, which was longlisted for the Bath Children's Novel Award.
Website: writeitandweep.home.blog

Inside the Wall
by C.L. Williams

They told us to build the wall. It was meant to protect us from the Mongolians and keep them from ever entering our country again. Little did we know, the tyrants were not the Mongolians, they were our own leaders.

"Do not stop until the wall is finished!" the commander yelled.

I saw someone fall inside the wall; the commander showed zero empathy. "Keep building!" he yelled.

Before I could do anything, I fell onto a now lifeless body.

"Keep building!" the commander yelled once more.

Nowhere to go, the wall meant to protect us will soon become my grave.

C.L. Williams is an international best-selling author currently living in central Virginia. He has written eight poetry books, four novellas, one novel, and a contributor to a multitude of anthologies and magazines. His most recent anthology appearance ANGELS: Dark Drabbles #2 from Black Hare Press became a number one in hot new releases. C.L. Williams is currently working on his second novel and a new poetry book.
Facebook: writer434
Twitter: @writer_434

A Penny for Your Thoth
by A.L. King

As Thoth ripped the heart from the latest applicant's chest, the man chained beside Penny watched her instead.

"Now I see," he finally said. "You're Penny Nettle, famous author. Did you know Thoth is also a writer?"

The still-beating organ smacked wetly onto the scale's plate. The baboon serving as judge for the dead observed the mechanism before issuing a frightful bark.

"He's a writer?"

"God of it or something. Say…maybe he's a fan of yours."

Thoth devoured the heart and shared a bloody grin. Applicants moved forward, and Penny wondered if perhaps the primate would like her autograph.

A.L. King *is an author of horror, fantasy, science fiction, and poetry. As an avid fan of dark subjects from an early age, his first influences included R.L. Stine, Edgar Allan Poe, and Stephen King. Later stylistic inspirations came from foreign horror films and media, particularly Japanese. He is a graduate of West Liberty University, has dabbled in journalism, and is actively involved in his community. Although his creativity leans towards darker genres, he has even written a children's book titled "Leif's First Fall". He was raised in the town of Sistersville, West Virginia, which he still proudly calls home.*

283

A Nice Day for a Stroll
by James Lipson

"You don't think it's a bit ostentatious? I mean seriously, look at how ridiculously big this thing is. It's a monstrosity, an affront to all things sane, Fercockt beyond reason. Who in their right mind needs something like this?"

"Lemuel! Uri! Stop chitchatting and get back to work. Don't make me call the whip master!"

"Sorry Haim!"

"That guy is such a shmuck. Big deal, we all know you only got the job because your cousin is one of Khufu's concubines. Anyway, a few of us are going for a hike on the beach with that Moses guy tomorrow. You in?"

James Lipson's debut book, Fallen and Other Stories, was published in 2019. His short stories have appeared in Black Hare Press Anthologies, Teleport Magazine, Inner Circle's Writers Group Anthologies, and others. With a background in art, James has naturally turned to illustrating as he writes, bringing many of his short stories to life with not only descriptive detail but also detailed visual imagery.
Website: www.jameslipson.com
Instagram: jameslipsonart

Clown
by David Wright

"Do you know where the first clowns came from?"

The fresh corpse didn't respond.

"Ancient Egypt. Four *thousand* years ago. Can you believe it?"

The newly dead body was silent.

"They were priests, too. All 'Ra this' and 'Horus that'. Crazy, huh?"

The deceased man said nothing.

"And they didn't have pretty makeup like me. Did my face really scare you?"

The recently murdered victim kept his own counsel.

"Humph! You're no fun. Don't you feel like talking without your organs?"

The clown continued to feast on the liver of his recent kill.

"Of course, I'm not *really* a clown…"

David Wright was once young and carefree. Once...

Physician Heal Thyself
by Dawn DeBraal

In ancient civilisations, medical cures were used to assist those who were afflicted.

Bloodletting was based on the belief that "bad blood" caused illness. Relief of this malady required the use of leeches or by cutting open a vein and draining blood.

Trepanation, or boring holes into one's skull, released the evil spirits of possession and reduced headaches, epilepsy, and blood clots.

Poisoning with mercury or animal dung cured a whole host of diseases such as syphilis and impaired libidos.

Let's not forget the cannibal cures—drinking the blood of gladiators cures epilepsy. The door opens and the physician calls out, "Next?"

Dawn DeBraal lives in rural Wisconsin with her husband Red, two rat terriers, and a cat. She has discovered that her love of telling a good story can be written. Published stories with Palm-sized press, Spillwords, Mercurial Stories, Potato Soup Journal, Edify Fiction, Zimbell House Publishing, Clarendon House Publishing, Blood Song Books, Black Hare Press, Fantasia Divinity, Cafelit, Reanimated Writers, Guilty Pleasures, Unholy Trinity, The World of Myth, Dastaan World, Vamp Cat, Runcible Spoon, Dark Christmas, Siren's Call, Iron Horse Publishing, Falling Star Magazine 2019 Pushcart Nominee.
Amazon: amazon.com/Dawn-DeBraal/e/B07STL8DLX

Prayers on Deaf Ears
by Paul Benkendorfer

Creon commanded his men to seal the cave.

Antigone prayed. The gods would save her. They must.

Her brother, Polynices, renounced as a traitor. Left to fester on the field of battle. Denied burial rights. All she needed was a handful of sand, and that's all she gave. A few grains of sand would suffice Polynices' passage to Hades.

Traitor. Creon rebuked her king and father-in-law. Pregnant with his grandchild, it did not matter.

The last vestige of sunlight waned.

The gods would save her. Her only crime was obeying their law.

The last stone dropped. Darkness enveloped everything.

Paul Benkendorfer *is an English and history teacher from Scottsdale, Arizona, who mainly writes historical fiction, poetry, and non-fiction. He is currently working on his novel A Bridge Outside of Limerick based on the events of his great-grandfather who fought in the Irish Revolution of 1916. Paul has nearly 15 years' experience working with at-risk youth and children with special needs and continues to primarily work with them to this day. In 2014 Paul received a Bachelors in Creative Writing from the University of Arizona and is currently process of obtaining his Masters in Teaching Writing from Johns Hopkins University.*
Twitter: @PBenkendorfer

Reign of War
by Monica Schultz

Flames flicker, dancing across my feathers, reducing them to ash. Smoke licks at my lungs—suffocating. Yet, it is a pleasure to burn.

After years of empty slumber, to feel anything is a delight.

They'd thought to lock me away for good. That it was the war to end all wars. Still, my iron chains are melting under the tension of "peace."

Through the cracks in my prison, I can see the threads of fate—the many roads to war. Already greed and anger twist the minds of men.

All they need is a spark.

The Mórrígan shall rise again.

Monica Schultz is a full-time Mathematics and History teacher from Ipswich, Australia, with a passion for writing fantasy. When she isn't busy finding "x" in the latest equation, you can find her curled up with a young adult book and a cat on her lap.
Website: https://monicaschultzauthor.weebly.com/
Instagram: @monicaschultzauthor

God or Angel: Hades
by Luis Manuel Torres

"I'm assuming you've heard what's been going on up above?"

"You mean about the new guy in charge," answered Hades. "Yes, I've heard. The new status quo says my family become either Guardian Angels or mortals." Hades laughed at the thought. "I take it you're one of these Angels."

"Not exactly, but what do you think about all of it?"

"It's hysterical. Never would've believed my brother would face my eternal punishment. Let your boss know he's doing a great job."

The dark winged man smiled. "I think we're going to get along quite well. You may call me Lucifer."

Luis Manuel Torres was born in Puerto Rico, lived in Boston Massachusetts for thirteen years and currently lives in Springfield Mass. He has a love for stories in all forms they come in, from books to television and video games. His work can be found in multiple anthologies with Zimbell House Publishing and Black Hare Press. He is always working on multiple writing projects. His debut short story collection Midnight Animals is now available on Amazon.
Blog: luisitowrites.wordpress.com
Twitter: Luis1989Manuel

Freyja
by Jim Bates

As if Norse winters weren't bad enough, her dullard of a husband, Oor, didn't help. Gone all the time doing his macho thing, he gave gifts like a Brisingamen necklace and a wild boar, thinking they would please her. But no. She wasn't easily bought off. She had a good life all her own, ruling over the heavenly fields of Folkvangr and taking care of her lovely daughters, Hnoss and Gersemi. So when he tried to placate her with a fancy chariot pulled by two cats, that was too much. A goddess like her? She at least deserved winged horses.

Jim Bates lives in a small town twenty miles west of Minneapolis, Minnesota. His stories have appeared online in CafeLit, The Writers' Cafe Magazine, Cabinet of Heed, Paragraph Planet, Nailpolish Stories, Ariel Chart, Potato Soup Journal, Literary Yard, Spillwords (December 2019, Author of the Month), The Drabble, The Academy of the Heart and Mind, and World of Myth Magazine. In print publications: A Million Ways, Mused Literary Journal, Gleam Flash Fiction Anthology #2, the Portal Anthology and the Glamour Anthology by Clarendon House Publishing, The Best of CafeLit 8 by Chapeltown Publishing, the Nativity Anthology by Bridge House Publishing, and Gold Dust Magazine.
Website: www.theviewfromlonglake.wordpress.com

The Nekomata
by Lyndsey Ellis-Holloway

Never trust the two-tailed cat.

An ancient Chinese warning, sadly the Japanese did not understand what it meant.

At first.

Cats are innately magical creatures, not to be trusted at the best of times.

The first two-tailed cat sauntered through the streets, jauntily passing by the potters. A fascination, *inspiration*.

Until night came.

The streets echoed with mewling laughter.

Spine tingling, a cacophony of feline wails.

Soon the laughter vanished, devoured by the crackling of flames. Their huts consumed by fire.

Never trust the two-tailed cat.

For they are wicked and full of mischief.

And they bring death in their wake.

Lyndsey Ellis-Holloway *is a writer from Knaresborough, UK. She writes fantasy, sci-fi, horror, and dystopian stories, focussing on compelling characters and layering in myth and legend at every opportunity. Her mind is somewhat dark and twisted, and she lives in perpetual hope of owning her own dragon someday, but for now she writes about them to fill the void...and to stop her from murdering people who annoy her. When she's not writing, she spends time with her husband, her dogs, and her friends enjoying activities such as walking, movies, conventions, and of course writing for fun as well!*
Website: theprose.com/LyndseyEH

Queen of the Damned
by Holley Cornetto

I'm remembered as a hapless child—ignorant, abducted, and tricked. But that wasn't the way of it.

The truth is that I chose Hades.

How could his heart, shrouded in darkness, fail to notice my light? He would love me in a way that no other god could.

It's written as if I were fooled, as if I didn't know what it meant to consume the food of the dead. Swallowing those seeds etched my future in stone. Persephone, Queen of the Damned.

I am the sculptor of my own fate.

I am not a victim. I am a goddess.

Holley Cornetto was born and raised in Alabama, but now lives in New Jersey. To indulge her love of books and stories, she became a librarian. She is also a writer, because the only thing better than being surrounded by stories is to create them herself.
Twitter: @HLCornetto

Date Night
by Brian Rosenberger

After dinner and drinks, wild sex at her apartment, he hoped. Fingers crossed.

Date number five.

They worked in the same office. He in HR. Her new to Accounting.

Date details to be shared with her Boss, his best pal, in the AM.

He adjusted his crotch, already hard.

But not as hard as the falling masonry that shattered his skull.

Sidewalks transformed to blood-splattered Jackson Pollock paintings.

Pedestrians, his date among them, screamed and fled as buildings fell apart.

Ancient gutter spouts toppled. Pushed.

Dormant no more. The Gargoyles returned, destroyed false replicas, invited survivors to their faith. Gargoyles rule.

__Brian Rosenberger__ lives in a cellar in Marietta, Georgia, USA, and writes by the light of captured fireflies. He is the author of "As the Worms Turns" and three poetry collections. He is also a featured contributor to the pro-wrestling literary collection "Three-Way Dance", available from Gimmick Press.
Facebook: HeWhoSuffers

God or Angel: Guatu
by Luis Manuel Torres

The Gods have lost their power. The Greek, Norse, and Egyptian Gods are no more. They've either turned into Guardian Angels and adapted to their new position in eternity or perish as mortals do.

Now it was the Taino Gods' turn to lose their power.

Unlike the other Gods, the Tainos have been good to their mortals. Guatu was their God of Fire and provided them with his flame for their welfare. His power was never used for punishment.

It is because of this, instead of becoming a Guardian Angel, Guatu became an Archangel and the hunter of old Gods.

Luis Manuel Torres *was born in Puerto Rico, lived in Boston Massachusetts for thirteen years and currently lives in Springfield Mass. He has a love for stories in all forms they come in, from books to television and video games. His work can be found in multiple anthologies with Zimbell House Publishing and Black Hare Press. He is always working on multiple writing projects. His debut short story collection Midnight Animals is now available on Amazon.*
Blog: luisitowrites.wordpress.com
Twitter: Luis1989Manuel

The Priest
by David Green

The moment of sacrifice. Osiris would judge those chosen worthy, taking their place in his Underworld kingdom, or cast out; their spirits cursed to wander the world ever westward.

At the outskirts of Abydos, his God's bountiful city, Adom suppressed a shiver, not from the midnight air. As the priests chanted, beckoning Osiris, Adom reflected that he himself had never witnessed the Judge of Death's glorious presence during any ritual throughout his years of service. Doubt assailed him, his limbs heavy.

"Wait!" he cried, too late. A blade carved through his throat, spilling his blood on to the silent sand.

David Green is a writer based in Co Galway, Ireland. Growing up between there and Manchester, UK meant David rarely saw sunlight in his childhood, which has no doubt had an effect on his dark writings. Published in places such as North West Words, The Devil Made Me Do It and Nymphs, David is aiming to release his debut novel in 2020.
Twitter: @David Green

The Hunted
by J.W. Garrett

The Cro-Magnons gathered around the fire at their cave. Their leader grabbed a torch attached to the wall, stomped inside. With a grunt and intricate hand signals, the men followed his lead to the side of the cave. The flame illuminated markings—actions the group was to take on the hunt.

Stealthily, they tracked the man doomed to die for his deeds against the clan, killing his mate. His one chance…slaying the hunters first.

The posse tracked him, spears and axes hefted, ready, invigorated for their battle.

Weapons flew, claiming the fugitive, his gaze frozen now on the night sky.

J.W. Garrett has been writing in one form or another since she was a teenager. She currently lives in Florida with her family but loves the mountains of Virginia where she was born. Her writings include YA fantasy as well as short stories. Since completing "Remeon's Quest-Earth Year 1930", the prequel in her YA fantasy series "Realms of Chaos", she has been hard at work on the next in the series, scheduled to release August 2020. When she's not hanging out with her characters, her favourite activities are reading, running, and spending time with family.
Website: *www.jwgarrett.com*
BHC Press: *www.bhcpress.com/Author_JW_Garrett.html*

Plagued

by Maxine Churchman

Apollo was bored. The war was stale, and he decided to stir things up a bit.

In the Greek encampment, Codras felt wretched. He was hit by a stray arrow; only a scratch but he fell sick. He ached and couldn't stop coughing.

Eos gasped when he saw him. "You look like death, my friend. I'll fetch the physician."

Codras shivered but his skin was slick with sweat. In his fevered mind, Aphrodite told him to prepare for death.

By nightfall, Eos, too, had fallen sick. The coughing spread quickly through the camp.

Apollo clapped. He was pleased with his work.

Maxine Churchman *lives in Essex, UK, and has recently started writing poetry and short stories to share. Her interests include learning to improve her writing, reading, knitting, walking, and teaching yoga. She is also planning a novel.*

The Bog Body
by Galina Trefil

The stench of the bog was exceptionally thick, she thought dismally, as the garrotte slipped around her neck. Hogtied on her knees and dizzy from being fed ergot, she glanced at the devout villagers around her, then grimly towards her own reflection in the acidic water inches away.

Her sixth finger had caused this. The Northern Gods preferred their sacrifices to be from among the different.

She'd heard stories horror stories of this ritual. The reality was worse. She finally sank, strangled, stabbed, and mutilated into the mire.

She hoped that her death would bring them all a good harvest.

Galina Trefil *is a novelist specialising in women's, minority, and disabled rights. Her favourite genres are horror, thriller, and historical fiction. Her short stories and articles have appeared in Neurology Now, UnBound Emagazine, The Guardian, Tikkun, Romea.CZ, Jewcy, Jewrotica, Telegram Magazine, Ink Drift Magazine, The Dissident Voice, Open Road Review, and the anthologies "Flock: The Journey," "First Love," "Sea of Secrets," "Coffins and Dragons," "Organic Ink volume One," "Winds of Despair," "Waters of Destruction," "Curses & Cauldrons," "Unravel," "Hate," "Love," "Oceans," "Forgotten Ones," "Dark Valentine Holiday Horror Collection," and "Suspense Unimagined."*
Website: galinatrefil.wordpress.com
Facebook: Rabbi-Galina-Trefil-535886443115467

The Truth in the Bones
by Chris Bannor

The tortoise shell gleamed after flesh and blood were stripped and cleaned. They drilled the proper pits into the surface. It dried as he sharpened his knife to make the inscription into the shell.

He carefully carved each line, meticulous but bold. The ancestors must recognise his need in the writing.

When it came time, he handed the tortoise shell to the chief diviner. He drove fiery brands into the hollows, and they watched as it began to crack and break.

After a moment, the diviner let out a heavy sigh. "This is not a battle he will return from."

Chris Bannor *is a science fiction and fantasy writer who lives in Southern California. Chris learned her love of genre stories from her mother at an early age and has never veered far from that path. She also enjoys musical theatre and roadtrips with her family but is a general homebody otherwise.*
Facebook: chrisbannorauthor
Website: ChrisBannor.com

Reawakening
by J.D. Doolan

Is that what I think it is? I scrape at the rusted dirt with my thick gloves. Granular sand shifts to reveal a perfectly straight edge of stone.

That's not possible!

No one had been here before me. No human hand has touched this wasted soil. How can there possibly be a straight line in the sand?

I dig around all the edges. A perfect square. Too perfect. In the middle of the square is a depression. A button of sorts. I press it.

Click.

The ground shudders. Olympus Mons is collapsing. And out of the rubble rises…a pyramid.

*This is **J.D. Doolan**'s first foray into fiction writing. He's into sci-fi, fantasy, and thrillers and hopes to finally finish procrastinating about his murder mystery trilogy that he's promised himself he will publish.*

Divine Wisdom
by Maxine Churchman

Odin approached the shadowy figure standing guard over the well—Mimir, wise counsellor to the gods. It was said his wisdom came from drinking the waters of the well.

"I would drink of your well," Odin said.

Mirmir drew himself up, narrowing his eyes. "To perceive the divine, you must sacrifice the profane."

Odin considered for a moment, before plunging his fingers deep into his eye socket and plucking out his eye. Ignoring the pain, he dropped the eye into the well and accepted, from Mimir, a horn filled with well water.

A small price to pay for such wisdom.

Maxine Churchman lives in Essex, UK, and has recently started writing poetry and short stories to share. Her interests include learning to improve her writing, reading, knitting, walking, and teaching yoga. She is also planning a novel.

Everything Has a Price
by Zoey Xolton

Idun wandered beyond the mighty gates of Valhalla, tending to the Golden Grove; the trees' boughs heavily laden with the golden fruit of the gods. The fruit of Idun was the fruit of immortality, and it was her sacred charge to keep the *Aesir* in their godhood.

Lurking in the shadows, as dusk set upon the halls of Valhalla, Loki stole into Idun's garden, and save all but one, poisoned the ancient trees, and took the goddess hostage.

In exchange for a place at the table of the gods, Idun was freed, and the last tree, *Glasir*, spared from destruction.

Zoey Xolton is an Australian speculative fiction writer, primarily of dark fantasy, paranormal romance, and horror. She is also a proud mother of two and is married to her soulmate. Outside of her family, writing is her greatest passion. She is especially fond of short fiction and is working on releasing her own themed collections in future.
Website: www.zoeyxolton.com

Remus et Romulus
by Umair Mirxa

Romulus felt the warm blood envelop his hand. Watched it drip across his dagger's hilt. Impaled on the blade's sharp end was his brother, Remus.

"Forgive me, brother," he said, tears flowing free down his cheeks. "I love you but for our people to rise, you have to fall."

He withdrew the dagger slowly and let Remus crumple with one final, agonised groan.

The deed was done. Heinous it may have been but necessary. So thought Romulus as he turned to face his generals.

"Gather the men. Prepare to march. Soon, the world shall tremble before the might of Rome!"

Umair Mirxa lives and writes in Karachi, Pakistan. His first published story, 'Awareness', appeared on Spillwords Press. He has since had stories accepted for publication in anthologies from Zombie Pirate Publishing, Blood Song Books, Black Hare Press, Iron Faerie Publishing, Clarendon House Publications, Fantasia Divinity Magazine & Publishing, and The ReAnimated Writers Press. He is a massive J.R.R. Tolkien fan; loves everything to do with mythology, fantasy, and history; and wishes with all his heart that dragons were real. When he's not writing, he enjoys reading novels and comic books, playing video games, listening to music, and watching movies, TV shows, and football as an Arsenal FC fan. Website: umairmirxa.com

Aboriginal Curse
by Dawn Knox

I was set aside in my youth because of my amber-flecked eyes. When the elders judged I was ready, they put me in a trance. Then throwing me on to a fire, they invoked the deities and spirits. When I came out of the flames, I was a Carradhy—worthy of carrying the femur and quartz crystal.

This is my first test.

I fix the sleeping man with my amber-flecked eyes and imagine the fat draining from his body. With my Carradhy powers, I will transform imagination into reality until the fat and the life are sucked out of him.

Dawn Knox enjoys writing in different genres and has had romances, speculative fiction, sci-fi, humorous, and women's fiction published in magazines, anthologies, and books. She's also had two plays about World War I performed internationally. Her current work in progress is a story set in Bletchley Park during World War II.
Website: dawnknox.com
Twitter: SunriseCalls

Rome's Pyre
by Trynda E. Adair

"What would you have us do, Cesar?" His secretary's voice trembled from behind.

Nero swallowed the last mouthful of sweet liquid with a satisfied growl. He straightened, dropping the limp female slave to the marble floor.

"Bring my cithara," Nero said over his shoulder.

"With respect, Ces—"

"My cithara, Epaphroditos," he snapped.

"Yes, Cesar." The freeman bowed without another word, snapping a finger at a nearby slave to fetch the instrument.

Nero turned back to the flames dancing through the buildings of the Palatine. They needed a melody to accompany the song of crackling wood sung by his majestic city.

Trynda E. Adair grew up in a small town in Manitoba, Canada, where she would pass her writing back and forth between her school friends. Since first being published in 2011, Trynda has continued to release eBook editions of the short stories online and is currently working on more stories from her fictional universe. When she is not writing, Trynda can be found developing websites and software for computers, playing video games, or reading about history.
Website: www.authortryndaadair.ca

The Mouth at the Well
by Jacob Baugher

The obsidian knife whispers about blood. Crimson screams stain its volcanic essence.

The drunk tourist groans on the stone table, bound with corded poison vines. A solstice summer sun sets on El Castillo. Sparkling skies fade to a wine-dark sea.

"It's time," Kukulcán hisses.

I strike. The tourist bucks. Blood wells. The Serpent sucks on his jugular, staining its rainbow feathers.

Power floods my waiting veins.

My wife holds our dead son in bloody rags. I touch his forehead. His body twitches, strangled cries echo hers, but fade. A dying fire at dusk.

Night falls and we are alone again.

Jacob Baugher can be found in the Cuyahoga Valley hiking with his wife and son or brewing beer on his front porch. He's received honourable mentions for his work in the Writers of the Future contest and he co-edits a series of Fantasy and Science Fiction anthologies titled Continuum. His work also appears in Black Hare's Deep Space and Area 51 anthologies, as well as in the Dark Drabble anthologies Worlds, Angels, Monsters, Beyond, and Unravel. He also hates pineapple on pizza.

A Stone-Cold Scam
by Abi Marie Palmer

Dumps, car boot sales…Nathan didn't care where his stock came from. His customers were so *gullible* he could glue googly eyes to a golf ball and some moron would believe it was a Viking talisman.

Today, it was the lawn ornaments he'd swiped from the charity shop. He listed them one by one on his website: The insipid cherub figurine would be a "Mesopotamian idol" (£299.99); the goat-headed statue would be…

The statue grinned.

Months later, the police came looking for Nathan. They didn't find him—only a junk-filled garage and a carving of a goat-headed monster eating a screaming man.

Abi Marie Palmer *is a freelance proofreader and editor with an English Literature degree from Cardiff University. She is training to become an English teacher and enjoys writing in her spare time.*
Instagram: abimariepalmer

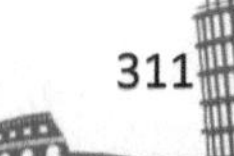

The God's Reckoning
by Michelle Brett

Flames flickered in her fingertips. She released. They launched at the figure, striking him. His cries shattered the silence as he fell. An arm rose, a clenched fist. Through gritted teeth, he called. A bolt of lightning erupted from above. It pierced her chest and she crumpled. They stared at each other through weary eyes. The same eyes.

The gods stared down from their tower, burning with rage. For all the gifts that they had bestowed on man, but mankind was toxic, poisoned inside. Enough! They would watch no more. They turned their backs, forsaking humanity. Magic vanished from earth.

Michelle Brett is a New Zealand-based writer and performer. She has a Diploma in Applied Writing and is working towards a Bachelor in Communication. In her free time, she likes to question the choices of horror movie characters and report on historic crimes for a local paper.

The Controller of the Mysteries
by Matthew M. Montelione

1266 BC.

Hot winds rushed over the desert sands of Egypt and into the wabet, where the embalmer Nes-shou prepared a courtier for the afterlife.

Nes-shou removed his sweaty jackal mask and carefully placed it down on the table. Grinning, he grabbed a canopic jar with a baboon-headed lid. "For your sins against me, I have filled the sacred jars with the organs of a servant." Nes-shou's dark eyes glared at the soon-to-be mummy. "Your *ka* will be forever confused, unable to recognise the foreign viscera. For I am the Controller of the Mysteries, and I take my *eternal* revenge."

Matthew M. Montelione is a horror writer born and raised on Long Island in New York. His work has been published in many titles, including MONSTERS: A Horror Microfiction Anthology and Quoth the Raven: A Contemporary Reimagining of the Works of Edgar Allan Poe. Matthew lives with his wife in New York.
Website: maybeevils.com
Facebook: maybeevils

Nazca
by L.P. Hernandez

He scrapes the top layer of desert soil free with cracked and bleeding hands. The efforts thus far have been futile. Their young heads purposefully deformed in tribute, expire with mother's withered breast in their mouths.

The tribe is dying.

The rains that seldom came never come.

So now this.

He squints towards an azure sky—the sun, a molten pearl—and hopes the gods see their likeness carved into the earth.

Night falls and he considers every twinkling star, searching for salvation, finding only a cold, dead moon, lifeless as the desert. No gods tonight.

Tomorrow, a new creation.

L.P. Hernandez is an author of horror and speculative fiction. His stories are featured in many collections, including Tavistock Galleria, Black Rainbow, and Monstronomicon. His work has also been adapted as audio productions on the NoSleep Podcast. He is an NYC Midnight Short Story Challenge Finalist and was awarded second place in the 2019 Writer's Digest Annual Writing Competition.
Website: www.lphernandez.com

The Voice of Volcanoes
by Clint Foster

The old woman and her dog skipped and danced a hula down the dirt path, her hair shining in the midday sun. "Soon it will be cloudy, and more than rain will fall!" She sang as she danced down the path, emblazoned on the backs of the eyelids of those who caught a fleeting glimpse. They cast questioning glances to one another, hoping someone else had seen it, but one of the elders made clear the truth.

"Pele offers warning."

Halema'uma'u shook, and in the distance, Kilauea burst. Sure enough, there fell lava, ash, and soot from hellish, black clouds.

Clint Foster *lives with his herd of four cats; beloved Basset, Zero; and wonderful wife, Nik. He loves to tell stories just as much as he loves to read them and is excited to share his work. A long-time consumer of media of all kinds, he enjoys giving back what he hopes everyone else thinks are good stories.*
Facebook: *ClintFosterAuthor*

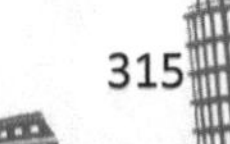

The Mummy's Curse
by Matthew M. Montelione

Menkhaf and Neferu walked cautiously past cold sandstone walls, their narrow path illuminated only by the soft orange glow of their torches in the otherwise pitch-black tomb. The cousins were silent; their hearts raced. They were risking their lives to steal the dead prince's riches; grain was scarce, and their families would starve if they could not afford to buy more.

Neferu suddenly lost his balance, falling into an unforeseen pit, screaming until he collided with the rocky ground.

Menkhaf panicked. He caught a whiff of spices and decay.

The mummy of the prince groaned, lurking behind Menkhaf's shaking torchlight.

Matthew M. Montelione is a horror writer born and raised on Long Island in New York. His work has been published in many titles, including MONSTERS: A Horror Microfiction Anthology and Quoth the Raven: A Contemporary Reimagining of the Works of Edgar Allan Poe. Matthew lives with his wife in New York.
Website: maybeevils.com
Facebook: maybeevils

Red Indian Devil
by Megan Willette

To show kindness to the pale men was to forfeit life. The young Beothuk hunter learned this the hard way as he was sacrificed to the spirits of the dead.

He watched as his body was buried carelessly in an empty, lakeside grave, left alone and barred from the country of the good spirit as a final punishment for his actions.

Just as the moon hit its zenith, the water rippled. Without any bone carvings, his spirit was left defenceless against the coming evil. A short, stocky figure wrapped in beaver skin emerged and the hunter became the hunted.

Aich-mud-yim.

Megan Willette is a registered cardiology technologist living in St. John's, Newfoundland. While most of the time she can be found reading various types of stories, she sometimes tries to write them. Fantasy themes come easiest to her, but she has attempted fiction, sci-fi, and mystery as well. There are currently two unfinished fantasy novels sitting on her computer, which may or may not eventually be shared with other people if she can ever manage to finish them.

Trireme
by Maxine Churchman

Teris strained against the oar, concentrating hard to keep in time. He was no longer aware of the water lapping close to his seat, nor of the odour from the feet of oarsmen above him.

He could see nothing of the battle—his first—but he was aware they were speeding up, ready to ram the enemy.

The impact was brutal, but not as expected. An enemy ramrod punched through their hull, crushing the oarsmen directly in front of him. The sea rushed in; he was trapped in his cramped seat. He thought of his mother. "Make me proud," she'd said.

***Maxine Churchman** lives in Essex, UK, and has recently started writing poetry and short stories to share. Her interests include learning to improve her writing, reading, knitting, walking, and teaching yoga. She is also planning a novel.*

A Warrior's Death
by Mikko Rauhala

There was a clank outside. Ulf arose from his mourning and looked his brother in the eye. Knut snuck beside the door, poleaxe at the ready.

The door burst in, revealing a warrior as pale as death standing in the doorway. "Draugr!" Ulf shouted. Without hesitation, Knut swung his weapon.

The revenant blocked the blow with his sword, but Knut managed to push it aside. Ulf lunged in, slicing the thing's head clean off. The dry mouth slowly twisted into a familiar smile.

Ulf wiped a tear of joy off his cheek. "Father will make it to Valhalla after all."

Mikko Rauhala is a Finnish author of speculative fiction with a national Atorox award nomination under his belt. Informed by his Master's degree in intelligent systems, Rauhala is most at home in hard science fiction settings, though he's not exclusive and likes to cross genres. Rauhala has dabbled in editing flash fiction for The Self-Inflicted Relative anthology, and some of his English science fiction can be found in the Infinite Metropolis short story and audio drama collection, co-authored with Edmund Schluessel.
Blog: rauhala.org
Podcast: infinitemetropolis.com

Old Croghan Man
by Chris Hall

He trudges barefoot through the thick black butter of the bog yet holds his head high, for he is a king. The year's great wheel has turned many times since he was crowned upon the hill overlooking the slough.

Many seasons, the land fed his people abundantly. But this summer, they starve.

As he stumbles, pitching forward into the mire, he muses: as kings may fail, so men may fall. His kinsfolk's blows grant him a crimson crown, yet he smiles. In order to feed his people, the land must be fed, and a king is the greatest of sacrifices.

Chris Hall is a creative writer trapped in the body of an English professor and academic. He was born in the Bitterroot Valley region of Montana and transplanted to the Yuba-Sierra Bioregion at the ripe age of one. Along with foxes, raccoons, squirrels, bears, and innumerable other non-human kin, he lives with his partner, their two-year-old daughter, and several cats in a house on the fringes of a deep, dark wood.
Website: chrishall.blog

Out of Mercy
by Shawn M. Klimek

Jutur squatted between water jars in the shade of the palace wall, pressing clay sheets onto stone slabs and then smoothing them for use by the royal scribes. The majordomo insisted they be perfect. Noticing a black beetle making tracks across one freshly completed, he plucked it aside before smashing it with a rock. "No mercy for mistakes," he taunted, imitating the majordomo.

Hearing his name shouted, Jutur looked up to see the enraged majordomo standing nearby. Raised above his head was a flawed stone slab Jutur had hidden too hastily. Jutur heard only the familiar words "No mercy—"

Shawn M. Klimek is the internationally published author of more than 170 poems and stories, in several genres. He is the author of Hungry Thing, an illustrated fantasy tale told in five poems. He lives in Illinois, USA, with his wife and their Maltese. Website: blog.jotinthedark.com
Facebook: shawnmklimekauthor

The Communal Cup
by Eddie D. Moore

Atan and Fati leaned against one of the statues scattered around the island of Rapa Nui and watched their recent guests sail away.

Fati motioned towards the ships. "At least these visitors didn't kill anyone."

"I'm glad they're gone. You never know if they are friendly. What did they call our island again?"

"Easter Island." Fati laughed at the absurdity of the name.

Atan suddenly emptied his stomach and groaned, "I'm not feeling so well."

"If you don't take the first drink of the communal cup at tonight's celebrations, the honour falls to me."

"Oh, I'm not passing that up."

Eddie D. Moore travels hundreds of hours a year, and he fills that time by listening to audiobooks. When he isn't playing with his grandchildren, he writes his own stories. You can find a list of his publications on his blog or by visiting his Amazon Author Page. While you're there, be sure to pick up a copy of his mini-anthology 'Misfits & Oddities'.
Website: eddiedmoore.wordpress.com
Amazon: amazon.com/author/eddiedmoore

The Dawning
by Cecelia Hopkins-Drewer

I am Ammi, trusted servant to the wife of the king of Ur. My mistress' husband is sick, and I pray to the gods he recovers. I wait on my knees, facing the window. I can see the ziggurat. The sun is rising.

If the king dies, I will not live to serve another day. I will be forced to drink poison and be buried alongside my mistress, the queen, to serve her in the afterlife.

There are shouts. The priest has an announcement. Footsteps sound on the stairs. The king is dead. I swallow the poppy powder.

Cecelia Hopkins-Drewer *lives in Adelaide, South Australia. She has written a Masters paper on H.P. Lovecraft, and her weird poetry has been published in The Mentor (edited by Ron Clarke) and Spectral Realms (edited by S.T. Joshi). Her novels include a teenage vampire series commencing with Mystic Evermore. Short stories have been published in Worlds, Angels & Monsters, Beyond, Storming Area 51, and Unravel (Dark Drabbles anthologies edited by Dean Kershaw).*
Amazon: amazon.com/Cecelia-Hopkins-Drewer/e/B071G968NM
Website: chopkin39.wixsite.com/website

Pandora's Treasure Box
by Umair Mirxa

Petra felt her excitement rise with each sweep of the brush. Ancient Greek letters revealed themselves but slowly from beneath centuries-old dirt.

Her colleague's excited yelp echoed through the Spartan vault as he peered over her shoulder; eyes squinted in an effort to read the faded inscription.

"We've found it," said Sotiris.

"We actually found it!" said Petra, looking back at him mischievously, and lifted the lid off the jar.

"Petra, no!"

Sotiris' shriek was a moment too late. Petra began to melt before his eyes even as his own throat became constricted and boils erupted all over his flesh.

Umair Mirxa lives and writes in Karachi, Pakistan. His first published story, 'Awareness', appeared on Spillwords Press. He has since had stories accepted for publication in anthologies from Zombie Pirate Publishing, Blood Song Books, Black Hare Press, Iron Faerie Publishing, Clarendon House Publications, Fantasia Divinity Magazine & Publishing, and The ReAnimated Writers Press. He is a massive J.R.R. Tolkien fan; loves everything to do with mythology, fantasy, and history; and wishes with all his heart that dragons were real. When he's not writing, he enjoys reading novels and comic books, playing video games, listening to music, and watching movies, TV shows, and football as an Arsenal FC fan.
Website: umairmirxa.com

The Sacred Cenote
by McKenzie Richardson

Jess peered over the dizzying drop.

"Careful," Hector said, pulling her from the cenote's edge. "They used to throw people in there as sacrifices to the gods."

"Stop trying to scare me."

"It's true. Loads of skeletons down there."

Jess shivered despite the scorching sun, then grinned. "Maybe I'll push you in to stop this awful drought then."

Their receding laughter echoed down into the darkness. Awakened by the faint smell of distant blood, Chaac, the rain god, yawned. It'd been ages since he'd received a sacrifice. He hungered.

Perhaps it was time he took matters into his own hands.

McKenzie Richardson *lives in Milwaukee, WI. Her horror stories have been featured in various anthologies including Evil Lurks, Pandemic, and After: Undead Wars. She has also published a variety of poems and flash fiction pieces.*
Facebook: *mckenzielrichardson*
Blog: *www.craft-cycle.com*

What the Seas Didn't Swallow
by Raven Corinn Carluk

Machu Pichu mourned the sinking of Atlantis.

Survivors arrived daily, bereft of hope, most of them with only the clothes upon their backs. Some searched for loved ones, but most were too deeply in shock, unable to believe *anyone* had survived.

The governors presented a calm façade, but they were as helpless and grief stricken as everyone. The airships had been the first technology to stop, stranding them in the mountain city. Communications slowly failed as the great city's crystals died on the ocean floor. Once the lights went out, control would be lost.

Was survival a blessing or a curse?

Raven Corinn Carluk writes dark fantasy, paranormal romance, and anything else that catches her interest. She's authored five novels, where she explores themes of love and acceptance. Her shorter pieces, usually from her darker side, can be found in Black Hare Press anthologies, at Detritus Online, and through Alban Lake Publishers.
Twitter: @ravencorinn
Website: www.ravencorinncarluk.com

Serpopard
by Beth W. Patterson

"Daddy, look at the funny giraffe!"

The older man blanched. He hadn't even noticed the long-necked feline creature lurking in the pen. He had described it many times in his lectures as a mythological zoomorphic symbol of chaos depicted on Mesopotamian palettes. *A serpopard?* How could the zookeepers have overlooked this intruder?

The fanged beast slunk to the edge of the bars. Its scaly jaw dropped, its hiss unscrambling itself into the professor's language.

"You never bothered to find out our true names, professor. But we are older than the gods, our appetites primal."

The child was a worthy sacrifice.

Beth W. Patterson *was a full-time musician for over two decades before diving into the world of writing, a process she describes as "fleeing the circus to join the zoo". She is the author of the books Mongrels and Misfits, and The Wild Harmonic, and a contributing writer to over forty anthologies. Patterson has performed in nineteen countries, expanding her perspective as she goes. Her playing appears on over a hundred and ninety albums, soundtracks, videos, commercials, and voice-overs (including seven solo albums of her own).*
She lives in New Orleans, Louisiana with her husband Josh Paxton, jazz pianist extraordinaire.
Website: www.bethpattersonmusic.com
Facebook: bethodist

The Beginning of the End
by Jim Bates

Atahualpa was ready to lead his men in the first battle against the Spanish, the Battle of Puna. The great Inca leader had 80,000 men who wore a kind of armour made from the wool of alpacas and were armed with only knives and clubs. The Conquistadors had 168 men armed with steel lances, rifles, bronze armour and long swords, one cannon, and twenty-seven horses. The fighting ended when the Spanish captured Atahualpa and held him hostage, demanding gold and silver. The Inca fulfilled the ransom, but Atahualpa was executed anyway. The fall of the mighty Inca civilisation had been.

Jim Bates lives in a small town twenty miles west of Minneapolis, Minnesota. His stories have appeared online in CafeLit, The Writers' Cafe Magazine, Cabinet of Heed, Paragraph Planet, Nailpolish Stories, Ariel Chart, Potato Soup Journal, Literary Yard, Spillwords (December 2019, Author of the Month), The Drabble, The Academy of the Heart and Mind, and World of Myth Magazine. In print publications: A Million Ways, Mused Literary Journal, Gleam Flash Fiction Anthology #2, the Portal Anthology and the Glamour Anthology by Clarendon House Publishing, The Best of CafeLit 8 by Chapeltown Publishing, the Nativity Anthology by Bridge House Publishing, and Gold Dust Magazine.
Website: www.theviewfromlonglake.wordpress.com

The Passions of the Lightning
by Clint Foster

"Can you imagine it? Lightning, with all its passions, made flesh."

"I prefer not to imagine such a thing."

"None of us want to. Yet each direction we turn, another statue, another reminder of Zeus."

Both women shuddered at the name, looking to the clear sky and smiling, hoping the thunder was nowhere near them at the moment. Together, they approached the altar, bowing their faces in the hope that Zeus would not recognise them from his bronze likeness that towered so far above. Their sacrifice was modest. They knew what it meant to be singled out for Zeus' passions.

Clint Foster *lives with his herd of four cats; beloved Basset, Zero; and wonderful wife, Nik. He loves to tell stories just as much as he loves to read them and is excited to share his work. A long-time consumer of media of all kinds, he enjoys giving back what he hopes everyone else thinks are good stories.*
Facebook: ClintFosterAuthor

Immortality is a Lonely Business
by Shelly Jarvis

"When I was a young man, they called me Alaric. Now I am neither young nor a man, and that name has fallen away. I answer to no name, only the sweet pump of blood through your veins."

"I was a soldier, a leader, the first king of the Visigoths. You haven't heard of me? Hmm. Your history books are sorely lacking. I destroyed Corinth and Sparta, I besieged and sacked Rome. Thrice!"

"Eh, fine. Pretend you're not impressed. Perhaps tomorrow, when you wake as mine and we face the long eternity together, you'll be a better audience. Now drink."

Shelly Jarvis is a speculative fiction author from West Virginia, US. She found a lifelong love of sci-fi and fantasy in the third grade when she found Madeleine L'Engle's "A Wrinkle in Time." Shelly is an avid reader, a Whovian, the ideal viewer of dog rescue videos, and undoubtedly Ravenclaw. She currently has three YA sci-fi books available for purchase on Amazon.
Website: www.ShellyJarvis.com

Scythian Servant
by Vonnie Winslow Crist

Lilliya cried softly in her tent-covered wagon.

She'd travelled the Black Sea steppes serving Taras her entire life. A ferocious Scythian warrior who wore cloaks made from his enemies' tanned skins and drank from their skulls, Taras seemed invincible. He wasn't.

"It's my honour to serve forever," whispered Lilliya as the tribe's shaman summoned her.

Lilliya left her tent and followed the shaman to Taras' corpse. It'd been gutted, stuffed with herbs, stitched together, then embellished with golden trinkets. Before being entombed in Taras' kurgan, Lilliya's body would be treated the same.

Always obedient, she knelt and awaited her beheading.

Vonnie Winslow Crist is author of The Enchanted Dagger, Owl Light, The Greener Forest, Murder on Marawa Prime, and other award-winning books. Her fiction is included in "Amazing Stories," "Cast of Wonders," "Outposts of Beyond," Killing It Softly 2, Defending the Future—Dogs of War, Midnight Masquerade, Chaos of Hard Clay, and elsewhere. A clover hand who has found so many four-leafed clovers, she keeps them in jars, Vonnie strives to celebrate the power of myth in her writing.
Website: www.vonniewinslowcrist.com

A Big Letdown
by John H. Dromey

A galley master inquired about an oarsman. "Why is Hannibal so blue?"

"What did you expect? He is, after all, one of the Purple People."

"A what?"

"A Phoenician."

"Ah. That explains why he's such a great sailor, but *not* why he's despondent."

"He's depressed for good reason. After Alexander the Great laid siege to Hannibal's home port—an island city—the inhabitants were either massacred or sold into slavery and the city was levelled."

"Hannibal's homesick?"

"Not exactly. He wonders how he can continue to be a carefree world traveller when he's plagued by thoughts of a 'flat Tyre'."

John H. Dromey was born in northeast Missouri, USA. He enjoys reading—mysteries in particular—and writing in a variety of genres. In addition to contributing to the Black Hare Press series of Dark Drabbles anthologies, he's had short fiction published in Alfred Hitchcock's Mystery Magazine, Martian Magazine, Mystery Weekly, Stupefying Stories Showcase, Thriller Magazine, Unfit Magazine, and elsewhere, as well as in numerous anthologies, including Chilling Horror Short Stories (Flame Tree Publishing, 2015).

Burnt Offerings
by S.O. Green

On Beltane Eve, they sent Aila away from MacDuff's Cross. A special duty. To deliver a sacrifice to the snake witch.

She took a bannock, a burnt oat cake, in a wicker basket. Just as they gave a lamb to the wolves and seed to the crows. Just as they stoked the needfire on the hill to prove their dedication to the gods.

She set out into the woods; the women wept and the men sighed, and all crossed themselves.

Because the basket was empty. Save for a note that read: *Take this, O Serpent. Spare thee my children.*

Simone Oldman Green *lives in the Kingdom of Fife with husband, John. They have been published in short story anthologies by Otter Libris, Rogue Blades and Dragon Soul Press. They also won Third Place in the British Fantasy Society's Short Story Contest 2018 for the feminist post-Apocalypse piece, 'Travesty'. Writer, vegan, martial artist, gamer, occasionally a terrible person (but only to fictional people). They thrive on the unusual, which might explain why there are so many cats.*
Website: https://thebasementoflove.blogspot.com/
Twitter: @SOGreenWriter.

From the Sky
by Thomas K.S. Wake

Frantic steps on a shining ebony floor, driven by regret and realisation. High Priest, rushing to make amends. Inside the ziggurat, impended in the altar, was the Stone of An. Surely an appeasement to the descending gods. They didn't know not to take it, to encase it in marble, to bow to it. To worship it. And now they were paying for the blasphemy.

The skies opened and chariots of shining rays and thundering roars appeared. An ocean of people screamed. Too late.

A blinding pillar of light from the sky. A nation cindered, sent to the realm of Irra.

Thomas K.S. Wake *was pushed into the world during the harsh winters of Finland. Tempered by the shamanic winds, a thousand lakes with a thousand stories, the whispers of the birch filled forests, he fell in love with horror at the tender age of 6 when he saw Re-Animator. That led him to search for the source story and that was it. The young man's mind was blown. Cosmic horror wrapped its nebulous tentacles around his imagination and it has been feeding it ever since. Eventually, driving him to write his own stories.*
Twitter: [@ThomasKSWake](#)
Facebook: [thomas.wake.963](#)

But This One Can Move
by Nikki DeKeuster

There is beauty in darkness.

That beauty is me.

Thought crumbles beneath the madness of ages, and when light shines into my blackhole prison, I seize it.

In a flash I'm cliffside, sneering at fragments of the obsidian mirror that once shackled me. A towering waterfall, only a trickle when last I stood here, rushes behind me. Crepuscular rays peek through the rainforest canopy. They've called me home.

Me! Ayautheotl! Goddess of mists!

I stretch my arms, legs, win…

…no wings.

My eyes reflected in that polished stone are human.

Thundering falls swallow my scream.

One prison traded for another.

***Nikki DeKeuster** devours souls. She spits them onto her glowing screen and toys with their lives for your amusement. Reading this story makes you an accomplice to their suffering. You're welcome. A storyteller with decades of experience crafting tales with her friends, she's bound some of them to bring into the wider world. The stories, not her friends. She enjoys throwing stones into Lake Michigan with her daughter and keeping her husband up past his bedtime with her ramblings. The first novel in her horror series will claw its way out of the earth in 2020.*
Website: NJDeKeuster.com

Silent Warrior
by Jo Mularczyk

Hanyu stretched. He'd been hunched over for so long that the movement was painful. Unclenching his hand from his awl, he regarded his work. The final terracotta warrior complete. Tomorrow they would be placed in the tomb of Emperor Qin Shi Huangdi. Hanyu felt honoured to have served his emperor.

"Hanyu!"

"Yes, Commander Xiu?" Hanyu murmured.

"You must carve one more warrior!" Xiu barked.

"It's impossible. I cannot complete another warrior in time."

"Then serve your emperor in another way!" Xiu cried, running Hanyu through with his sword.

Xiu dropped Hanyu's body at his servant's feet.

"Cover him in terracotta!"

Jo Mularczyk*'s stories and poems appear in magazines and anthologies including - The School Magazine's Blast Off and Touchdown; One Surviving Story; fourW thirty; Wonderment; Zinewest; Short and Twisted; several Storm Cloud Publishing anthologies; Daily Science Fiction; the US magazine Cricket; an upcoming UK collection; other Black Hare Press publications and several upcoming anthologies. Jo mentors a gifted and talented students' writing group, runs writing workshops and is a co-author with the student literacy program, Littlescribe, providing writing tips and story starters for students to complete. Jo lives in Australia with her husband and three children.*
Website: www.jomularczyk.com
Facebook: jo.mularczyk.author

Chosen
by Elin Olausson

We call her Mother. She loves us and we love her, as children must. Nerthus, goddess of life. Nerthus, whose face we can never see. The creaking of her cart causes whispers and wonder. Her blessing means prosperity, a bearable winter. Us boys are chosen, following the cart, never once peeking under the cloth. Wreaths are placed on our heads like crowns.

Lastly, the priest takes us to her lake and unveils her. We wash the goddess, avoiding her wooden gaze. *Now come*, she sings. *Come to me.* We walk into the water. Our brothers' bones reach out, taking us home.

Elin writes psychological horror and weird fiction. Her works have appeared in anthologies by Eerie River Publishing, Belladonna Publishing, and others. When she's not writing, Elin works as a librarian. She lives in Sweden.

Buried Treasure
by Peter J. Foote

Ma'ii, called Coyote the Trickster by some, listens to the prospectors.

Vigilant of the failing lamplight, Ma'ii works its magic to alter another mark on the cave's wall.

"I'm telling you Clancy, the entrance isn't this way, and the lamp is going dry."

"Amos, will you shut up! See, there's my chalk mark. We must be close, just think about the silver we found!"

The lamp flickers; Ma'ii pauses and listens.

"Clancy, I'm telling you we're moving in deeper into the caves."

The lamp flicker and fails, the prospectors falter in the dark, and Ma'ii leaves them to their fate.

Peter J. Foote is a bestselling speculative fiction writer from Nova Scotia. Outside of writing, he runs a used bookstore specialising in fantasy and sci-fi cosplays and alternates between red wine and coffee as the mood demands. His short stories can be found in both print and ebook form, with his story "Sea Monkeys" winning the inaugural "Engen Books/Kit Sora, Flash Fiction/Flash Photography" contest in March of 2018. As the founder of the group "Genre Writers of Atlantic Canada", Peter believes that the writing community is stronger when it works together.
Twitter: @PeterJFoote1
Website: peterjfooteauthor.wordpress.com

ANCIENTS

Garden of the Fugitives
by James Lipson

"Pliny, are you sure we should stay? I'm worried."

"Trust me, the tremors aren't particularly alarming, they happen quite frequently in this area. As a matter of fact, last month alone, Campania experienced over 100 earth shakes."

"But don't they seem to be getting stronger?"

"Not really, the one we had back in 62 was by far the worst. Granted we've had a plethora since then, but none have been nearly that strong. I think that's the worst we're going to see."

"You're absolutely sure? You really don't think we should leave?"

"Why? Pompeii is magnificent this time of year."

James Lipson's debut book "Fallen and Other Stories" was published in 2019. His short stories have appeared in Black Hare Press Anthologies, Teleport Magazine, Inner Circle's Writers Group Anthologies, and others. With a background in art, James has naturally turned to illustrating as he writes, bringing many of his short stories to life with not only descriptive detail but also detailed visual imagery.
Website: www.jameslipson.com
Instagram: jameslipsonart

The Silk Road
by D.J. Elton

I turn in my seat, third in the line, and see the great camel train as it winds and dips down over desert. Sands are blowing and the cool night air is chilling my back.

"We'll stop soon," my brother Jin speaks. Always short, no need for conversation. I know he is drinking on the journey. Father forbade this but I will not tell him, as it could cause Jin to be set aside. I don't want that on my conscience.

There is much dust, horses coming fast, furious. The Mongols, shouting, screaming, have come for our silk and gunpowder.

D.J. Elton is a writer living in Melbourne's west. As a child, she came from England to Australia, on the last boat down the Suez Canal, where she underwent a sacrificial dunking ritual in the court of King Neptune and has never looked back. She likes creating speculative microfiction and short stories, as well as random essays. Her work has been published in several anthologies, and she has written a historical fantasy novella, 'The Merlin Girl.' When not playing with a pen, she likes most of all to go to the green country.

Asherah's Score
by Beth W. Patterson

As with most power couples, the male tends to get all the glory.

Mortals removed the name of Asherah, wife of Yahweh, from all sacred texts. They destroyed her trees next to sacred sites. But you cannot obliterate a goddess from existence.

If anyone remembers her, they might fancy Asherah the mere tambourine player to the bandleader that they believe Yahweh to be. They don't know that she is the one who composed the music and arranged the score. Hell hath no fury like the woman forgotten, especially a deity.

Her signal's feedback shrieks across the earth's magnetic fields.

Beth W. Patterson *was a full-time musician for over two decades before diving into the world of writing, a process she describes as "fleeing the circus to join the zoo". She is the author of the books Mongrels and Misfits, and The Wild Harmonic, and a contributing writer to over forty anthologies. Patterson has performed in nineteen countries, expanding her perspective as she goes. Her playing appears on over a hundred and ninety albums, soundtracks, videos, commercials, and voice-overs (including seven solo albums of her own).*
She lives in New Orleans, Louisiana with her husband Josh Paxton, jazz pianist extraordinaire.
Website: www.bethpattersonmusic.com
Facebook: bethodist

River Indus
by Vonnie Winslow Crist

"Mohenjo-Daro," said Nana.

Uzma studied the ruins.

"River Indus gave life to Mohenjo-Daro. A grateful daughter, the city honoured her mother."

Nana patted Uzma's shoulder. "Mohenjo-Daro's streets were straight, crossing one another like finely woven linen. Constructed of hard, well-burnt bricks, her buildings were strong. But as centuries passed, Mohenjo-Daro forgot whose water was used to make bricks, float boats, and quench thirst."

Nana sighed, "Ignored, the goddess Indus angrily overflowed her banks, washing away walls, fields, livestock, people."

"Then, she changed course," said Uzma, "and Mohenjo-Daro died…"

"For a goddess' revenge is swift, brutal, and forever," finished Nana.

Vonnie Winslow Crist *is author of* The Enchanted Dagger, Owl Light, The Greener Forest, Murder on Marawa Prime, *and other award-winning books. Her fiction is included in* "Amazing Stories," "Cast of Wonders," "Outposts of Beyond," Killing It Softly 2, Defending the Future—Dogs of War, Midnight Masquerade, Chaos of Hard Clay, *and elsewhere. A clover hand who has found so many four-leafed clovers, she keeps them in jars, Vonnie strives to celebrate the power of myth in her writing.*

Website: www.vonniewinslowcrist.com

City of the Ancients
by J. Scott Hill

In a dream, I walked beneath the cyclopean walls of an ancient city. I found remains of travellers who passed this way; their bones encrusted in tombs of dust. Others of some prominence to this place, rest in catacombs.

I wandered maddening streets twisting without reason, untouched by the sun. Where grim-decayed machines of some unimaginable advancement mingled with primitive tools like monuments to timeless travellers.

Then I heard them. Whispering. The dwellers called to me in a vile language I did not understand. Cold pallid hands clawed at my flesh dragging me into darkness.

I dared not wake.

J. Scott Hill is a sometimes writer, avid gamer, and IT professional in his spare time. He lives with his wife and two furry kids in Columbia, MO. He once received a Silver Honorable Mention for a short story, The Black Grave, entered in the L. Ron Hubbard Writers of the Future contest.

The Folly of Achilles
by Joshua E. Borgmann

Priam begs for his son's body, but with the blood of his beloved Patroclus still staining his armour, Achilles cannot forgive Hector. Anger replaces Achilles' grief, and he murders the old man, placing his head upon his table.

Enraged Apollo bargains with Hades, and the world changes.

As Achilles sleeps, Hector rises. The fallen hero draws his sword and takes his revenge.

At dawn, the Greeks find Achilles' head impaled at the edge of camp and Hector leading an army of corpses towards their ships. Defence is futile. The ships burn, the victorious dead feast, and Troy does not fall.

Joshua E. Borgmann *holds degrees from Drake University, Iowa State University, and the University of South Carolina. He grew up on horror and science fiction and had long intended to become a great master of the art form before he was sucked into the bottomless pit of academia. He toils away his days as an English instructor at a small community college and dreams of being able to escape into a world of fantasy and terror where there are no student papers to grade. He and his wife reside in a nameless rural Iowa town surrounded by terrible cornfields where he is terrorised by several felines who have taken refuge in his home.*

Pyramid Scheme
by John H. Dromey

A powerful pharaoh toured the remote site of a large pyramid under construction. Pleased by the mathematical precision of the foundation, he offered a reward to the man responsible for its design.

"Tell me, Ammon. What is your greatest desire?"

"An isosceles triangle."

"What's special about those?"

"Two of its sides are exactly alike."

"That should be feasible. I have skilled craftsmen who can shape you a three-sided obelisk. Would you like it made of stone, mud bricks, papyrus? Or what?"

"Not that kind of triangle. I want mine to consist of nubile identical twins—Rana and Nanu—and me."

John H. Dromey was born in northeast Missouri, USA. He enjoys reading—mysteries in particular—and writing in a variety of genres. In addition to contributing to the Black Hare Press series of Dark Drabbles anthologies, he's had short fiction published in Alfred Hitchcock's Mystery Magazine, Martian Magazine, Mystery Weekly, Stupefying Stories Showcase, Thriller Magazine, Unfit Magazine, and elsewhere, as well as in numerous anthologies, including Chilling Horror Short Stories (Flame Tree Publishing, 2015).

A Flower on a Grave
by Chisto Healy

As a botanist, this hidden Mayan temple was exciting for Addy, who looked at the strange flowers with wonder. She had heard that there was life that grew only in these temples, entirely unknown to the rest of the world.

The goal was to transport one alive, study it, reproduce it, and introduce a new species to the world. Addy would find fame and money. She removed one carefully, coughing at the strange pollen.

A week later, they ruled her death, poison. To honour her after, they placed the strange flower that she had in her hand by her tombstone.

Chisto Healy *has been writing since childhood, but he only started following his dreams and writing full time in 2020. On top of the award nominated self published novels from his earlier days, he now has 50 published stories. You can find out what is out to read at his blog or follow him on Amazon as there is new stuff constantly coming out. He lives in NC with his fiance and her mom, his daughter Ella who has inspired stories that have been published, and his daughter Julia who has been published alongside him, and his son Boe who thinks the world is his drum.*
Blog https://chistohealy.blogspot.com

Bad Blood
by Sue Marie St. Lee

Rowdy lines formed outside the coliseum whenever Spartacus fought. Men paid to drink gladiators' blood and sweat for increased virility. Women used it for perfume and face cream. Attilus wanted five vials of Spartacus' blood for longer-lasting erections.

The day's last fight ended when Spartacus struck Barnabas' throat—blood sprayed everywhere.

At the bath house, servants used strigils to scrape and collect Spartacus' blood and sweat before his bath. The scraping revealed no bloody lesions. The blood scraped from Spartacus belonged to Barnabas.

That night, Attilus drank five of the vials, collapsed and writhed in pain when his testicles exploded.

*Born in Chicago, **Sue Marie St. Lee** currently lives in Oklahoma with her husband and Manx cat. A storyteller since learning to talk, her wild imagination caused reprimands from her mother. Her imagination persevered. Retired from Finance Management, Sue began ghostwriting until 2019, choosing to have works published internationally, in print and online, under her own name. Black Hare Press, Fantasia Divinity, and Spillwords Press are some of the publishers to feature Sue's work to date.*
Blog: suemariestlee.home.blog
Amazon: amazon.com/Sue-Marie-St.-Lee/e/B07WJFRF1L

The Latest Poop
by John H. Dromey

Cleopatra's handmaids were prone to gossip.

"Did you hear about Ana? While her fiancé was away with the army, a virile young man—the spoiled son of a very wealthy grain merchant—tried to steal her affections. He even threatened to sully her reputation if she didn't give in to him. Finally, she agreed to a clandestine meeting on condition he supply her with an organic contraceptive."

"Do tell! Was it effective?"

"I'll say. She won't have a child with him. Ahead of their rendezvous, Akhon was intent on obtaining the freshest dung possible when the crocodile turned on him."

John H. Dromey was born in northeast Missouri, USA. He enjoys reading—mysteries in particular—and writing in a variety of genres. In addition to contributing to the Black Hare Press series of "Dark Drabbles" anthologies, he's had short fiction published in Alfred Hitchcock's Mystery Magazine, Martian Magazine, Mystery Weekly, Stupefying Stories Showcase, Thriller Magazine, Unfit Magazine, and elsewhere, as well as in numerous anthologies, including "Chilling Horror Short Stories" (Flame Tree Publishing, 2015).

The Worm
by S. Mudita

It was an unexplored site. The findings were usual. More cattle seals. Until the pickaxe popped a "worm" seal with strange ominous glowing markings. The crew huddled together to scrutinise it. Real? or Fake? If fake, then who'd…if…

They heard the ground shake and a shape crawl. With an explosion came out a humongous worm. Big, white, with mountain range teeth, sharp and unforgiving. They tried to run. But the worm caught up and slurped them. It picked on their flesh and their bones. They were there, and then they were not.

Thus quenched, it returned whence it came from.

S. Mudita is a storyteller from India and is working on his short story collection.

Penthesilea
by Mark Kodama

Calliope, muse of epic verse, sing the song of Queen Penthesilea, in dulcet metre of poetry, and how she killed herself, by the hand of another, the great killer Achilles.

Penthesilea rode through Scaean Gate, with her retinue, at windy Troy by the mouth, of the Hellespont where the north wind blows south. The hapless thirteen Amazonian maids from River Thermadon had a date with Death at the hands of the long-haired Achaeans.

Queen Penthesilea, regal and fair, why so melancholy? What is in your stare?

You hurled your ash spear at a stag, accidently slaying your sister Hippolyta instead.

Mark Kodama is a trial attorney and former newspaper reporter who lives in Washington, D.C. with his wife and two sons. He is currently working on Las Vegas Tales, a work of philosophy, sugar-coated with metre and rhyme and told through stories. His stories and poems appear in Apocalypse, Blaze, Cadence, Unravel, Dragon Bone Soup, Enigma, Hate, Tall Tales and Short Stories, Gleam, Fireburst, Latin Anthology, Maelstrom, Pride, Tempest, and What Sort of Fuckery Is This? "Land of the Pharaohs" won Story of the Month at World of Myths and "The Summer Camp" will appear in the Best of Potato Soup Journal.
https://www.facebook.com/xkodama
http://www.amazon.com/-/e/B07Z2HHKR6

Getting Blood into Stone
by Frances Tate

"Blood!" Thorn's voice, the High Priest, rolled down the pyramid and settled on fellow Mayans bowed in the dust.

The rains had not come. Crops failed. Even the most precious sacrifice—a first-born child—hadn't swayed the Gods to make clouds. Send water.

What more could the Gods ask? The starving people, panicked and devout, looked around them.

"Blood," Thorn said. "The Gods want more blood!"

Who had more blood on his hands than anyone?

Who sacrificed nothing while they gave all?

The people swarmed up narrow steps.

Thorn retreated. Implored the heavens for help. Bled.

Fed his deaf, thirsty God.

Frances Tate is a British self-published writer of vampires and drabbles who lives in the north west of England. She enjoys gardening, exploring historical sites, cinema, reading, and travelling. She's taken pleasure in flight planning a cabbage white butterfly approach to careers, preferring to generalise rather than specialise. She trained as an Economics high school teacher and has a private pilot's licence amongst other things. Currently she writes (very restrained) overhaul instructions for an engineering company.

Yonaguni
by Charles Reis

Yonaguni stood in the centre of a large flat square structure playing a bamboo flute; the sandstone monument floated in a desolate ocean. Hundreds of human-like amphibians called kappas climbed onto it, approaching the priest like moths to a flame. They had ravaged Japan, but Yonaguni's music lured them here.

Once the creatures exited the water, he dropped the flute and reached into his robe. His heart throbbed as he took out a conch and blew on it. Massive square blocks appeared, trapping them in darkness within a pyramid.

Tears formed in his eyes, but he smiled knowing he saved his people.

Charles Reis *was born and raised in Coventry, Rhode Island, but currently lives in neighboring West Warwick. He graduated from the University of Rhode Island with a BA in English Literature in 2012 and currently works as a museum tour guide. Additional works of his have appeared in "One Night in Salem", "Trembling with Fear: Year 1", "13 Postcards from Hell", and "Coffins & Dragons".*
Facebook: charles.reis.35
Instagram: cthulhudawn1979

Burnt Offerings
by Jasiah Witkofsky

The Inferno changed everything.

The opening of the mines brought an opportunity and its dark tunnels blind ignorance about the world above.

Reborn from the abyss into a home ravaged by continental fires where flora and fauna no longer remain, I stumbled hoarse and bleary upon a dead planet. Spent blazes revealed ancient artefacts: spearhead, obsidian scrapers, and the shaped wood known as the rabbit stick. I knew enough to see that the chert knapping was crafted before the previously displaced tribe, from the time of the mammoth hunters. A breakthrough discovery and no one to share of cultures lost.

*Nature enthusiast, dabbler of the arts, and multicultural advocate, **Jasiah Witkofsky** has never published his works but has edited the writings of local authors.*
He resides in the majestic Sierra Foothills of California tending to the gardens and woodlands of his community, further distilling his pragmatic philosophy.

The Wisdom of the Ancient Ones
by Paula R.C. Readman

Before the tomb I stood, deciphering the ancient carvings. Excitement bubbled as each notch explained the symbolism of the treasures that lay beyond. I lifted my chisel and pried open the lid.

Staleness choked the air from my lungs as the tomb's lid creaked and shuddered back into place behind me. Within an array of sparkling stars, the wisdom of the ancient ones filled my labouring heart as the chisel clattered to the ground.

In the darkness, I dropped to my knees knowing death was the only escape, as my greed had snatched the greatest wealth of all from me.

Paula R.C. Readman learnt *"how to write" from books that her husband purchased from eBay. After 250 purchases, he finally told her "just to get on with the writing." Since 2010, she's had 34 stories published.*
Blog: paulareadman1.wordpress.com

Midwinter at Dun Skeig
by T.M. Brown

Tasgall's harvest was late and meagre. Frost had already formed on the barley heads before he and his sons could bring it in. His heart sank the morning he found the Cailleach doll lying in his field. He didn't have enough to pay the Old Hag her due.

Her gaunt silhouette now perched upon his threshold like a scavenging crow. His wife cried. Tasgall clenched his fists. Cailleach, the ancient and ravenous, walked amongst his brood. She selected Lilias, the copper-haired youngest. She took the child and departed into the softly falling snow.

Tasgall worked even harder the next season.

*Captain **T.M. Brown** is a Space Operations Officer in the United States Army. He currently lives with his wife, Anna, and their two dogs, Fry and Zapp, in Colorado Springs. Although he has long held a passion for dark fantasy, cosmic horror, and speculative fiction, he has only recently taken up writing for publication.*

Manos
by Denver Grenell

Hands. Everywhere he looked, the walls waved at him. Red hands. White hands. Taunting him. Mocking him.

His younger brother gazed proudly at his latest work. A fresh white hand. He offered the spray pipe to his older sibling, who just stared blankly at the tool. White paint dripped from one end. He looked back at the cave wall. The hands kept waving.

He took the pipe and swung it down. His brother's skull caved in. He punched his fist deep into the red hole. Withdrawing his hand, he pressed it against the rock. One more red hand amongst many.

Denver Grenell *is a writer of horror & dark fiction who lives with his family in the small rural town of Featherston, New Zealand. A life-long horror hound who got back into writing after a long break, he is now making up for lost time, furiously expelling every idea that has collected inside his skull over the years. His stories are soon to be featured in Crystal Lake Publishing's Shallow Waters anthologies and Black Hare Press' Ancients & School's In anthologies.*
Instagram: *@beware.the.moon*
Instagram: *@degrineer*

The Emerald Isle
by Raven Corinn Carluk

Nuada disembarked the crystal ship and inhaled the heavily scented air. Rich with growth and flowers and animal life, it reminded him of home.

Those breezes never carried the odours of death and rot and violence, however.

Danaa approached, armour gleaming. "The locals call those giant things fomori and swear there is no way to stop them. Holding them at bay is the best they do."

Nuada smiled and rested a hand easily upon his sword. "Unstoppable monsters, eh?" His blood stirred at the thought of battle and slaughter and bloodshed. "Exactly how I want to found my new kingdom."

Raven Corinn Carluk *writes dark fantasy, paranormal romance, and anything else that catches her interest. She's authored five novels, where she explores themes of love and acceptance. Her shorter pieces, usually from her darker side, can be found in Black Hare Press anthologies, at Detritus Online, and through Alban Lake Publishers.*
Twitter: @ravencorinn
Website: www.ravencorinncarluk.com

Prophecy of Destruction
by Zoey Xolton

I am against you, Tyre, and I will bring many nations against you, like the sea casting up its waves.

"So is the prophecy of our Sovereign Lord," declared Ezekiel.

The King of Babylon crushed the mainland, putting all to the sword. Seeing the destruction, the King of Tyre prostrated himself and made peace with Nebuchadnezzar. The price was his exile, but his island kingdom was saved.

Years later, Alexander the Great used the remnants of the mainland to build a causeway to the island, plundering it without mercy… Tyre's citizens were slaughtered; the prophecy of the vengeful Hebrew God fulfilled.

Zoey Xolton is an Australian speculative fiction writer, primarily of dark fantasy, paranormal romance, and horror. She is also a proud mother of two and is married to her soulmate. Outside of her family, writing is her greatest passion. She is especially fond of short fiction and is working on releasing her own themed collections in the future.
Website: www.zoeyxolton.com

The Heir's Duty
by Dawn Knox

She watched the priest lay fingertips on her husband's eyelids and close them for the final time. A stone was placed on his lips.

Now, it would be the king's son who held the power of life and death over his people.

Her son.

His face impassive, the boy watched the priest perform the last rites on his father, the man who'd beaten the tears out of him many years ago.

She felt his eyes alight on her and both knew the young king would preside at the burial when his dead father and living mother would be interred together.

Dawn Knox enjoys writing in different genres and has had romances, speculative fiction, sci-fi, humorous, and women's fiction published in magazines, anthologies, and books. She's also had two plays about World War I performed internationally. Her current work in progress is a story set in Bletchley Park during World War II.
Website: dawnknox.com
Twitter: SunriseCalls

First Kill
by Eddie D. Moore

Luta shouted with the other men of his tribe as the giant beast lifted his long nose and roared. Blood ran steadily down each of its sides. Luta was determined to place the killing blow before the monster collapsed from blood loss. He had to prove himself.

The beast swiped his tusks to the right, and Luta stuck his spear deep into the creature's neck. When the monstrous animal collapsed, Luta shouted, "Today, I am a man!"

The other tribesmen snickered and tossed several sharp stones at Luta's feet. "You killed it; you clean it. Then you'll be a man."

Eddie D. Moore travels hundreds of hours a year, and he fills that time by listening to audiobooks. When he isn't playing with his grandchildren, he writes his own stories. You can find a list of his publications on his blog or by visiting his Amazon Author Page. While you're there, be sure to pick up a copy of his mini-anthology 'Misfits & Oddities'.
Website: eddiedmoore.wordpress.com
Amazon: amazon.com/author/eddiedmoore

Prayer to the Black Dragon
by K.T. Tate

"Zir, the great sorcerer and teacher of mankind, hear me.

Bless this ink that I mix and all that will stand under your draconic flag.

I know that they are coming. Visions of horror filled my dreams, blessed as I am by you. My black eyes a reflection of your scales.

They convert by right of the sword. Crosses burning with more hatred than the hell they claim we are doomed to. Our warriors are brave, but our people are scared.

May our sacrifices be enough.

May the way you've shown me be true.

May the Wends win this day."

K.T. Tate *lives in Cambridgeshire in the UK. She writes mainly weird fiction, cosmic horror, and strange monster stories. Website:* *www.eldritch-hollow.com*

When They Dig Me Up
by Shelly Jarvis

The last time I arose, it was 1922. They dug too deep, their pride overwhelming their sense. It took years to make each pay for the disturbance; but pay they did. With their lives.

I have guarded the Valley of Kings for thousands of years, protecting each dynasty laid to rest in these lands. When someone, anyone, disrupts a Pharaoh's rest, I come for them. I am the barrier between this world and the next.

My own slumber is restless as they burrow into the land nearby. They will know the curse of the Pharaohs when they dig me up.

Shelly Jarvis is a speculative fiction author from West Virginia, US. She found a lifelong love of sci-fi and fantasy in the third grade when she found Madeleine L'Engle's "A Wrinkle in Time." Shelly is an avid reader, a Whovian, the ideal viewer of dog rescue videos, and undoubtedly Ravenclaw. She currently has three YA sci-fi books available for purchase on Amazon.
Website: www.ShellyJarvis.com

Demon of Passion
by Paul J. Scribbans

Mike felt the warm breeze lick his naked body. He stroked her long black hair and inhaled her sweet essence.

He'd insisted on this Mayan trail stag holiday to avoid intimate encounters. Leaving camp to take a leak, he'd seen her leaning against a tree, dressed in white. Her dark eyes gazed into him. She looked stunning, intoxicating; he couldn't resist her. She'd lead him farther into the jungle where they made love.

Whispering into her ear, "What is your name?"

"Xtabay," she replied as she tore his chest. He died in agony as she mutilated and devoured his body.

Paul J Scribbans is a writer who has lived his entire life in the Lake District, UK. His working background is in Information Technology and he didn't start writing seriously until his early forties. Apart from writing, he enjoys reading and absorbing himself in the local countryside with hobbies such as trail running and hiking. His genres are fantasy, sci-fi, and horror which adopt strong environmental and survival themes.

Dragons of Hurukan
by Joachim Heijndermans

"There! Nice and pretty for the people outside," I say to my dragon, as I drape the golden ornament upon its nose horn. He growls a bit but does not resist. "They wait. Come."

I take him by his leash and walk onto the platform. Our new pyramid stands tall among the old ones, where those of the Maya paid tribute to me before. Now, a crowd of people so new and varied cheers at our debut. I have returned to them this tri-horned thunder lizard. More will come. Tyrant kings and winged ones for all.

Hurukan loves. Hurukan provides.

Joachim Heijndermans writes, draws, and paints nearly every waking hour. Originally from The Netherlands, he's been all over the world, boring people by spouting random trivia. His work has been featured in a number of anthologies and publications, such as Mad Scientist Journal, Asymmetry Fiction, Hinnom Magazine, Ahoy Comics' Edgar Allan Poe's Snifter of Terror, Metaphorosis, and The Gallery of Curiosities, and he's currently in the midst of completing his first children's book.
Website: www.joachimheijndermans.com
Twitter: @jheijndermans

From Warrior's Slumber
by Radar DeBoard

The Melsoupati were a civilisation of ruthless warriors. From the coastline of what is modern day Spain to the beginnings of the Gobi Desert, they levelled all who stood in their way.

They had special powers that made them stronger and faster than any normal man. They trampled thousands of civilisations under their feet. Though eventually, like all things, their power faded away.

The Melsoupati were forced into a long slumber to try to regenerate their powers. Now, we have awakened them, and they are ready for blood. With several millennia of rest, they will cover the world in war.

Radar DeBoard is a horror movie and novel enthusiast who resides in the small town of Goddard, Kansas. He occasionally dabbles in writing and enjoys making dark tales for people to enjoy. He has had drabbles and short stories published in various electronic magazines and anthologies.
Facebook: WriterRadarDeBoard

A Ghost and a Bear Cult
by Paul Carberry

Members of the bear cult had sworn an oath of silence. To honour their vow, they had removed their tongues at an early age. They hid behind their silent rituals. Hatred filled the mother as they prepared the young adolescent for sacrifice to the ghost. Coins placed over the eyes so the child could not see; their lips stitched shut so they could not scream. The alabaster demon approached, the ice groaning in protest as it circled. Forced away from the light, the cult dragged the mother into the blackness. A spirit emerged from the darkness; the feast greedily received.

Paul Carberry is the author of the Zombies on the Rock series. His tales of the zombie apocalypse in Newfoundland are inspired by George A. Romero's Living Dead series. He has also published several short stories over three "from the Rock" anthologies including "Halloween Mummers", "The Light of Cabot Tower", "Into the Forrest", and "Harmon Field". His Zombies on the Rock series currently has three novels, "Outbreak", "The Viking Trail", and "The Republic of Newfound" and is currently working on the fourth novel "Extinction". Most recently Paul has been accepted in Black Hare Press' Oceans Anthology. Paul is from Newfoundland and is currently living in Shearwater, Nova Scotia.

Blood for the Corn
by Ava Montes

The Elders say last year marked the last sacrifice since Farming began, but the Corn *perpetually* hungers. Only after Feeding does it provide crops. From my Ohioan town, I am Harvested; my scoliosis prevents sufficient Devotion.

My blood saturates the gluttonous Dirt beneath my rope-bound feet, attracting the Corn. Roots like blackened tongues slither close in the cloying dusk, but I have a buck knife hidden up my sleeve. I ignore the harsh echoes of ancient custom and cut my bonds. Slash the roots. They scream.

The River—freedom—I fight the field.

I will not die for the Corn.

Ava Montes is a senior at the Franciscan University of Steubenville studying English writing and Theology; her home is O'ahu, Hawaii. She enjoys drawing (@doodle_baron on Instagram), all sunsets, aesthetic photographs, classical literature, fat cats, and large salads. She wants to one day travel the world and write about it. When she was a child, her ideal career was piratical adventure on the high seas, but she has since settled for studying diligently until more sensible opportunities arise.

The Battle of Lake Texcoco
by Jim Bates

The Aztecs were ready for Cortes with canoes, and they attacked, wave upon wave of them, pulling soldiers and their horses off the causeway. The water was soon filled with bodies sinking in the lake under the weight of the gold they had tried to carry out. Some of the soldiers were captured and sacrificed in full view of the survivors, their screams filling the air. That night lives in history as the Noche Triste—The Sad Night—a sad night for the Spanish, but not for the natives. It was a joyous night for them because they'd been so victorious.

Jim Bates lives in a small town twenty miles west of Minneapolis, Minnesota. His stories have appeared online in CafeLit, The Writers' Cafe Magazine, Cabinet of Heed, Paragraph Planet, Nailpolish Stories, Ariel Chart, Potato Soup Journal, Literary Yard, Spillwords (December 2019, Author of the Month), The Drabble, The Academy of the Heart and Mind, and World of Myth Magazine. In print publications: A Million Ways, Mused Literary Journal, Gleam Flash Fiction Anthology #2, the Portal Anthology and the Glamour Anthology by Clarendon House Publishing, The Best of CafeLit 8 by Chapeltown Publishing, the Nativity Anthology by Bridge House Publishing, and Gold Dust Magazine.
Website: www.theviewfromlonglake.wordpress.com

Dimaryp of Neverwhere
by Joachim Heijndermans

"What's inside?"

"Some bones. A sarcophagus or two."

"And it just hovers upside down like that? What's keeping it up?"

"We were hoping you could tell us."

"I'm more of a pyramid expert. This is the opposite. A dimaryp, I suppose. Plus, what do I know about sudden unexplainable appearances?"

"Funny you should say that. Because lab analysis says it's been here for hundreds of years."

"Wait, what? There were only the Neverwhere temples yesterday. How is that possible?"

"You want to argue the lab?"

"No. I want to go in."

Joachim Heijndermans *writes, draws, and paints nearly every waking hour. Originally from the Netherlands, he's been all over the world, boring people by spouting random trivia. His work has been featured in a number of anthologies and publications, such as Mad Scientist Journal, Asymmetry Fiction, Hinnom Magazine, Ahoy Comics' Edgar Allan Poe's Snifter of Terror, Metaphorosis, and The Gallery of Curiosities, and he's currently in the midst of completing his first children's book.*
Website: www.joachimheijndermans.com
Twitter: @jheijndermans

Day Dreams
by Andrew Kurtz

"Please show the plumbers where to go," Jane told her husband Max.

The Egyptian Pharaoh, whip in hand, led the slaves to the area where the pyramid needed to be repaired due to flooding.

Next, Jane wanted Max to review their children's homework.

The wise Greek philosopher gathered his students in the arena to discuss their lessons.

Finally, Jane informed Max that she was going to lie down for a while in bed because she was dead on her feet.

The Aztec priest approached the sacrificial victim on the stone slab with his sharp flint to cut out her heart.

Andrew Kurtz is an emerging writer of horror, influenced by Stephen King, H.P. Lovecraft, and Wells. He has stories published by Black Hare Press, Eleanor Merry, Renaimted Writers, and R.J. Roles.

Asgard by the Ash
by Joachim Heijndermans

Hello. Yes, they're all dead. Aesir, Jötunn, and the Skye Walker's children, together in death. But I am still here, the messenger of the Ash, where ruins lie.

This place, you ask? Well, it's what's left of Asgard. During the battle, they broke it in the process and it fell here, around our dear world tree.

But it's still good. Do you want to see it? I know all the good spots. All the secret rooms and where the interesting things are hidden. The spot where I've buried the bodies. Let Ratatoskr be your guide.

You gonna eat those nuts?

Joachim Heijndermans writes, draws, and paints nearly every waking hour. Originally from The Netherlands, he's been all over the world, boring people by spouting random trivia. His work has been featured in a number of anthologies and publications, such as Mad Scientist Journal, Asymmetry Fiction, Hinnom Magazine, Ahoy Comics' Edgar Allan Poe's Snifter of Terror, Metaphorosis, and The Gallery of Curiosities, and he's currently in the midst of completing his first children's book.
Website: www.joachimheijndermans.com
Twitter: @jheijndermans

A Heady Solution
by Jim Bates

The Aztecs tried to remain calm when Cortes and his soldiers inhabited their lovely city, but when one of his commanders opened fire on an innocent celebration, killing over one hundred men, women, and children, all polite détente ceased. In retaliation, the natives captured a soldier a day, cut off his head and displayed the bloody thing on a tall pole. When one of the younger soldiers saw the head of his friend towering above a chanting crowd, he cried out, "You'll never get me. I'm never coming back." To which an officer said to him, "That's using your head."

Jim Bates *lives in a small town twenty miles west of Minneapolis, Minnesota. His stories have appeared online in CafeLit, The Writers' Cafe Magazine, Cabinet of Heed, Paragraph Planet, Nailpolish Stories, Ariel Chart, Potato Soup Journal, Literary Yard, Spillwords (December 2019, Author of the Month), The Drabble, The Academy of the Heart and Mind, and World of Myth Magazine. In print publications: A Million Ways, Mused Literary Journal, Gleam Flash Fiction Anthology #2, the Portal Anthology and the Glamour Anthology by Clarendon House Publishing, The Best of CafeLit 8 by Chapeltown Publishing, the Nativity Anthology by Bridge House Publishing, and Gold Dust Magazine.*
Website: www.theviewfromlonglake.wordpress.com

Rebellion on Ynys Mon
by Bec Lewis

She entered the shack. "Tad? I'm back from the North."

"Olwen? Daughter, must be twenty summers…"

"Since you sold me to Druid Dewain, yes. He's joined the rebellion on the beach, chanting spells at the Romans. Their boats approach our beloved isle."

"They'll slaughter us all."

"Not you." She lunged, her knife piercing his belly. "They won't take this moment from me."

He fell, gasping.

"Can you imagine what Dewain did to me, Tad? For years?" She severed his heels to further limit movement. He shrieked.

Then Olwen shovelled hot embers on dry straw and headed back to the beach.

Bec Lewis lives in Kent, England. She's had stories published in a number of e-zines and print magazines. Website: www.beclewisfiction.com

The Final Winner
by Olivia Arieti

"I'll prove that I can do better than you," boasted Arachne to Minerva, before being challenged to the weaving contest.

Competing with the gods was dangerous and the envious deity on realising how skilful the girl was, destroyed her work and hit her.

No sooner the maiden full of shame had hanged herself than the furious goddess sentenced, "You shall hang and spin to the last generations."

Then she turned her into an ugly spider unaware that one day, the scary descendants would beat her by spinning the most intricate and beautiful web that would entangle the whole wide world.

Olivia Arieti has a degree from the University of Pisa and lives in Torre del Lago Puccini, Italy, with her family. Besides being a published playwright, she loves writing retellings of fairy tales and, at the same time, is intrigued by supernatural and horror themes. Her stories appeared in several magazines and anthologies like Enchanted Conversations, Enchanted Tales Literary Magazine, Fantasia Divinity Magazine, Cliterature, Medieval Nightmares, Static Movement, 100 Doors To Madness Forgotten Tomb Press, Black Cats Horrified Press, Bloody Ghost Stories Full Moon Books, Death And Decorations Thirteen O'Clock Press, Infective Ink, Pandemonium Press, and Pussy Magic Magazine.

She Waits
by Brian Rosenberger

We were at war. War changed people quicker than evolution. Honest men became thieves, wives were recast as whores, and farmers transformed into soldiers.

Grandmother told tales of Ungaikyo, a simple midwife that became a caretaker of orphaned children.

Our soldiers invaded her home. The soldiers executed her orphans when she refused to cooperate.

Desperate, Ungaikyo fled with the surviving children into a haunted mirror.

My only daughter, Yui, went missing weeks ago.

Grandmother reminded me of Ungaikyo, how she and her orphans waited in mirrors, waited for revenge.

Now I wait in front of the mirror to see Yui again.

__Brian Rosenberger__ lives in a cellar in Marietta, Georgia, USA, and writes by the light of captured fireflies. He is the author of "As the Worms Turns" and three poetry collections. He is also a featured contributor to the pro-wrestling literary collection "Three-Way Dance", available from Gimmick Press.
Facebook: HeWhoSuffers

The Music Master
by Lynne Phillips

Phalaris scoffed, "I don't believe the pipes in your bronze bull will transmit the screams of our victims the way you propose."

"I promise they will sound like a bull roaring," Perilaus replied.

"Prove it," the ancient Greek leader demanded.

Perilaus climbed inside his invention.

The door slammed. A fire raged underneath it. Perilaus' screams sounded just like a roaring bull.

"It's true," Phalaris marvelled, "Receive the due reward of your wondrous art. Let the music master be the first to play." He laughed.

Still alive, Perilaus' charred body was pulled from the bronze bull and tossed off a cliff.

Lynne Phillips, *a retired teacher, lives in the beautiful Northern Rivers Region of New South Wales, Australia. Her stories, across all genres, have been published in anthologies and various online magazines. Her priority is spending time with her family. Her passions are reading, writing, and keeping fit.*

383

Torn Utopia
by C.L. Williams

Land Between Rivers is what it was once called
A war between two tyrants led to its downfall
Though the first to civilise the human race
A utopia about to become disgraced

Before they knew it, Romans were ready to seize
Land ruled by tyrants cared for no pleas
Before the people could take their stand
The Persians arrived, also wanting their land

A war was fought with the people not involved
All they could do is watch their world dissolve
A land that was once rich, is now torn in two
With the people themselves unsure what to do

C.L. Williams is an international best-selling author currently living in central Virginia. He has written eight poetry books, four novellas, one novel, and a contributor to a multitude of anthologies and magazines. His most recent anthology appearance ANGELS: Dark Drabbles #2 from Black Hare Press became a number one in hot new releases. C.L. Williams is currently working on his second novel and a new poetry book.
Facebook: writer434
Twitter: @writer_434

Ancient Doesn't Mean Gone
by Wondra Vanian

"Ancient doesn't mean gone. Remember that when you go poking around another culture's sacred sites."

Misplaced hope flashes across the invader's face and I smile. As I heft him up roughly, his safety helmet clatters to the ground.

Plastic. He brought that poison here, to my temple…

My smile fades.

"There's a reason we endure while you find yourselves on the brink of extinction time and again."

He sputters.

I don't wait for him to find his voice.

It'll give me indigestion for a decade but will be worth it. Letting my jaw fall open, I stuff the invader inside.

Wondra Vanian is an American living in the United Kingdom with her Welsh husband and their army of fur babies. A writer first, Wondra is also an avid gamer, photographer, cinephile, and blogger. She has music in her blood, sleeps with the lights on, and has been known to dance naked in the moonlight. Wondra was a multiple Top-Ten finisher in the 2017 and 2018 Preditors and Editors Reader's Poll, including the Best Author category. Her story, "Halloween Night," was named a Notable Contender for the Bristol Short Story Prize in 2015.
Website: www.wondravanian.com

A Late-Night Feast
by Stuart Conover

For centuries, the Norse Gods fed upon Sæhrímnir's flesh.

Each night, Andhrímnir would slay the cosmic boar.

After, he would prepare their bounty.

The great Chef always made the same thing.

Humans claimed variety was the spice of life.

He craved originality.

When hunting the majestic creature, he aimed his bow.

As he had done for a millennium.

Only tonight, his arrow struck one of the lesser Vanir.

With this one act, everything would be different.

After all these centuries, it wouldn't be the boar he killed.

No, tonight the Pantheon would have something new.

The flesh of the Vanir.

Stuart Conover is a father, husband, rescue dog owner, published author, blogger, journalist, horror enthusiast, comic book geek, science fiction junkie, and IT professional. With all of that to cram in daily, we have no idea if or when he sleeps or how he gets writing done! (We suspect it has to do with having evil clones.) Stuart is a Chicago native and runs the author resource Horror Tree.

Demon Wind
by J.D. Bell

For centuries, monks in the monastery had warned of the evil in the Irish wind. Do not submit to temptation for air demons will take your soul and curse you to eternal suffering.

Seamus O'Malley ignored such malarkey. Walking home one night, after betting on horses at his local pub, a fierce wind rose in the surrounding darkness. Shrill cries, evil laughter, and agonising screams filled the air. A black cloud filled with hideous, tortured faces cried out to him. Dark, swirling arms lifted O'Malley high into the air as his tormented soul became one with the demon wind.

J.D. Bell is an award-winning, internationally published author of flash fiction and short stories. He recently retired from the world of writing advertising copy and is now enjoying the universe of creative fiction.
Facebook: jim.writes.stories
Twitter: @JimBell58

The Sacrifice
by Destiny Eve Pifer

Up the stone path they walked. Guiding the young woman past the dark shadows of the forests and the slithering snakes that hid beneath the tall grass. Higher they climbed with lit torches in hand. Through every doorway they came closer. When finally they came upon the slab of stone, the young woman knew it was time to meet her fate. She laid upon the cold dark slab and stared up at the moon above. No matter what terror her trembling body felt, she would not flinch. Not even as the dagger plunged into her heart.

Destiny Eve Pifer is a published author whose work has appeared in numerous anthologies and magazines. Her stories have been featured in Fate Magazine, True Confessions, Spotlight on Recovery, and Country Magazine. A lover of all things supernatural and spooky, she resides in Punxsutawney, Pennsylvania, with her son Dartanyan.

Boudicca
by Stacey Jaine McIntosh

The battlefield was littered with fallen soldiers. Blood and dirt mingled together to form a slurry in the rain that fell in sheets upon the ground.

"We can't hold out much longer!" the commander shouted. "We must retreat!"

"Never!" Queen Boudicca roared.

"Then you shall die at the hands of my blade as you should have done on the day we killed the King," said the enemy.

"Leave Prasutagus out of this!"

"Aye."

A single caress meant to distract as he raised his sword and drew it across her throat.

Blood flowed freely. The Queen of the Iceni was dead.

Stacey Jaine McIntosh *was born in Perth, Western Australia, where she still resides with her husband and their four children. Although her first love has always been writing, she once toyed with being a Cartographer and subsequently holds a Diploma in Spatial Information Services. Since 2011, she has had a vast number of stories and a few poems published online as well as in various anthologies. Stacey is also the author of Solstice, Morrighan, Lost, and Le Fay and she is currently working on several other projects simultaneously. When not with her family or writing she enjoys reading, photography, genealogy, history, Arthurian myths, and witchcraft.*
Website: www.staceyjainemcintosh.com

Forests Precede Us; Deserts Dog Our Heels

by Chris Hall

When Sargon the Great stood atop the ziggurat at Akkad surveying the verdant croplands below, Inanna whispered to him a vision of the changes to come.

He watched as his skin sluffed off like soil washed away by the Tigris waters, the very waters that nourished the crops which fed his empire. He watched as those same waters deposited salt upon the earth, voiding the soil of its life-giving boon.

He stood revealed—a skeleton king reigning over a desert. Finally, he watched a thousand other kings standing on towers that quickly crumbled to dust beneath the weight of centuries.

Chris Hall is a creative writer trapped in the body of an English professor and academic. He was born in the Bitterroot Valley region of Montana and transplanted to the Yuba-Sierra Bioregion at the ripe age of one. Along with foxes, raccoons, squirrels, bears, and innumerable other non-human kin, he lives with his partner, their two-year-old daughter, and several cats in a house on the fringes of a deep, dark wood.
He has published essays, reviews, and short stories in markets as diverse and divergent from one another as The Pacific Crest Trailside Reader (2011), Resilience: A Journal of the Environmental Humanities, Ecozon@, and Swords and Sorcery Magazine (swordsandsorcerymagazine.com).

Forgemasters' Vault
by Daniel Bagley

Here lies a repository of ancient, powerful artefacts sealed away from those who once tread the earth, ravaged by centuries of war.

Mortals who hear of such tales are fuelled by their desire to find them, not knowing of the consequences that would soon follow. A fool's gambit, no less.

The Forgemasters predicted this destructive path and sought to contain the weapons' horrible power. At the expense of their physical bodies, the makers' souls now reside within tempered steel, hoping to dissuade its influence, far from the curious eyes of mortal kind. From truth to myth, as the historians would claim…

Daniel Bagley has spent the last three years finding his way through the world of literacy, to understand different styles and its various audiences. Dark fiction, for him, is a rarity among genres, because not many will explore its crevices. Of course, he sees it as a reflection of one's life, the journeys we have to take to seek redemption. Through the power of words, he finds it easier to unleash his emotions to convey my point. Despite its name, it's a genre worth exploring.

Liquid Gold
by J.W. Garrett

The Indus citizen, Eshiram, plodded down the series of steps into the maze of tunnels. Their drainage systems were well planned, due to his skill and the other's years of expertise. The younger man followed the older deep into the drainage system. The stores of water held there were liquid gold due to the long-term drought that sucked the life from the people.

Eshiram turned, confronted. "You've had your portion."

"Move old man; I'll end you before thirst will."

Eshiram grabbed his club, plunging it into the man's head, spilling red. Eshiram chuckled. *Keep 'em coming. Less for tomorrow's count.*

J.W. Garrett has been writing in one form or another since she was a teenager. She currently lives in Florida with her family but loves the mountains of Virginia where she was born. Her writings include YA fantasy as well as short stories. Since completing Remeon's Quest-Earth Year 1930, the prequel in her YA fantasy series, Realms of Chaos, she has been hard at work on the next in the series, scheduled to release August 2020. When she's not hanging out with her characters, her favourite activities are reading, running, and spending time with family.
Website: www.jwgarrett.com
BHC Press: www.bhcpress.com/Author_JW_Garrett.html

Heaven on Earth
by Simon Clarke

Ai Fan wept at her mother's grave.

"Write on the Joss paper," said grandmother, "Something she would want."

Ai Fan sat quietly, then started to write. She set alight the list and smiled as her gaze followed the smoke into the afterlife.

"What did you write?"

"After what my stepfather did, I sent mother my request to the Gods."

Hiding in a filthy apartment in Hangzhou sits the stepfather. Suddenly the room dissolves. He is chained to a table and screams in agony as a giant saw begins ripping him in half. The first of Eighteen Hells wished upon him.

__Simon Clarke__ lives and writes in Norfolk, United Kingdom. His first published microfiction story, 'Loss', appeared on Black Hare Press. His first short story appeared in What If? on Black Hare Press. He enjoys writing fiction and poetry. He regularly submits to UK and international publications and enjoys reading short pieces and poetry at open mic events. He is currently working on his first novel. His main influences reflect authors he read as a teenager: J.R.R. Tolkien, Ian Fleming, Peter O'Donnell, H.P. Lovecraft, Raymond Chandler, and Sir Arthur Conan Doyle. He loves Gothic literature and all things mystical and mysterious.

Catal Huyuk
by Vonnie Winslow Crist

Though Mama birthed many children, Bahar was the only one to reach eleven.

As Father again carried bones stripped clean by sacred vultures through their mud home's roof entrance and down the wooden ladder, Bahar wiped her tears. Like all her dead siblings, Azian would be buried below Bahar's sleeping platform.

"Catal Huyuk is cursed. We should leave," cried Mama as she helped place Azian in his grave.

"Foolishness," scoffed Father. "A streetless city like Catal Huyuk is difficult to conquer. We're safe here."

Witnessing dozens of ghosts rising from beneath her bed, Bahar whispered, "I agree with Mama."

Vonnie Winslow Crist is author of The Enchanted Dagger, Owl Light, The Greener Forest, Murder on Marawa Prime, and other award-winning books. Her fiction is included in "Amazing Stories," "Cast of Wonders," "Outposts of Beyond," Killing It Softly 2, Defending the Future—Dogs of War, Midnight Masquerade, Chaos of Hard Clay, and elsewhere. A clover hand who has found so many four-leafed clovers, she keeps them in jars, Vonnie strives to celebrate the power of myth in her writing.
Website: www.vonniewinslowcrist.com

God or Angel: Ares
by Luis Manuel Torres

Ares, the God of War, stood in front of a battlefield with two armies fighting each other. Ares was one of the most respected Gods around and you wouldn't go to battle without giving a prayer to the mighty War God.

But time passed and people stopped worshipping the old Gods.

With no more worshippers, Ares was given two options by the Archangel Uriel. He could either become a mortal and eventually die, or he could become a Guardian Angel and keep his immortality.

Reluctantly, Ares became a Guardian Angel and now is stuck babysitting a child playing with bugs.

Luis Manuel Torres *was born in Puerto Rico, lived in Boston Massachusetts for thirteen years and currently lives in Springfield Mass. He has a love for stories in all forms they come in, from books to television and video games. His work can be found in multiple anthologies with Zimbell House Publishing and Black Hare Press. He is always working on multiple writing projects. His debut short story collection* Midnight Animals *is now available on Amazon.*
Blog: luisitowrites.wordpress.com
Twitter: Luis1989Manuel

Righting Babylon
by K.T. Tate

They killed you. Great mother who was dismembered to make this world. They call me a monster for my visions and ghastly appearance. One of your children. But then, if that's true, perhaps my blood can wake you.

You gave everything to protect your children, your family. I was powerless when they took mine. I was just trying to help the girl. She had no one, like me.

Thus, I gather these artefacts of your soul. Piece by piece finding you, knowing you. I will be your vessel. Soon you shall return, great Tiamat, mother of monsters, and they will pay.

***K.T. Tate** lives in Cambridgeshire in the UK. She writes mainly weird fiction, cosmic horror, and strange monster stories. Website: www.eldritch-hollow.com*

Awaiting Dawn Among the Stones
by Hayley Arrington

We keep vigil near bonfires as the longest night darkens. Stars seem brighter as we wait for the first glimpse of the sun to meet the lintel's cold stone. Bright eyes stare from beyond the stones' perimeter. The dark figures venture forth on these liminal nights to claim a soul, switch a child, or aid healing. Their hands, like vines, quietly claim theirs as we shiver at bonfires and pray that we will see the coming dawn.

We begin our low chant. Ululating syllables crescendo as the flames leap higher. We know day follows day but, on nights like this, who can tell?

Hayley Arrington is a writer of mythological and dark poetry and prose. Her writings have appeared in various publications online and in print, including Circe's Cauldron: Pagan Poems and Tales of Magic and Witchcraft, Eternal Haunted Summer, Folk Horror Revival: Corpse Roads, Witch Lit: Words from the Cauldron, Liminality, and Fantasia Divinity anthologies Elemental Drabbles Volume I. Hayley is from the greater Los Angeles area, where she lives with her husband, David, and their son, Stevie.

Ubaid's Missing Brides
by Monica Schultz

Abida runs through the wheat fields, tears streaming down her face. She isn't ready to marry, to please a man thrice her age. Yet her first blood suggests otherwise.

Abida stills. Reptilian figures fill the field ahead. Their tongues scent the air, flickering from scaled mouths. She's heard the legends but hasn't hoped until now.

Abida falls to her knees, begging their assistance. The gods crowd around her, their eyes cold and calculating. Such youth and warmth could sustain them for several winters.

"Risssse child," the gods hiss as one, "Join ussss and forget all your fearssss."

Enthralled, Abida obeys.

Monica Schultz is a full-time Mathematics and History teacher from Ipswich, Australia, with a passion for writing fantasy. When she isn't busy finding "x" in the latest equation, you can find her curled up with a young adult book and a cat on her lap.
Website: https://monicaschultzauthor.weebly.com/
Instagram: @monicaschultzauthor

Axes, Swords, Wind, and Wolves
by Clint Foster

A crack of thunder shook the mountains free of their snow, unmooring the winds from their tethers that they might howl across the world. It sent men and beasts alike into a frenzy, and the storming feet of the Einherjar made the very earth rock. Valkyries flew overhead as giants and the foul wolf of Hel's domain swarmed. Like the rest, I took up my axe, standing upon the threshold of Valhalla to be torn to ribbons by the claws of fell beasts. Ragnarök will claim the world, no matter how hard we struggle, but we shall struggle, nonetheless.

Clint Foster lives with his herd of four cats; beloved Basset, Zero; and wonderful wife, Nik. He loves to tell stories just as much as he loves to read them and is excited to share his work. A long-time consumer of media of all kinds, he enjoys giving back what he hopes everyone else thinks are good stories.
Facebook: ClintFosterAuthor

The Bean-Nighe
by Bec Lewis

She was washing a shroud in the roadside stream when Mike approached.

"Three questions," she said, "and ye answer three."

"Car died a mile back." God, she had webbed feet! "How far's town?"

"Five miles. Ye'll nae get there."

"Why not?"

"Folks see me, they don't last long… Why's ye here?"

"Celebrating promotion. Thought I'd visit the Highlands."

"D'ye deserve it?"

"Of course."

"Then why d'ye kill for it?"

Mike gasped. "Who are you?"

"Bean-Nighe, the Washerwoman. Messenger from the dead."

"Crazy hag." Mike ran till he felt safe.

High on the mountain above him, a rain-loosened boulder gathered speed.

Bec Lewis lives in Kent, England. She's had stories published in a number of e-zines and print magazines.
Website: *www.beclewisfiction.com*

Visiting the Tourist Sites
by Gabriella Balcom

Toga-clad people walked around the Acropolis, talking about Rome's glory days, advances, and military successes. They'd even defeated invaders from Carthage, despite their maritime prowess.

Natalie listened raptly, but Wendell grimaced, angry she'd insisted he accompany her.

They visited the Parthenon, Colosseum, and more, ending up at Circus Maximus, where chariot races were being enacted.

Wendell wandered away, scowling when helmeted, armour-clad "gladiators" appeared, battling one another. "Stupid projections," he snorted, seeing the walls through their bodies.

A gladiator stalked towards him, running him through with a sword.

Gurgling noises escaped Wendell's lips, and he collapsed, blood pooling around him

Gabriella Balcom *lives in Texas with her family, loves reading and writing, and thinks she was born with a book in her hands. She works in a mental health field and writes fantasy, horror/thriller, romance, children's stories, and sci-fi. She likes travelling, music, good shows, photography, history, interesting tales, and animals. Gabriella says she's a sucker for a great story and loves forests, mountains, and back roads which might lead to who knows where. She has a weakness for lasagne, garlic bread, tacos, cheese, and chocolate, but not necessarily in that order.*

Facebook: GabriellaBalcom.lonestarauthor

Sacrifice to the Moloch
by D.M. Burdett

Wind whistled through the trees, rustling branches—eerie sounds in the moonless night. Silent shadows huddled together, their steps a steady rhythm to Tophet.

Candles flickered in the breeze.

Abijah stood in line, motionless bundle in his arms, trying to hide his dirty tears—he didn't want to anger Kronos.

When it was his turn, Abijah held the child aloft for Kronos to see.

Kronos' bronze face was impassive.

Abijah tenderly placed the bundle in Kronos' hand. It rolled, shroud unwrapping, into the fiery pit below.

"I see your tears, Abijah," boomed Kronos.

Mothers wept—it would mean more sacrifices.

D.M. Burdett *initially roamed as an army brat, but now lives in Australia where she spends her days avoiding drop bears and killer spiders. She has published a Sci-Fi series, has short stories in various anthologies, and has published two children's series. She is currently working on the first book in a dystopian series.*
Website: www.dmburdett.com
Facebook: DMBurdett

Aztalan
by Dawn DeBraal

In Lake Mills, Wisconsin, huge glacial boulders were rolled to the shallow area of the Crawfish River. Ancient Indians created a weir where fish were driven through the narrow opening to be captured. The remnants of thirty watchtowers grace the walls surrounding the twenty-two-acre city.

Upon excavation, the Princess Burial Mound revealed the only remains left behind, that of a woman wearing 1978 clamshell beads.

The ruins of Aztalan tell the story of a thriving ancient Native American civilisation. No explanation has ever been offered as to why the Woodland Tribe suddenly vanished. It is a mystery to this day.

Dawn DeBraal lives in rural Wisconsin with her husband Red, two rat terriers, and a cat. She has discovered that her love of telling a good story can be written. Published stories with Palm-sized press, Spillwords, Mercurial Stories, Potato Soup Journal, Edify Fiction, Zimbell House Publishing, Clarendon House Publishing, Blood Song Books, Black Hare Press, Fantasia Divinity, Cafelit, Reanimated Writers, Guilty Pleasures, Unholy Trinity, The World of Myth, Dastaan World, Vamp Cat, Runcible Spoon, Dark Christmas, Siren's Call, Iron Horse Publishing, Falling Star Magazine 2019 Pushcart Nominee.
Amazon: amazon.com/Dawn-DeBraal/e/B07STL8DLX

The Sybil Scythes
by Hari Navarro

The General strides into the trapezoidal passage and inhales the heady thickness of its sulphuric breath. He, who feels nothing and fears even less, shudders at the amber dribble snaking his thigh, curling down, and pooling in the arch of his sandalled foot.

"Women are but son bearers, cooks, and warmers of cock. But you're special, celestially chosen. A nothing girl, and yet I quake and piss as you impart my true fate from the leaves. Praise me, for all I fear is you."

The Oracle raises her eyes to her finger, pointing to his groin with a simper.

"Castrātus."

Hari Navarro has, for many years now, been locked in his neighbour's cellar. He survives due to an intravenous feed of puréed extreme horror and absinthe-infused sticky-spiced unicorn wings. His anguished cries for help can be found via 365 Tomorrows, Breachzine, AntipodeanSF, Horror Without Borders, Black Hare Press, and HellBound books. Hari was the winner of the Australasian Horror Writers' Association (AHWA) Flash Fiction Award 2018 and has also succeeded in being a New Zealander who now lives in northern Italy with no cats.
Amazon: amazon.com/Hari-Navarro
Tumblr: harinavarro.tumblr.com/

No Mentioning
by Radar DeBoard

There is a very strange phenomenon that seems to occur when experts talk about ancient, abandoned civilisations. They sit and give their opinions on what could have caused the people living there to disappear.

Whether it be the Anasazi and their stone dwellings or the Polynesians of Easter Island, the experts only speculate. They even give ridiculous theories for what happened in Roanoke.

It never fails that they never mention the spider people that lived in those areas. Simple people who were normally very passive. That is, until they run out of food. Like what happened to the Mayans.

__Radar DeBoard__ is a horror movie and novel enthusiast who resides in the small town of Goddard, Kansas. He occasionally dabbles in writing and enjoys making dark tales for people to enjoy. He has had drabbles and short stories published in various electronic magazines and anthologies.
Facebook: WriterRadarDeBoard

A Legacy Bestowed
by Joshua Gessner

Never had I seen a god before. A thing so great you huddle beneath it, but now I have. It stood far above me and stretched across the sky and covered all of Mesopotamia. It was Anu, our Sky Father, a man—no, a god—with a crown-like headdress of horns curling towards its tip. Off him dropped a giant staff of gold, and as it fell far from the sky above me, it shrunk and shrunk and shrunk. Now at my feet, it had landed, the size of a mere twig. It's golden glow tempting. Its ownership given.

Joshua Gessner is a full-time college student, enrolled under the English major at his local community college. He is nineteen years old and lives with his family in Manchester. Joshua Gessner has been published for the first time ever in January of 2020 and was published again one month later in February of 2020! He now continues working diligently on his craft, hoping to enter literary contests. In the future, he also hopes to publish novels, novellas, short stories, and poetry!
Facebook: joshua.gessner.98
Twitter: @joshuagessner41

Emer's War
by Nikki Foster

Slowly, then all at once, light came to her, revealing it to be much more than the mere dream. She had long revelled in an altogether different dream. Alas.

He was beautiful, and his steady breathing nearly hypnotised her to stay. She pinned her hair back and remembered her life until this moment.

Her husband, somehow more beautiful than the man she was trying not to wake, would be the one cast aside now. Eyes closed, breath held, she opened the door.

"Sweet Ferdia, tomorrow you shall make my vengeance. Tomorrow, you make a war between brothers. Aife, be damned."

Nikki Foster loves her husband, the Earth, and all of the animals, but none more than her own four-legged fur children, including her most beloved Basset, Zero.

The Outlaw God
by A.R. Dean

Hiding in our mud huts from the new arrivals. They follow the outlaw god. The screaming starts as the strangers drag women from their homes and disappear. The village priest prays to the gods for those lost.

I ask my father, the elder, why we do not rescue them. I don't understand why no warrior from the tribe can be spared to fight such evil.

"Those villains are protected by the outlaw god. Only death awaits those who try to fight them," he sighs. "The outlaw god demands the eating of flesh and souls. There is nothing left to save."

A.R. Dean is a dark and twisted soul. Dean has spent their whole life spreading fear with the tales from their head. Best known for stories that terrify and show the evilest side of human nature. So, look for Dean haunting your local cemetery or under your bed, because they're here to spread the fear. Turn off your lights and enjoy a scare. Dean is being published in Black Hare Press' Beyond and Unravel Anthologies. Keep a lookout for more stories.
Facebook: A.R. Dean Author & Ghoul

The Deal
by Jacek Wilkos

The snake's head fell with a hiss to the ground. He raised his burned head and smiled with the healthy part of his mouth. The figure standing before him held a burning sword; six pairs of black wings obscured the sky.

Another flaming slash and the chains bounding the giant fell on the stones.

"I hope you'll fulfil your part of the deal," the angel rather stated than asked.

Loki got up from his knees.

"Of course. You'll help me unleash Ragnarök and I'll help you in your crusade against Yahweh."

Samael nodded.

"And now let's go free my children."

Jacek Wilkos is an engineer from Poland. He lives with his wife and daughter in a beautiful city of Cracow. He is addicted to buying books, and he loves coffee, dark ambient music, and riding his bike. He writes mostly horror drabbles. His fiction in Polish can be read on Szortal, Niedobre literki, Horror Online. In English, his work was published in Drablr, Rune Bear, Sirens Call eZine, and Trembling with Fear.
Facebook: Jacek.W.Wilkos

Blood Makes the Sun Shine
by Clint Foster

I do not cower as I walk the slick steps, following in the path of hundreds, of thousands before me to do the same. Once I reach the top, I will meet my end as a hero before Huitzilopochtli, but first I must walk the smooth stones. Worn round by innumerable feet, they tell the tale of the pyramid just as well as the priests who dance upon the altar, whipping the crowd into a frenzy for blood. My blood. Proud, strong, I do not grimace as the obsidian knife opens me up and the priest hands me my heart.

__Clint Foster__ lives with his herd of four cats; beloved Basset, Zero; and wonderful wife, Nik. He loves to tell stories just as much as he loves to read them and is excited to share his work. A long-time consumer of media of all kinds, he enjoys giving back what he hopes everyone else thinks are good stories.
Facebook: ClintFosterAuthor

Time to Die
by A.R. Johnston

They always think they have all the time in the world. How wrong people are. Time is not everlasting; time is fleeting. Watching the ongoing battle, seeing another, a goddess descends onto the battlefield; I chuckle. She is the goddess of war and battle, but I too am a god.

A god most don't pay attention to, unfortunate for them. Only in their last minutes, as they feel the sands of their lives flowing away, vanishing, do they think to pray to me. I decide how much time you have. I am the god of time; I am Kronos.

A.R. Johnston is a small-town girl from Nova Scotia, Canada. She is known to write mostly urban fantasy, though she goes where the muses lead her and you never know where that may be. She is a lover of coffee, good tv shows, and horror flicks and a reader of good books. She pretends to be a writer when real life doesn't get in the way. Pesky full-time job and adulting!
Facebook: arjohnstonauthor
Website: arjohnstonauthor.wordpress.com

Keeping Score
by G. Allen Wilbanks

"He called my name," said Huracan. "Did you hear?"

"I did."

"He called out for help in my name. He prays to me, that makes him one of mine."

"He is spread out on my altar," said Chaac defiantly. "He is under a knife held by a priest of the Rain God. I say that makes him mine. Unless you are planning to interfere?"

Huracan waved the suggestion away as if it was unworthy of consideration.

"Of course not. I am merely pointing out the obvious."

"Which is?"

Huracan smiled, storm light flashing in his eyes. "You owe me one."

G. Allen Wilbanks is a member of the Horror Writers Association (HWA) and has published over a hundred short stories in various magazines and online venues. He is the author of two short story collections and the novel "When Darkness Comes".
Website: www.gallenwilbanks.com
Blog: DeepDarkThoughts.com

ACKNOWLEDGEMENTS

When we embarked on DARK DRABBLES—the first set of anthologies from BHP—we never envisioned the huge support we'd get from the writing community. We have been truly humbled by the number of submissions (more than 500 for WORLDS alone!) and have loved reading every single one of them. So, to everyone who crafted a tiny tale just for us, we thank you from the bottom of our hearts.

To everyone who has helped us on the way—our families and friends, collaborators, and random strangers who took pity—we couldn't have done it without you. Thank you all.

www.blackharepress.com

A BLACK HARE PRESS ANTHOLOGY
WORLDS
DARK DRABBLES #1
ANCIENTS
ALIENS
LOVE
APOCALYPSE
UNRAVEL
BEYOND
MONSTERS
ANGELS
WORLDS
10
9
8
7
6
5
4
3
2
1
Edited by D KERSHAW
edited by D KERSHAW

www.ingramcontent.com/pod-product-compliance
Lightning Source LLC
Chambersburg PA
CBHW030355200726

48286CB00014B/1435